"I couldn't sleep last night at all."

Ryder murmured the words against her temple, making Lauren shiver with desire. "I kept remembering you, hearing the broken little sounds you make in your throat when I hold you. I wanted to get up and come over here."

She smiled, nuzzling her face against his neck. "You could have."

He lifted her hair, catching it so that he could tilt her head and look into her eyes. Long seconds passed, as though he couldn't quite believe what he'd heard.

"You could have," Lauren repeated softly.

"One of these days," Ryder said, a huskiness lingering in his voice, "it's going to be the two of us...alone, nobody else around. I'm going to kiss you the way I've always wanted to. But until I can take a long, long time—until I can savor every beautiful inch of you, we both know I can't do what you suggest."

ABOUT THE AUTHOR

Still passionately in love with her husband of thirty-two years, Karen Young has always been an incurable romantic who firmly believes in happy endings. A native of Mississippi, Karen has moved more than twenty times since her wedding. She began plotting her first novel when her husband suggested that "being a writer is the perfect profession for a nomad." Now settled in Kansas, this proud mother of two grown daughters is hard at work on her third Superromance.

Books by Karen Young

HARLEQUIN SUPERROMANCE
341–ALL MY TOMORROWS

Compelling Connection

KAREN YOUNG

Harlequin Books

TORONTO • NEW YORK • LONDON
AMSTERDAM • PARIS • SYDNEY • HAMBURG
STOCKHOLM • ATHENS • TOKYO • MILAN

Published September 1989

First printing July 1989

ISBN 0-373-70371-6

To Evan Marshall,
my agent and friend
who is the real Justin's daddy

PROLOGUE

1975

IT WAS EARLY, but Baby's Bar was smoke filled and crowded as usual. For once, conversation was possible, a circumstance brought about by the end of exam week. Like soldiers suffering battle fatigue after narrowly escaping disaster, weary students huddled around tiny tables. Over the rise and fall of hushed voices, the audio system pulsed with the rhythm of the Rolling Stones. Mick Jagger's wail blended with the muted clink of glasses and weary laughter.

Ryder Braden stared into his beer. *Thank God, it's over,* he thought. Graduation was only a week away. It had taken six years—six long, hard years—but now he could begin to reap the rewards. He savored his satisfaction for a long moment before lifting his head to look at his former roommate across the table.

Neil Putnam was finishing off his sixth beer. Or was it his seventh? Ryder hid a smile, shaking his head. Laid-back, low in his chair, he decided it didn't matter. It was over for Ryder but Neil, poor devil, still had three or four more arduous years of medical school to go followed by his residency. In spite of all that, tonight Neil still had the look of a man with cause to celebrate. Along with everyone else in the bar—Ryder included—Neil suffered from end-of-semester fatigue. But that circumstance was eclipsed by the momentous event which has just transpired. Tonight, Neil had become a father.

"Twins! Jeez, Ryder, I still can't believe it!"

Ryder chuckled, watching Neil gulp more beer. "These things aren't supposed to be a surprise to a man in your profession, buddy. Seems to me pretty difficult to keep two five-and-a-half-pound babies a secret. Didn't you have just a tiny hint from Patti's size?"

Neil ran slightly shaky fingers through his hair and shook his head. "There aren't any twins in either family," he said, looking dazed. "I haven't figured out how it happened yet."

Ryder laughed outright, drawing curious stares their way. "If you really mean that," he said dryly, "then we're having a serious talk . . . soon." The waitress appeared, and he ordered a refill for Neil, but nothing for himself. At the rate Neil was going, he thought, one of them would have to be sober enough to drive. Still smiling, he lifted his empty glass along with one dark eyebrow and acknowledged Neil's next toast.

He stretched out his long legs and considered his friend's proud look. Something akin to envy stirred briefly, and then he shook his head. Either the beer or the profound nature of the day's event was beginning to get to him. Before a man started thinking like that, he needed a home and a wife, neither of which were in Ryder's immediate future plans.

"I'm a father," Neil said, still awed and slightly drunk. He peered earnestly at Ryder. "You know something, Ry? At first I worried that we'd sorta jumped the gun. Hell, I've still got half a dozen years of med school and residency to go, but, by God, I forgot all that when I looked at the twins."

Smiling faintly, Ryder said nothing. Neil was beginning to sound a little fuzzy, but what the hell. A man didn't become the father of twin sons every day.

Neil inched his chair a little closer and brought Ryder into clearer focus. "You'd make a wonderful fam'ly man, Ry. Hell, I wish we were celebratin' the same thing."

Ryder's grin flashed again. "I don't know, buddy. Twins are pretty heavy. I think I'll start out a little more conservatively. Besides, there aren't any genes for twins in my family that I know of." He caught the eye of the waitress and signaled for coffee. While Neil was still mobile, they'd better wrap this up. The hour wasn't too late—probably about ten—but they'd left the hospital at three in the afternoon and had been drinking every since.

Neil reared back and studied Ryder solemnly. "You may not have twins in your genes, my man, but you've still got exceptional genes."

Ryder made a rueful face. "And you ought to know, roomie."

Neil looked momentarily gratified. He lifted his glass again and saluted Ryder. "It was a fine thing you did, my man. I told you how long we searched for a good match for that guy and you were perfect in every way." He sat up straighter, blinking. "Did I ever tell you just how well you matched up with Ho—uh . . . um, with the father?"

"Neil, why don't we change the subject?" Ryder suggested, shifting uneasily in his chair. He looked around impatiently for the waitress. Where was his coffee? He was always slightly uncomfortable talking about this subject. He just couldn't think of his sperm in scientific terms.

Ryder hadn't had any real objection when the topic of artificial insemination had first been broached. At the time, Neil had been studying infertility and was participating in a university-sponsored project at a nearby clinic. He'd approached Ryder, then his roommate, with the idea of contributing sperm. Ryder, it appeared, was an exceptional match for a particular infertile couple. He had refused at first, but Neil had encouraged him to think of being a donor as a humanitarian deed. After weighing the pros and cons and his own conscience, Ryder found he had no real objection to assisting a couple so eager to have a child. Such a child would be part of a loving relationship, truly wanted. But he had never quite managed to adopt Neil's casually sophisticated attitude. And he damn sure didn't consider his sperm something to discuss at Baby's Bar.

Neil screwed up his face, thinking. "Not that the, ah...recipient was the man you are, buddy."

Ryder groaned. "Neil—"

Neil studied him with a kind of alcohol-induced detachment. "'Course the similarities were there...brown hair, sorta like yours, blue eyes kinda like yours. That is, they're blue, but not as...blue," he finished, at a loss. "As for height..." he laughed shortly and shook his head. "He wasn't as tall or as tough, but who the hell is? The best way I can describe it, he was a sorta...pale imitation of you, Ry."

Ryder reached for the coffee which had finally been placed in front of him. "Yeah, well, I'm glad I was able to oblige. Now, could we drop the subject, Neil?"

"About the only place you two are equal is—Whoa!" Beer sloshed over the rim of his glass onto the table. Conscientiously Neil mopped it up with the tiny bar napkin. "Is intellectually. The guy's a genius, Ry."

Resigned, Ryder rubbed a palm over his face and swallowed more black coffee. He was definitely going to be the one behind the wheel of Neil's Corvette when they finally got around to leaving. Seated, Neil was still okay, but once he tried to stand, or when he hit fresh air...Ryder shook his head.

Warming to his subject, Neil screwed up his face again, concentrating. "His bloodline, now. It's interesting, too.

He's from a very old family. Aris-to-cratic, you might say," Neil said, enunciating carefully.

Ryder rolled his eyes and decided it was time to go. He motioned to the waitress for the check. "Well, if that's the case, I'm surprised you guys at the clinic didn't throw out my contribution on a technicality, buddy."

Neil blinked and looked confused. "Whash that supposed to mean?"

Ryder stood up and tossed some bills onto the table. "Don't tell me you didn't notice the discrepancy in the subject's blood and my own." He shook his head and made a tsking sound. "I'm surprised it took, considering."

Neil struggled to his feet, frowning blearily. "Considering what, Ry? What're you talkin' about?"

Ryder grinned and wrapped an arm around him when it was obvious Neil's legs weren't cooperating. "You mean you didn't notice my blood was red and his was blue?"

Neil laughed loudly and hiccuped. He landed a playful punch on Ryder's shoulder and then slumped against his friend, who half carried him out of the bar. Neil continued to talk non-stop as Ryder struggled with him. "Nah, we didn't quibble over technicalities. Eyes and hair and brains and brawn seemed enough. Clay Holt better consider himself lucky that—"

Ryder looked startled. "Clay Holt? You mean the Holts of Mobile society? *The* Holts? That's who they gave my...uh, I mean, you're saying those people are going to be the parents?"

"Yessirree, they're the lucky ones," Neil said with satisfaction, stumbling a little. "And they're already parents. It's a boy!"

Ryder groaned again. "Hell, Neil, you weren't supposed to tell me that."

"Maybe I didn't really," Neil said, obviously addressing himself out loud. He leaned heavily against Ryder as they negotiated a path down the steps of the bar and through the parking lot.

"You did really," Ryder muttered beneath his breath, holding Neil upright. "But maybe you won't remember it in the morning." He propped Neil's dead weight against the passenger side of the sleek Corvette and put out his hand. He'd been right about fresh air. The proud new daddy was wiped out. "The keys," he demanded.

Obediently Neil dug in his jeans and pulled them out. Ryder took them and unlocked the car. "In you go, buddy."

Happily obliging, Neil crawled halfway in, then gave Ryder a happy smile when he bodily picked up his legs and stuffed them under the dash.

"Buckle up."

Hiccup. "Right."

Ryder slammed the door and stalked around the front of the car. As he was ready to pull out of the lot, he saw that Neil hadn't moved an inch. His seat-belt wasn't fastened and he seemed to be sleeping. Sighing, he leaned over and secured his friend.

"Thanks," Neil murmured, turning his head on the back of the seat to look at Ryder. "You're a great humanitarian, my ol' buddy, ol' pal."

"Don't mention it." The Corvette's three hundred horses roared to life.

Neil blinked gravely, his eyes on Ryder's profile. "No, I mean it. You helped that couple immensely."

"I was glad to do it," Ryder returned dryly.

"See," Neil said with satisfaction, "A great humanitarian. What'd I tell you?"

"I've got to get you home," Ryder muttered, turning out of the parking lot onto the street. "I hope you don't suffer brain damage. Patti would never forgive me."

He was barely a block from the apartment when Neil suddenly made an attempt to sit up. "Stop, Ry! We need to talk."

"No way am I stopping until I get you home, buddy," Ryder stated in a tone that was unmistakable even to a drunk. "But go ahead, talk anyway."

"I think the circumstances are such," he said, trying to sound stern, "that you should just forget that you are the natural father of Clay Holt's child."

Ryder threw him a wry glance. "Don't you worry, friend," he said grimly. "It's forgotten. It's history."

With great effort Neil kept himself upright as he considered Ryder's words solemnly, then nodded once. Bestowing a beatific smile on his friend, he relaxed in the luxurious depths of the Corvette's contoured seat.

After putting Neil to bed, Ryder prowled around the apartment feeling unsettled. *Too much coffee,* he decided, debating whether to just spend the night on Neil's couch or to go home. He turned the television on, flicking through all the channels before turning the set off. He wandered into the kitchen and checked the contents of the refrigerator. Nothing but rabbit food, he discovered, slamming the door with a disgusted mutter. Apparently Patti was still trying to reform Neil's eating habits. Finally he decided to go home even if it meant traveling on foot. He had his running shoes on, anyway. He went to the bedroom and checked Neil, who was passed out and snoring. No doubt exhausted from all that labor Patti went through, Ryder thought dryly. Daddy would pay for his celebration tomorrow with a world-class hangover. Shaking his head, he began turning out lights as he passed through the apartment heading for the door.

Outside, he checked the lock and stood a moment in the stillness of the spring night. The sky was clear and starlit. The beach was only a couple of blocks away, and the smell of the Gulf was heavy in the air. He swore softly but fervently, driving the fingers of one hand through his hair. Dammit! Why hadn't Neil kept his mouth shut? He didn't want to know the name of the couple.

The couple. That was the way he always thought of them. He never expected to know any details about them—certainly not their names! And that was the way it should be, the way he'd been assured it would be.

Ryder broke into a jog. His feet pounded rhythmically on the sidewalk, each stride on the hard concrete jarring him all the way to his teeth. He welcomed the distraction, hoping to push the events of the evening out of his mind. Until now he'd managed to convince himself that what he'd done was indeed a humanitarian act. Somehow, knowing the name of the couple and the sex of the child took the deed out of the altruistic never-never land where he'd mentally consigned it and made it all too real. Now he felt a stirring of curiosity, a sort of compelling interest in the lives of two people who, ordinarily, he would never have the slightest chance of meeting. At least in this life.

His laugh was short and humorless. No, in this life he'd never meet Clay Holt and his wife, whoever she was. His destiny and theirs were worlds apart. He thought of his interview with an international firm scheduled in just five days. If he got an offer, who knew where he would land—Saudi Arabia, Japan, Europe—the possibilities encompassed the whole free world. Meanwhile, the Clay Holts would stay in Mobile, Alabama, and enjoy a way of life almost extinct except in the Deep South, their little family complete.

He slowed suddenly as a new and good feeling stirred. Why was he having these second thoughts? His original reasons for donating to the clinic were unchanged. The only thing different was that he now knew the name of the couple, a couple who would otherwise have remained childless. Reflecting on his decision was a useless waste of time and energy. It couldn't be altered, and furthermore he discovered he had no desire to rewrite history. He was still confident the child would be loved and nurtured—probably even more than most. Smiling slightly, Ryder fixed his sights on a point high in the starry night. His own destiny was waiting.

CHAPTER ONE

LAUREN HOLT PAUSED a second with her palm on one panel of the massive double doors of the courtroom. She was dreading confronting the mob of reporters with their cameras and tape recorders on the other side. Maybe she should wait for Jake, she thought, frowning slightly, but she didn't think she could bear another moment inside the dark, oppressive chambers. When this ordeal was finally over—and please, God, she prayed, let it be over soon—she honestly didn't think she would ever enter a courtroom again. So far, all she'd ever heard from a judge was bad news.

Taking a deep breath, Lauren lifted her head and pushed the door open. She tensed, taking in the sea of bodies who turned as one toward her. Eyes straight ahead, her shoulders rigid, she moved forward, only dimly aware of the popping of flashbulbs and the intense light of a minicam zeroing in on her. There appeared to be dozens of reporters lying in wait for her. The questions were fired at her thick and fast.

"What was the judge's ruling today, Mrs. Holt?"

"Have you decided on your next move against NuTek-Niks?"

"Would you consider a settlement offer, Mrs. Holt?"

One overweight, rumpled reporter, chewing a repulsive cigar stub, shoved an expensive tape recorder in her face. "Are you ready to admit your husband was a lousy manager, Mrs. Holt?"

Lauren felt like crying. Instantly the firm hand of her attorney settled at her waist.

"No comment," Jake Levinson barked, shouldering aside a long-haired youth who was scribbling on a notepad. Jake turned Lauren so that his elbow struck the tape recorder and knocked it out of the hand of the fat reporter. "Sorry about that," he snapped, unaffected by the man's outraged reaction.

"Okay, let the lady through." Jake used his imposing height and a fierce look to part the crowd. To Lauren's relief he whisked her through the marble-floored foyer of the courthouse and down the steps without further delay.

Both were silent as they crossed the parking lot. Lauren matched her steps to Jake's and let him guide her to his car. He stopped at a dark green Mercedes. "You okay, hon?"

She inhaled a shaky breath. "I'm fine, Jake, just a little disappointed. In spite of everything, I'd counted on the judge seeing things our way."

Jake unlocked the door on the passenger side and seated her with the courtliness instilled in him by his Southern upbringing. Closing the door, he went around and got behind the wheel of the Mercedes. "We didn't provide enough evidence to convince him that Clay's designs were original. The attorneys for NuTekNiks argued that their engineers had been developing those procedures for a couple of years before Clay died."

"It's a lie, Jake. It's all lies. NuTekNiks pirated those designs from our company and I'm going to prove it somehow."

Jake started the car. "That's what it's going to take, Lauren—proof, solid evidence. Not a well-written brief stating our opinion that Clay's designs were ripped off, but proof from some source that they were so innovative nobody else could possibly have them."

Lauren sighed and rubbed her forehead. They'd played their last card by requesting the court to restrain NuTek-Niks from the use of the systems that Clay had designed, but they'd failed to present a convincing argument. She knew they hadn't failed because of any lack of expertise on Jake's part. But he could only work with the information she'd furnished him. And she could only give him what she had from the company's records, records that were sometimes spotty and incomplete. Only Clay Holt fully understood his designs. And Clay was dead. She'd been a widow for over a year.

"What are we going to do, Jake?" She looked at him, her amber eyes troubled.

Jake reached over and gave her hand a reassuring squeeze. "Don't worry about it right now, Lauren. Between the judge's ruling and that scene at the courthouse, you've had a trying morning. Why don't you lean back and try to relax while I drive you back to your office? There'll be time enough when we get there to rehash everything. We need a new game-plan."

"But what else can we do, Jake? We've already—"

Jake gave her hand a little shake. "Forget it for a few minutes, Lauren. Trust me, we've just begun to fight."

Unconvinced, but too frazzled to argue, Lauren subsided. She didn't want any more battles. She'd never been an aggressive person, even though it seemed that all she'd done since Clay's death was fight.

Her husband had been an engineer with special abilities. Singlehandedly he'd developed sophisticated robotic techniques that simplified and streamlined a variety of manufacturing tasks. After struggling on a shoestring, the Holt Company had just begun to reap the benefits of Clay's research and development. But immediately after his death, NuTekNiks, a rival firm, began marketing equipment using exclusive designs that could only have come from Clay's confidential records. Lauren was shocked when she finally recognized what was going on. Industrial espionage was an ugly possibility she'd never expected to have to consider.

And she probably never would have had to if Clay hadn't died. Her own position in the Holt Company had been restricted to marketing and public relations. She'd enjoyed her work, but much of her energy and time had been devoted to her role as a wife and mother. Upon Clay's death, the reins of the business fell into her hands. After an initial period of panic and insecurity, she'd quickly adjusted to her new responsibilities and had discovered the surprising steel in her backbone. She was absolutely determined to protect the legacy left to her by Clay, not for herself, but for their son, Justin.

Again, Lauren was swamped with the familiar sense of pain and loss. Clay had been her best friend in all the world. Their relationship had been rich in so many ways. They'd come from the same social background, enjoyed the same friends, politics, music and books. Both had been born to old, once-monied Alabama families. Lately, however, the Holts and the Buchanans were rich only in tradition rather than wealth, a circumstance that didn't bother either Clay or Lauren. In fact Clay had often joked about it. All he'd really cared about had been Lauren and Justin and his work. In that order. A pang struck her heart. *Oh, Clay, I miss you so much.*

"Here we are," Jake said, pulling the Mercedes into the curved driveway of the Holt Company's front office.

Lauren uncrossed her legs and was opening the door to get out before Jake reached her. Smoothing her skirt down over her knees, she stood up, then passed one hand over the sleek fall of her hair and squared her shoulders. Her face reflected none of the uncertainty and fear she felt, as she fell into step beside Jake. Her people would have heard about this latest setback. When she went into her office, she didn't want to alarm them. Already the notoriety of the situation had given birth to a spate of rumors, which was understandable; three hundred employees were dependent on a successful resolution of the whole mess.

As they entered, Cheryl Biggs, Lauren's secretary, was chatting with a young receptionist. Both women looked up questioningly, but from Lauren's expression no one could tell how grateful she felt at the feel of Jake's firm grip on her elbow. She forced a confident smile and made her way down the hall, greeting the employees she met, heading straight for the sanctuary of her own office.

Turning the corner, she nearly collided with Michael Armstead, the plant's general manager. His clerk, Jimmy Johns, was with him. Michael was a tall, slightly built blonde with a pencil-thin mustache and a ready smile. Sometimes a little too ready, it seemed to Lauren. Then she chastised herself for the uncharitable thought. She didn't have to love Michael, she reminded herself. As the former chief of sales, he had done a super job. In fact the company's phenomenal growth of the past two years was due as much to Michael's salesmanship as to Clay's creative genius. No, she didn't have to love him, but she did know his value to the company and she appreciated it.

"Hello, Michael…Jimmy." She nodded politely to both men.

"Morning, Lauren." Armstead's pale blue gaze rested for just an instant on her breasts before he smiled into her eyes. "How did it go in court this morning?"

"Not well, I'm afraid."

"Anything I can do?" he asked sympathetically. Michael divided a look between Jake and Lauren. "Technical input, that sort of thing?"

Jake touched Lauren's arm to ease her away. "We'll keep that in mind, Armstead," he said, allowing Lauren to precede him into her office. He followed her inside and closed the door firmly.

Armstead stood for a moment studying the pattern on the door of Lauren's office, his eyes cold and hard. He reached into his pocket for a cigarette.

"Looks like the pretty lady doesn't need you anymore, boss." Jimmy Johns's knowing cynicism grated.

"She needs me, Jimmy." The sound of Michael's lighter was loud in the silence of the corridor. He inhaled deeply. "She needs me all right. She just doesn't know how much yet."

Jimmy glanced at the other man's hard features. "You ain't afraid that fancy lawyer'll upset your plans?"

Impatiently Armstead released a stream of smoke. "Nah, he's just doing his job. Things keep going from bad to worse around here, but Levinson doesn't know jack about the inner workings of the plant, so he can't help her." Smiling faintly he gazed at the glowing tip of his cigarette. "But I can. She'll turn to me because I'm all she's got."

Johns simply stared, impressed as much by his boss's audacity as by his arrogant self-confidence.

"And then—" Armstead's tone softened and his pale eyes took on an avaricious gleam "—I'll have it all right here in the palm of my hand, Jimmy-boy." He slapped Johns on the shoulder, and laughing together, they headed on down the corridor.

In her office Lauren went to her desk and sank into the chair that Clay had once occupied. She linked her hands together to keep them from shaking and looked up at Jake. "Okay, coach, what's the new game plan?" she inquired.

Jake seated himself opposite her. "We've got a major problem here, Lauren. The next time we go into court, we've got to have an expert witness whose credentials can't be questioned. It must be somebody who can state from a position of authority that Clay's designs were original state-of-the-art innovations in the use of robotics—designs that NuTekNiks couldn't possibly have formulated on their own.''

Lauren laughed shortly and waved the fingers of one hand. "Sure, no problem. We'll just put an ad in the paper.''

"Well, not exactly." Smiling, he shifted in his chair and propped one ankle on the opposite knee. "Actually we're in luck for once in the matter of the expert, Lauren.''

Lauren gave him a puzzled look. "How, Jake? We haven't had any kind of luck except bad so far in this whole fiasco.''

The lawyer leaned forward and Lauren sensed a sort of restrained excitement in him. "Lauren, does the name Ryder Braden ring a bell?" Without waiting for a reply, Jake continued. "It was about five years ago. That was when you met him, I think. At a New Year's Eve Party. Do you remember? You and Clay went with Clare and me.''

"What?" Lauren said, momentarily thrown off track. As close as their friendship was, Jake *never* mentioned his ex-wife.

"A New Year's Eve party, five or six years ago," Jake repeated patiently. "Ryder Braden was there with Neil and Patti Putnam. He and Neil and I went to high school together and then he and Neil went on to college. They were roommates at Alabama. Anyway, Ryder graduated as an electrical engineer and was recruited by half a dozen companies. He went with a big international firm and his career took off like a rocket.''

Lauren leaned back slowly in her chair. "And just exactly how does all this tie in with our problem?''

"He's a manufacturing expert and he's been in on the ground floor in the use of robotics since the concept was first introduced." He stared at her. "Do you remember him?"

"I remember him," Lauren said cautiously.

Jake hesitated at something in her tone, then went on. "Yeah. Well anyway, lucky for us he's still in town, has been for two or three months. Could be he's between assignments right now."

"Oh, Jake, do you really think he's the man we need?" Lauren stood up suddenly and walked to the window looking doubtful.

"Believe me," Jake said firmly, "he's an engineering expert with an impressive background in high-tech manufacturing. He'll be very convincing to a judge. Ryder's particular brand of expertise is exactly what we need at this point."

"I don't know, Jake."

"You don't know? What the hell does that mean? People with experience in robotics aren't exactly growing on trees, in case you haven't noticed, Lauren."

Lauren wondered how to explain. She was going to sound like an idiot. She remembered Ryder Braden all right. Vividly. She also remembered that New Year's Eve party.

Lord, was it five years ago? Lauren stared out of the window, blind to the lacy pink beauty of a crepe myrtle directly in her line of vision. Braden must have been "between assignments" then, too. He'd been the star topic of conversation at that party, she recalled. He and Jake had been old friends and Jake apparently still thought highly of him, because he'd certainly grabbed the first opportunity to introduce him to Clay and her. Apparently everybody else in their crowd already knew him. Lauren, however, had al-

ready noticed him. Somehow Braden was the type of man
who stood out, even in a crowd.

When Jake made the introductions she'd sensed a certain
something in his cool acknowledgment as he'd looked into
her eyes. When they danced—only once—he'd seemed literally wired with tension. He'd held her like a live coal and
had been unresponsive to her efforts to make friendly conversation. When the music stopped, he'd walked her back
to the table with almost indecent haste. She'd never seen him
again.

For some reason that experience with Braden had been
one that had stuck in her mind, a little glitch in her memory bank. It was like a close call on the expressway or a
particularly embarrassing moment that one would dearly
love to forget. The trouble was, Braden wasn't easily forgotten. Just the opposite. Lauren flicked the drapes with her
fingertips and sighed. Jake seemed confident, but personally she wasn't going to count on Braden coming to her rescue.

She bent her head and kneaded her temples where a tiny
ache nagged. She felt Jake waiting and inhaled deeply. "I
don't think you should count on Braden's cooperation too
much, Jake."

He searched her face, frowning. "Why not?"

"This is going to sound stupid, but..." She looked at
him. "Have you spoken to him yet?"

"Not yet, but—"

"I hope he doesn't remember me."

Jake looked startled. "Doesn't remember you? What—"

"I only met him that one time, but for some reason I felt
that he...well, that he..."

"That he...what?"

"I told you, this sounds ridiculous, but I got the strong-
est feeling that the man disliked me."

Jake looked at her. "He disliked you.... Five years ago you met a man once and you think he disliked you on sight?"

"I told you it sounded stupid."

Jake arched his black brows but said nothing.

Lauren sank back into her chair. "Everybody left the table and it was just the two of us. He had to ask me to dance and he acted as if I was Typhoid Mary."

"It must have been your imagination, Lauren. You're a beautiful woman. No man with half his hormones in working order could be indifferent to you. And believe me," Jake added dryly, "all Ryder's hormones are in excellent shape."

Lauren was unconvinced. "I didn't expect you to believe me, but I still remember it, even after all these years. I even mentioned it to Clay that night after we got home, and he brushed it aside, too."

"With good reason," Jake said, standing up suddenly. "I assume, then, that you haven't any real objections to my contacting Braden to sound him out?"

"Well..."

"We need him, Lauren."

"In the words of your own profession, Jake," she said with her usual good humor, "I think the question may be moot. The man's going to refuse."

THE TELEPHONE WAS into the ninth ring before Ryder Braden managed to climb down from the roof and drop onto the white pine boards of the porch. He moved quickly across the new floor, to the open window where he'd placed the phone. The sound was a jarring intrusion into the peaceful atmosphere of the old place. A few more months of nothing but his own company and he'd turn into a real hermit, he decided as he picked up the receiver.

"Hello?"

"Ryder?"

He shifted his weight onto one leg and squinted across the yard to the dappled shade under a pecan tree. "Yeah, who is this?"

"It's Jake Levinson, Ryder. How the hell are you, man?"

"Not bad, not bad. How 'bout yourself, Jake?"

"Fine. Still working on my first million."

"Hell, I thought you'd passed that point the last time I was home."

"Not quite." Jake paused a second. "I ran into Neil Putnam and he told me you were in town and that you'd lost your grandmother. I was sorry to hear that."

"Yeah, thanks. I'm going to miss her." Ryder could hear the creak as Jake leaned back in his chair.

"I never eat seafood gumbo that I don't think of her, you know that? Mama Jane sure had a way with shrimp. I remember how she'd feed about half a dozen of us after football practice and never complain." He fell silent remembering. "She was one sweet lady."

Ryder nodded. "She was that," he said huskily.

Jake cleared his throat. "So, I guess you're knocking around that big old house looking for something to do."

"I'm knocking around all right, but I'm sure not looking for something to do," Ryder said, eyeing the pile of old roofing shingles that had taken him two days to remove. "I've been doing some work on the house."

"Getting it in shape to sell, huh?"

"I don't know, Jake. Maybe, maybe not."

"Are you serious? You haven't got anything pressing in some far-off corner of the manufacturing world?"

Ryder eased down onto the windowsill and crossed his legs in front of him. "Not yet. I guess you could say I'm sort of on sabbatical."

Jake was silent a second or two. "In that case, this could be my lucky day. You suppose I could persuade you to take on a project here?"

Ryder swatted at a mosquito. "What kind of project? I didn't know you legal eagles were into high-tech manufacturing."

"I'm not, but a client of mine is and we need an expert witness before the next court date. We couldn't ask for anybody better qualified than you, Ryder. It's a great stroke of luck that you happen to be in town," Jake said with genuine feeling. "And it's about time Lauren got a break."

"Who?" Ryder had picked up a towel and was wiping sweat off his face and neck.

"Lauren Holt. You met her and Clay, her husband, about five years ago. He designed some pretty sophisticated robotics which you might be familiar with in your line of work."

Ryder went still, one hand on the towel. "Holt," he repeated.

"Yeah," Jake said, encouraged, since Ryder hadn't refused outright. "Clay was killed about a year ago in an accident at the plant. Lauren's had her hands full trying to hold everything together."

"Clay Holt is dead?" Ryder repeated blankly.

"Right, and his designs have been pirated by a rival firm, NuTekNiks. You haven't got any connections to them, have you?"

"No." Ryder absently smoothed a hand over his chest, his blue eyes fixed on the tips of his worn Nikes.

"Ryder? You still there, Ryder?"

"Uh, yeah. I'm still here."

"So, whadda ya say? Think you can take on a little project like this? It'll be a piece of cake for you, Ryder, but to Lauren it may mean the difference between keeping her company in one piece or losing everything to a bunch of thieves."

"I don't think so, Jake. It's like I said, I'm not locked into another assignment yet, and I don't think I want to be right now. The old place got run down these past few years and I've been spending a lot of time on it. I—"

"Ryder," Jake broke in, "we're not talking about a simple medical malpractice suit where I can call in any doctor as an expert. Not a hell of a lot of people know anything about robotics. Lauren's predicament is unique. You won't find a more astute businesswoman, either, considering the way she's had to pick up and keep going in a very sophisticated environment." He paused a moment before adding, "She's a great gal, Ryder."

"Look, Jake..." Ryder rubbed the towel across his face. "I'm sure Mrs. Holt is everything you say, but I'm just not the man for the job. Tell you what, I know some top-notch robotics people. They'll do a good job for you."

"But they're not right here in town, Ryder," Jake pointed out. "We'd have to fly them in, maybe more than once, put them up, pay them expenses. They'd cost an arm and a leg and Lauren just doesn't have it."

Ryder narrowed his eyes. "Is she in financial difficulty?"

"Well, yeah, didn't I mention that? With the rights to the designs on the street, her company's being screwed out of thousands in royalties."

"I don't know, Jake—"

"That's for sure, Ryder," Jake put in quickly. "You really don't understand what Lauren's going through. It isn't just the company's problems and the weight of knowing all her employees are counting on her. On top of all that, the case has become a media circus. I guess there's something about her and the situation Clay left her in that fascinates the public. Every little ripple in the case is splashed on the front page or aired on the evening news. Like today, for instance..."

"Today?"

"Yeah, the press was waiting for her outside the court-room. I had to strongarm our way through; all the while they're yelling questions at her, some of them in pretty bad taste, I can tell you." He paused. "Well, hell, you can judge for yourself. Turn on the news tonight. You'll see."

Ryder's fingers flexed on the receiver. "It's really that bad, Jake?"

"It's that bad. She needs you, Ryder."

Ryder took a deep breath, wrestling with a multitude of thoughts that would have astonished his old friend if Jake had had an inkling as to what he was asking.

"Look, don't give me a definite answer right now," Jake said, shrewdly backing off. "Lauren's pretty strung out over this last setback. I wanted to give her the weekend to put the whole thing out of her mind, so I set our next appointment for Monday morning." He hesitated. "How does this sound, Ryder? Just meet her, get a fix on the problems she's up against, get a fix on Lauren herself. Then if you still feel reluctant, I'll understand."

"I'm telling you, don't get your hopes up, Jake."

"I hear you," Jake said amiably. "But Lauren Holt is a special lady, Ryder. You'll see."

Right up until a minute before six o'clock, Ryder planned to skip the evening news. It didn't take any special insight to figure out why, either, he thought, as he paced restlessly around his grandmother's outdated kitchen. He did not trust himself to see Lauren Holt's face again, not even on television. Once had been more than enough and even though it was over five years, he could still envision her with crystal clarity.

Damn it to hell! Why did Neil have to tell him? He raked a frustrated palm against the back of his neck, barely aware of the tense pain deep in his muscles. For the thousandth time, he cursed that night fourteen years ago when Neil had breached the confidentiality of the medical program. Now the woman was widowed and in trouble. And, heaven help him, Jake wanted him to be the one to run to her rescue. Ryder groaned and stared at the blank screen of the television. He'd never dreamed he'd be faced with a situation like this. He did not want to get mixed up with Lauren Holt. Even the most superficial association with her could become extremely complicated. Damn Jake for destroying his peace!

Almost as though someone else pulled the strings to manipulate his body, Ryder took a step forward and bent over to turn the set on. The Middle East and Washington politics took up the first ten minutes of the newscast. Bored, Ryder helped himself to a beer and sat down, crossing his legs in front of him. He was popping the tab when the words of the anchorman brought him straight up in his chair.

"We'll be right back with the latest wrinkle in a local woman's attempt to challenge a company she claims has ripped off of her dead husband's ideas," the newsman said. "Stay tuned."

With a sense of fate Ryder put his beer down and fixed his eyes on the screen. Impatiently, he endured sixty seconds of commercials. Then Lauren's face appeared and the muscles in his stomach tensed. The minicam followed her leaving the courtroom, catching every nuance of expression on her beautiful face. He sucked in a quick breath and watched her instantly besieged by a knot of reporters. *Jake should be with her,* Ryder thought with sudden concern, feeling an unusual sense of outrage at the reporters' callousness.

"What was the judge's ruling..."

"...your next move against NuTekNiks?"

"...settlement offer..."

"Mrs. Holt—"

"Lauren—"

In the chaos and distortion from the microphones, Ryder couldn't hear the demands of the media clearly, but Lauren's distress was obvious. In the artificial lighting of the minicam, her expression appeared vulnerable, he thought, staring intently at her. Why had Jake allowed her to face the press alone?

"Are you ready to admit your husband was a lousy manager, Mrs. Holt?"

When he heard the question, Ryder was surprised at the depth of his anger on her behalf. Was nothing sacred to those vultures? He watched her as she fixed her gaze straight ahead and attempted to make her way through the maze of bodies and journalistic paraphernalia. Suddenly one reporter elbowed aside his colleagues and thrust a microphone in her face. Lauren put out an unsteady hand to fend him off. Some emotion, something deep and elemental, flared in Ryder. Abruptly, he got to his feet to pace the length of the room, keeping an eye on the television screen.

"Where the hell is Jake?" he muttered, agitated. Then, to his relief, Jake's tall spare frame materialized at Lauren's side and began to sweep her through the crowd.

With swift strides Ryder reached the television and snapped it off. He gazed around the kitchen feeling a host of unfamiliar conflicting emotions. He cursed Jake for calling him and laying this burden on him. He damned Neil Putnam for his indiscretion fourteen years ago. He railed at fate for the uncanny trick it had played on him. The woman was not his responsibility, he told himself. Jake could find another expert. Then he remembered Lauren's circumstances and muttered an obscenity. Between her and Jake

Levinson, they probably knew everybody in the state of Alabama who was anybody. Someone would come through for her.

The old screen door banged behind him unnoticed. He went to the edge of the porch and propped an arm on one solid heart-pine support. He groaned, wiping a hand over his face, and stared blindly into the night. He didn't want this.

Without warning Lauren Holt's classic features swam into focus, and on the heels of that another image tantalized him, one that was never very substantial, one that Ryder never allowed himself to dwell on.

The boy. His son.

He had no responsibility in this situation, Ryder told himself again fiercely. There was no shame in what he did all those years ago. The act placed no obligation on him. Only through a twist of fate was he even aware of any connection to this woman and her child. He should just pack up and leave town. Right now. Today. Everyone would be better off even though he might be the only one who knew that. He pushed away from the stout column with a motion that was slightly savage. Definitely the smart thing to do was just to forget this.

But how could a man forget his own son?

A FEW MILES AWAY, at the Holt plant, another man sat patiently at his desk waiting as the activity signaling the end of the work day slowed and then stopped altogether. When there was only silence, he looked at his watch. Six-fifteen. He would have plenty of time. She was only half an hour away.

He got up slowly and made his way to the bank of files against the far wall. The drawer opened quietly, but his own anxiety magnified the sound in his ears. With a quick, furtive look around, he began riffling through the plans and specifications until he found what he was looking for. Bending, he squinted at the color-coded tab and then straightened with a grunt. Mislabeled, as he'd known it would be. As he'd made certain it would be. He pulled out a set of prints and folded them into a neat square before slipping them under his jacket, making sure they were secure. It would never do to have them fall out as he was leaving the plant. No, that would never do.

He closed the drawer after making sure nothing appeared out of order, and then glanced at his watch. He had thirty minutes before he was due to meet her. For a moment he was still, his gaze unfocused. His hand unconsciously sought the plans folded tightly, securely, against his heart. Surely this would satisfy them. Surely this would be the last time.

Daydreaming of Anna, he left the building.

CHAPTER TWO

THE OFFICES OF Levinson, Rayne and Javits were carefully designed around three ancient live oaks. Natural cypress siding and the lavish use of smoked glass enhanced the rustic effect. Inside, no expense had been spared to create an atmosphere of confidence and comfort. The window where Lauren stood served as a frame for a shaded courtyard dominated by one of the moss-draped oaks. But the view was wasted on her, and the expensive decor failed to reassure her. She wrapped her arms around her middle and turned to Jake.

"I spent the weekend sorting through Clay's records trying to uncover something that might buy us a little more time, Jake, but I drew a blank." She gave her lawyer a bleak smile. "I know it sounds incredible. Clay was so special, a creative genius, but he apparently kept very little documentation. You'd think a scientist would be more conscientious about that sort of thing."

Jake rubbed a hand over his chin, silently acknowledging the truth in Lauren's statement. Why the hell had Clay been so cavalier about safeguarding his work? No man expected to die, of course, but with the prudent instincts of a lawyer, Jake couldn't help feeling put out with Clay for failing to secure the future of his wife and son, even if he was the proverbial absentminded scientist. His gaze was troubled as he studied Lauren. Her composure seemed far too fragile this morning. She'd shown extraordinary courage and strength so far, but weeks of unrelenting stress were telling on her.

She turned, plunging her hands deep into the pockets of her skirt. "So, did you have any luck contacting Mr. Braden?"

"I called him and filled him in on the situation," Jake said, wondering how to tell her that he'd struck out with Ryder.

"He refused, didn't he?"

Jake shook his head wryly. "I'll be honest, babe. He wasn't exactly eager."

Lauren's expression revealed nothing as she absorbed the news. She would not have to deal with Braden after all. She immediately dismissed the curious little pang of... something. Certainly not disappointment, she told herself.

"Well, I'm hardly surprised," she said.

Jake leaned back in his chair, his disappointment plain. "Hmm, it looks as though you read the situation correctly. He didn't give me a definite no when we talked, but since he hasn't shown up, I guess we'd better regroup." Jake glanced at the digital clock on his desk. "It's unfortunate. With his practical experience he would have made us a first-class expert. Here's a partial listing of his credentials." He pushed a paper across to her.

Lauren looked it over. "Surely there are others?"

"Well, yes. Ryder mentioned he'd give me the names of some qualified people. It'll take a little time, but..."

"But what, Jake?" Lauren asked just as the intercom sounded on the desk.

Jake lifted one hand to stay her, then answered the summons. After a couple of quick questions, he stood up and motioned toward a thermos decanter on a credenza against the wall. "Have some coffee while I take this call. It's confidential—No, no, don't get up." He waved Lauren back into her chair as she began to rise. "I'll take it in the other office. You wait right here. We've still got to map out some strategy. Back in a minute, I promise."

Lauren's brief smile faded as Jake disappeared. She was frightened. This morning, alone in the bedroom she'd shared with Clay, she'd faced up to the very real possibility that she might lose the company. She might not be able to ensure Justin's future, let alone banish the uncertainties of the three hundred employees who were counting on her.

Blindly she stared out the window to the courtyard, feeling none of the peace and satisfaction that the sight of the ancient, massive oaks usually produced. Wearily she kneaded the back of her neck. How long since she'd felt truly at peace? Lately time was measured in the number of days or weeks before some new disaster. Fatigue and the ugly reality of her situation washed over her and she felt the sting of tears behind her eyes.

RYDER HAD NO TROUBLE locating Jake's office. He reached the door and stopped, his palm flat against the sun-warmed surface, unable to explain the compulsion that had brought him this far, overruling his better judgment. One hand went to his sunglasses. He pulled them off and slipped them into his breast pocket. He could feel his heart thudding in his chest. He was as nervous as a boy on his first date. Again he realized the irrevocability of this meeting. He'd done some foolish and impetuous things in his time, but nothing to compare with this. He drew a deep breath and then pushed the door open.

Inside he was directed to Jake's office by a fresh-faced receptionist. The door was open. Ryder's gaze flicked over the unoccupied desk, going directly to the solitary figure at the window. It was Lauren Holt. Deliberately he studied her.

Her pale gold hair was caught up and secured with a tortoiseshell comb, but several silky tendrils had escaped, giving her a slightly disheveled look. He frowned. He hadn't thought her the type to have a hair out of place.

She was simply staring out the window, shoulders slightly drooping. As he watched she brought one hand up and wiped at her cheek. It was then he realized that she was crying. Her cheeks were wet with tears even though she wasn't making a sound. Ryder's breath caught in his throat. Something about her weeping silently, alone, touched off a feeling that was both unfamiliar and disturbing. He had to consciously restrain himself from going to her. Where the hell was Jake?

His expression gentled as she suddenly drew in a deep breath and squared her shoulders. Sniffing, she wiped her cheeks with the heels of both palms. Ryder backed away from the door, his expression thoughtful. The last thing he'd expected to see was a vulnerable Lauren Holt giving in to a moment of despair. Her emotional reaction just didn't fit in with the way he thought of her—always composed, slightly aloof, more than capable of handling the stress in her world. He leaned against the wall, intrigued with his discovery.

A picture of Lauren's expression as she'd tried to fend off the reporters flashed in his mind, followed by a surge of protectiveness. Ruthlessly he closed off the feeling. He was not going to get personally involved with this woman. If his professional expertise could be helpful, fine—so be it. But that was where he drew the line. He wasn't even totally convinced that Lauren Holt needed him, no matter what Jake said.

So why am I here? he asked himself for the tenth time.

"Ryder! I'd just about given you up," Jake said, appearing from the opposite end of the hall. He put out his hand, grinning. "What are you doing out here propping up my wall? Come in, Lauren's already here.'' The attorney stepped to the open door and motioned Ryder inside.

Ryder tensed with anticipation at the prospect of once again facing Lauren Holt. In his travels he'd dined with royalty and parleyed with men who wielded enough power to change the destiny of nations, but he couldn't remember ever feeling quite this way.

Television didn't do her justice, he decided, looking at her closely. His recollection of her from that brief encounter five years before had always been colored by forbidden emotion. Her eyes were a pale, gold brown, fringed with long, dark, lush lashes; her features even; her makeup subtle. He wondered why she even needed it when her skin had the flawless look of magnolias. Except for a soft, vulnerable look to her mouth, he could detect no hint of whatever emotion had made her weep.

Jake made his way toward the credenza and the coffee carafe. "You remember Lauren, Ryder.''

"Hello, Mr. Braden,'' she said in a low, husky voice. She extended her hand.

Ryder took it, bracing against the allure of that voice, determined not to be affected by it or the slight tremor he felt in her hand. "Mrs. Holt,'' he responded with a brief nod of his dark head, wondering at the clear, cold clarity of her eyes. He glanced at Jake, whose black eyebrows went up blandly before bringing his attention back to Lauren.

"Here we go,'' Jake said with determined cheerfulness, pouring coffee and offering it to Ryder. "Hot and black, Ryder. Unless you have a taste for something stronger?''

Ryder shook his head, managing to tear his gaze away from Lauren's face long enough to accept the coffee, then move to the chair Jake indicated. He waited for Lauren to sit first.

"Lauren's familiar with your professional background, Ryder," Jake said, leaning back and smiling at them. "Our case is more or less stymied unless we can convince the court of the originality of Clay's designs. I've assured Lauren that you're the man for the job."

Lauren met the look Braden sent her head-on, braced for more of the brusque, almost rude treatment he'd subjected her to the only other time they'd met. She still smarted a little from that, she realized with a start. She recalled feeling somewhat testy about it at the time. Now, she ran a dubious eye over his ancient Nikes and well-worn jeans. Even five years later, something about him still definitely put her back up.

His hair was a dark tobacco brown, thick and crisp looking, just a little too long. Sunglasses were casually anchored in the pocket of a white pullover, a color that emphasized his deep tan and the startling effect of his eyes. She gazed into them, expecting a conventional brown. Instead, she found them to be a deep, dark blue. His face was rugged and angular with high cheekbones and a strong chin. He had a tiny scar at the edge of one dark eyebrow. All in all, his features were too harsh for him to be considered handsome in the conventional sense of the word. His mouth, in contrast, was oddly sensual.

"Take a look at this," Jake said.

Ryder leaned lazily forward to accept the papers Jake handed him, and she caught the scent of soap and warm-blooded male. Ryder Braden might look laid-back and slightly worn around the edges, but he also looked powerfully, uncompromisingly masculine. Dangerous. Unconsciously she wrapped her arms around her middle.

Averting her gaze, Lauren edged back into her chair, feeling slightly stunned by her reaction to him. It had never occurred to her that she would be aware of him as a man.

She thought about it, then decided it shouldn't surprise her that his appeal extended to women as well as men. Even Jake and his circle of friends—whom she considered sophisticated and discriminating for the most part—had reacted like starstruck boys, recounting Braden's exploits. She glanced at him, sprawled in the chair looking too confident, too at ease in the restrained decor of Jake's office. She felt certain that a law office in Mobile, Alabama, was as far removed from Braden's usual habitat as a zoo would be to a panther. He hadn't gotten that teak-dark tan behind a desk, that was for sure.

Was it safe to place the company's secrets in this man's hands? Her mouth compressed with sudden doubt. With that question in mind, Lauren concentrated on Jake's words as he briefed Braden on the status of their case.

Ten minutes later she had to admit that the man knew high-tech engineering. But still, when Jake sent a questioning look her way, she could not give him the nod of approval he sought. Seeing her uncertainty, Jake confined himself to a discussion of a few problems he was having with some of the technical aspects of the case. Ryder's responses were concise and knowledgeable. Lauren decided that though he might drift from job to job, he seemed to be an expert, overall.

Lauren wondered about his personal life. Why was he still lingering in Mobile? According to Jake, it had been more than three months since his grandmother's funeral. She frowned, thinking back to something Jake had said. Wasn't he living in a ramshackle old house he'd inherited from his grandmother? It sounded as though he hadn't had enough self-discipline to manage the huge salaries he must have earned in the past dozen years if Jake's glowing professional assessment was to be believed.

Her thoughts were interrupted by the sound of Jake's intercom. After a quick word he stood up. "Another urgent call which I can take across the hall. You two have more in common than most of my clients," he added with total disregard for the fact that neither of the two people in front of him had spoken over two words to the other, "so I won't worry about leaving you alone together."

In the wake of Jake's departure, total silence filled the office. Ryder tossed the yellow notepad on the desk, his mouth twisted with the irony of the lawyer's casual remark. Purposely he hadn't allowed himself to think of what he and Lauren Holt *did* have in common. The moment he'd looked into those unique eyes, he'd felt the compelling connection pulling at him. Suddenly Lauren Holt was not just an appealing woman beset by a tangle of legal circumstances. And she was definitely not some unnamed female who'd received his sperm in some clinic. She was suddenly a very real, live, breathing woman whose destiny was linked with his whether he wished it or not.

He leaned back, extending his long legs and crossing his feet, his dark gaze intent upon her. For a woman who needed his expertise, she certainly wasn't going out of her way to charm him. He wasn't sure what he'd expected, but it wasn't this cool, deliberate assessment. It was as though he was a bug under glass. Had she taken a dislike to him? Feeling strangely affronted, he reminded himself that she needed him, not the other way around.

Rejection was a unique experience for Ryder, and under the circumstances, he could almost see the humor in the situation. Almost. But not quite. He was too aware of her— her subtle perfume, the near-perfection of her feminine shape, the sleek, satiny look of her skin. He was suddenly very curious about her reasons for choosing a clinical pregnancy.

"I suppose you've done this sort of thing often, Mr. Braden."

Startled, his eyes locked with hers. It took him a second to realize their thoughts were on different wavelengths. She was sitting very straight, her gaze clear and steady. "You mean the expert witness thing?"

Her mouth compressed with impatience. "What else?"

"I've done it a few times."

She inhaled deeply. "I understand you're a native of Mobile."

He withdrew his gaze from her long shapely legs. "Yeah, Alabama born and bred, like the song says."

She looked blank.

"It's a country song, Mrs. Holt," he drawled.

"Oh, I see."

She didn't, he knew. "Do you get back often?"

He stared intently into her eyes, intrigued by the way she had of looking at him while at the same time keeping him at a distance. It was almost as if a brick wall stood between them. "Not as often as I would've liked in the past few years," he told her.

"Your work must take you all over."

"I just wrapped up a job in Japan."

"How interesting," she remarked, managing to make it seem just the opposite. "Troubleshooting, didn't Jake say? How did you drift into that?"

Ryder stared into her beautiful eyes a beat or two, absorbing the subtle insult, watching as she had the good grace to color faintly. He couldn't remember when he'd been put down quite so ruthlessly, that is, without bleeding a little at the same time. This lady wasn't going to have any difficulty holding her own with the sharks who were trying to steal her precious husband's designs, he decided, torn between irritation and admiration. Jake must be totally dazzled by the genteel look of her to think anything else. If he hadn't seen her crying . . .

"I . . . ah . . ." She cleared her throat delicately. "I didn't mean that the way it sounded," she said.

"No kidding?" One dark brow arched skeptically. "Actually, instead of focusing directly on a single element, the bulk of my work for the past couple of years seemed to be getting the bugs out of my clients' operations. I guess I did, as you say, sort of drift into it."

"Would I recognize any of your clients?"

"It's possible."

When he didn't elaborate, she made a clicking noise with her tongue. "Well?"

"Jake has a list somewhere."

"Which *you* conveniently furnished."

His eyes narrowed. "Are you suggesting I lied?"

Lauren's gaze slipped from his. "No, of course not."

"Well, what then?"

"I just meant—"

He was still a second, waiting, before getting up out of his chair. "Look, maybe this whole thing is a bad idea. I guess you have a right to be suspicious of people considering what you've been through since your husband died. But I didn't volunteer for this, Mrs. Holt. Jake called me." He moved to place his coffee cup on the credenza, then straightened, pinning her to her chair with a look. "Or did you forget that?"

Disconcerted, Lauren could think of no ready reply. Then, fortunately, she didn't have to because Jake chose that moment to return.

"Okay, gang, ready to talk turkey?" He went directly to his chair, but when he glanced at the two faces before him, his smile faltered.

"I don't think Mrs. Holt is desperate enough to need me, Jake," Ryder said, reaching for his sunglasses. He shot her a piercing look. "Or maybe my credentials don't impress her. Whatever. I'll be seeing you around, buddy." He put on the sunglasses and, without glancing toward Lauren again, walked out.

Jake turned to her slowly, his eyebrows lifted in silent query.

"Please, Jake, not just now, okay?" The words came out low and slightly uneven. She stood up and set her coffee cup on the tray, hoping the tremor in her hands would go unnoticed by her sharp-eyed lawyer. Setting the strap of her bag on her shoulder, she walked quickly to the door. "Let me know when the next disaster occurs."

HOURS LATER, BACK at the old house, Ryder was still smarting from the encounter with Lauren in Jake's office. Standing in the middle of Mama Jane's outdated kitchen, he chewed thoughtfully on his bottom lip and wondered why. He reminded himself that he'd been reluctant to get involved in her affairs in the first place. But, hell, that was a dead issue now. She obviously didn't have any intention of retaining him even though she had been impressed with his professional know-how. He knew that; he'd felt it as they talked. No, the problem was something personal. He felt that, too.

He stalked out of the house, slamming the screen door, and stood on the porch, his hand clamped at the back of his neck. Why did he care anyway? He had absolutely no obligation to assist her even if he was, by a strange quirk of fate, eminently qualified. He had made a respectable effort, and she had done everything except throw his offer back in his face. His duty was done.

Ryder stripped off his shirt and slung it over the porch rail. His body demanded physical release for the tension that was eating at him. He'd been tied in knots from the first moment he'd looked into her frosty, amber eyes. Now was the perfect time to rip out that section of the porch roof. He'd been thinking about it long enough. The old house could keep ten men busy. His renovation efforts had been on-going for months now with no end in sight.

Frustration and some other emotion he was unwilling to examine drove him to attack the porch with a ferocity that couldn't be sustained very long with the temperature nearing ninety. Doggedly, his thoughts went back to Lauren. For the tenth time he wondered why he was so bothered, because she obviously didn't want help from him. Scowling, he climbed up on a ladder to get to the aged joists of the porch roof. Hooking one leg over the top of the ladder, he sat for a minute, recalling how she'd looked, nodding in curt dismissal. He knew it wasn't reasonable, but something deep inside him leaped at the challenge of that gesture.

Ryder stared unseeing over the familiar territory that had once been Mama Jane's property. The sensible thing was to stick to his original plan and steer clear of Lauren Holt. Mutual avoidance would suit her just fine, judging by her attitude of that morning. Again he felt a stirring of some emotion he couldn't identify and knew that instead of washing his hands of Lauren, he was probably going to act like a damn fool. Muttering an oath, he grabbed a hammer and ripped at nails that had been in place more than sixty years. Somehow he couldn't forget how she'd looked when she was alone and crying.

Working with his hands eased the turmoil inside him after a few minutes. Actually he liked working on the old house with his own hands. It was the only home he'd ever known. He wasn't certain why he'd stayed on after Mama

Jane's funeral except that the place offered some kind of anchor that he seemed to need in his life right now. Board by board, nail by nail, restoring Mama Jane's was a way of taking apart and examining the pieces of Ryder's own life: his failures, successes, losses, his loneliness and isolation. Ryder was almost forty years old, but hardly a soul would miss him if he disappeared tomorrow. It was a chilling thought.

He picked up a crowbar and began prising at a board. It was pure cypress, solid enough to weather another six decades. He ripped it from the overhead joists supporting the porch. Instantly half a dozen wasps swarmed in all directions. Swearing, he threw the board one way and leaped off the ladder, diving for the screen door.

Safely inside, he headed for the refrigerator and got out a can of beer, shaking his head. It would take a few minutes for the wasps to settle down before he could resume work. He drifted to the door and instantly Lauren Holt was back in his mind. The beer was cold and he was hot and thirsty. For several minutes he was still, thinking. Then he tossed the empty can into the trash and picked up the phone.

He punched out a number and slouched against the kitchen wall, waiting for an answer.

"Jerry? Ryder Braden." He tucked the receiver between his chin and shoulder and reached for a pad that lay on the counter, exchanging small talk with Jerry Lynch, the manufacturing manager at Hy-Tech Products, in nearby Pensacola, Florida. The company had retained Ryder as a consultant several times over the past few years.

"You're going to sub out some of the work on that job Hy-Tech landed to build electronic ignition assemblies, aren't you, Jerry?" He squinted through the window at the fierce noonday while Jerry responded.

"I've got about four possible suppliers," Jerry said. "The only drawback is distance. Most of them are on the east or west coast."

"Why don't you look into the Holt Company right here in Mobile?" Ryder suggested, running a finger down the pad. He stopped at a number. "I'll bet they could compete with the other sources, especially since they wouldn't have the shipping costs."

"Hey, sounds good," Jerry said, repeating the phone number Ryder supplied.

"You might ask for Lauren Holt," he said, shifting so that his weight was on one leg.

Jerry was silent for a moment, then asked, "That's the woman who's been in the news lately, isn't it? Legal trouble, something about claims against the competition, as I recall."

"Something like that."

Jerry cleared his throat. "We don't have to worry that the company might fold halfway through the contract, do we, buddy?"

"You don't have to worry," Ryder said.

"Okay, if you say so."

"I say so." Ryder looked up just in time to dodge a wasp that had followed him inside. Casually he added, "No need to mention my name, Jerry."

"Hey, no problem. Take care now, you hear?"

CHAPTER THREE

AFTER LUNCH LAUREN was back in her office trying to concentrate on the papers in front of her when a small sound at her door made her look up.

"Got time to take a little break?" Clancy St. James smiled into Lauren's eyes. Leaning slightly on a cane, favoring her left leg, the petite redhead entered the office without waiting for permission and sat down.

"Oh, hi, Clancy." Lauren pushed the papers aside. "Please. A break sounds fine, since I wasn't accomplishing much anyway."

"Well then, maybe you can understand how utterly boring my life has been lately." Clancy cautiously stretched out her left leg, revealing a knee wrapped with elasticized bandaging.

Lauren was sympathetic. "It's only temporary, Clancy. As soon as that knee can support the weight of your knapsack, you'll be off again." She waved a hand. "Where will it be next time—the Mid-East? El Salvador? Northern Ireland?"

"Uh-uh." Clancy shook her head. "I'm home for good, Lauren. I've covered my last political coup and reported my last bloody revolution."

Lauren glanced at the exotic black and gold walking cane resting across Clancy's lap. Ten to one she hadn't bought it in the continental U.S. "Remind me to throw those words back at you as soon as you can hobble around without that thing. Who're you trying to kid, Clancy? Reporting's in your blood.''

"I'm not giving up reporting," Clancy told her. "I'm just staying home to do it from now on."

Lauren felt slightly alarmed. Clancy was a journalist with an impressive reputation earned during ten years of reporting from the world's trouble spots. After being injured on a foreign assignment somewhere in Central America, she'd chosen to recuperate at home. She was one of Lauren's oldest friends, but she was still a reporter, and Lauren had had her fill of the Fourth Estate lately.

Correctly interpreting Lauren's wariness, Clancy put out a hand. "For heaven's sake, get that look off your face. I'm not doing an interview. I've just been thinking over my options if I decide to stay in town. There's TV and the newspaper free-lancing. But even if I were working again, surely you know you don't have to be concerned about privacy. You're one of the few friends I've got left at home, Lauren."

Lauren shook her head. "I'm sorry, Clancy. I guess I'm getting a bit paranoid lately. I was almost mobbed by reporters as I was leaving the courthouse yesterday."

"Where was your hero?"

"I assume you mean Jake Levinson."

Clancy's shrug was a little too nonchalant. "Who else?"

"He's my lawyer, Clancy, not my lover. Yes, of course he was there and he fended off the media. He even let me cry a little on his shoulder."

"Humph." Clancy made a face and looked unimpressed.

Lauren eyed her thoughtfully. Clancy and Jake Levinson had once been engaged, but that had ended ten years before when Clancy left for Washington. Although she'd been back in Mobile for several weeks, Jake had not appeared to notice. On the surface she appeared to be the same free spirit she'd always been. Suddenly Lauren wondered about Clancy's decision to settle down. She leaned back; an eyebrow quirked. "You just missed him."

Clancy busied herself suddenly by propping her injured leg on the seat of the chair beside her, arranging the folds of her denim skirt, positioning her cane just so. Hiding a smile, Lauren watched her, not fooled for a second by the studied nonchalance. Clancy was irritated by Jake's indifference.

"Well, aside from playing the hero to the hilt, did he do his job?" Clancy's tone had a little bite in it. "Did he conjure up a miracle?"

Lauren thought of Ryder Braden, engineer extraordinaire, adept and dark and dangerous. "He tried."

"No miracles, hmm?" Suddenly Clancy's attitude became one of genuine concern. "I was hoping you'd look a lot more optimistic this afternoon than you do. I'm almost afraid to ask, but how bad is it?"

"It's not good, I'm afraid," Lauren said. "As for Jake doing his job, as I told you, he tried. I'm the one who flubbed up, not Jake." She'd been feeling unsettled ever since her encounter with Braden that morning and no matter how she played and replayed the scene in her head, Lauren couldn't explain her reaction to the man. Or her behavior. Jake had persuaded Ryder to come around and talk, and she'd alienated him in two minutes.

"Whatever happened must have been upsetting," Clancy observed, looking at the hodgepodge of papers on the desk. "I thought I was the only one whose desk got in that shape. Can't you delegate some of that?"

Lauren shook her head. "I'm afraid not, but that's not the problem." She searched a moment for a way to describe her dilemma. Maybe telling Clancy would help her put the whole episode into perspective.

"A funny thing happened at Jake's office this morning," she said finally. "Our case needs an expert witness and Jake managed to locate someone here in town who's qualified."

"Well, great, what a lucky break. Anyone we know?"

"I don't think you know him, but I do. At least, I met him. Once."

Clancy looked intrigued.

"His name is Ryder Braden. We met at a Mardi Gras ball about five years ago."

"Ryder Braden." Clancy repeated the name thoughtfully. "No, doesn't sound familiar. He lives here, in Mobile?"

Lauren shrugged. "He doesn't appear to live anywhere, at least permanently. He manages a stop in Mobile every few years. Jake told me his grandmother died about three months ago which seems to be his reason for being here right now."

"A rolling stone, hmm?"

"Apparently, but one whose career makes him tailor-made for our expert witness."

Clancy leaned back and crossed her bad leg over her good one. "So what's the problem?"

Lauren hesitated before drawing a deep breath. "Clancy, have you ever done something that you looked back on later and wondered what had come over you?"

Clancy grinned. "No, never."

Lauren stared at her. "Do you want to hear this story, or not?"

The grin vanished from Clancy's face, but laughter lingered in her blue eyes.

Lauren's half smile was fleeting. She turned her gaze to the window, looking thoughtful. "I don't know why,

Clancy, but I had my back up from the minute he sat down in Jake's office.''

"That I can certainly understand," Clancy said dryly.

Lauren ignored her. "I practically picked a fight with the man over nothing. I was rude and arrogant and..." She brought her gaze back to Clancy who wore a look of amazement.

"*You*, Lauren Holt, the very essence of polite southern womanhood, were rude? I don't believe it!"

"It's true. I don't know what got into me, Clancy. He looked like some battle-scarred drifter who'd been around the block so many times that nothing much could shock him, and—''

"Wow, he sounds pret-ty interesting to me.''

"Well, he isn't. I mean—'' she hesitated and then smiled "—actually, maybe he is. Slightly.''

Clancy's sandy eyebrows went up.

"The point is," Lauren continued, ignoring her friend's expression. "I'm not sure about turning the records of the company over to a man like that.''

"You mean because he wasn't wearing a three-piece suit and carrying a briefcase?''

"No, of course not. But, we'd have to turn over all Clay's designs. Whoever the expert is will have full access to the company's files and records.''

"He could hardly testify to their authenticity otherwise," Clancy observed, still looking a little baffled. "You said you'd met him before. Do you know much about him? I can't believe Jake would recommend him if he had any reservations.''

"Oh, Jake's practically ecstatic over him falling in our laps like this," Lauren said wryly. "I didn't tell Jake, but some of the things I heard that night make me extremely nervous about putting the fate of our case in the hands of some vagabond engineer with a taste for life in the fast lane.''

"What makes you say that?" Clancy carefully set her foot on the floor.

Lauren made a face, beginning to feel as though she was digging a hole and sinking in it. "It was nothing in particular. Naturally I'm cautious about trusting someone with such a—such a colorful reputation."

"This is getting more and more interesting," Clancy responded. "Exactly what makes his reputation colorful?"

"Oh, Clancy—"

"Well, what?"

Lauren looked at her. "You'll probably love it."

"Try me."

"According to Jake, Ryder had an impoverished youth with few advantages except for an exceptional grandmother. He worked to pay for his own education and landed a plum job at graduation, then he launched a successful business as a troubleshooting consultant."

"So," Clancy nodded, urging her on. "I can't believe you have a problem with a self-made man."

"I don't. If anything, it's just the opposite," Lauren said. "I admire that kind of strength. Oh, I don't know what I think. Why in the world did I act like such a bitch, for heaven's sake!"

Clancy leaned back in her chair watching Lauren closely. "You know, Lauren, maybe you're looking at this thing from the wrong angle. Maybe you're trying to figure out a reason to reject this man professionally because your reaction to him was extremely personal."

"Don't be ridiculous, Clancy. I've only met the man once. Well, twice." But the minute the words were out of Clancy's mouth, Lauren knew they were true. There was something about Ryder Braden that put her uncharacteristically on edge. Deep down she trusted Jake not to turn over company secrets to a man he had any doubts about. No, her problem with Braden wasn't anything to do with the company or questions about his career. Far from it. He had somehow managed to disturb something deep inside her that had gone undisturbed for years. All the way back to her senior year in college.

She'd been engaged that year to a handsome, charming, intelligent, ambitious man. Unfortunately she hadn't realized how ambitious he was until he'd abruptly broken off their engagement a few weeks before their wedding. Lauren's family, the Buchanans, were an old and respected family. Old Buchanan money and connections would have been tremendous assets to his career. The problem was that at that time, Buchanan tradition and connections were still intact, but there was not much money left. The humiliation of his rejection still made Lauren's face burn.

She shifted suddenly, with a fervent wish that she'd never started this conversation. It wasn't like her to react so emotionally, let alone to tell anyone about it. Not even Clancy. Stress must be taking more of a toll than she realized.

Clancy rose, favoring her left leg. "Okay, babe, I'm out of here. Just one thing..." She grinned at the wary look in Lauren's eyes. "If this guy really is the perfect expert and he seemed willing enough before you...ah, insulted him, then maybe you ought to consider giving Jake a call and asking him to try and pour a little oil on troubled waters. Aren't lawyers good at that sort of thing?"

JAKE WASN'T HAVING any part of it. Lauren put down the receiver with a sigh and spent a fleeting moment remembering how uncomplicated her life had been before the responsibility of the whole company had landed in her lap.

Her lawyer certainly hadn't hesitated to let her know how disgusted he was with her. She winced, recalling his words.

"What the hell happened, Lauren? I leave you alone for three minutes with the one man within a thousand-mile radius who just might possibly make a difference to our case. I come back and he's walking out looking like a man who wants to hit something."

"Do you think he might reconsider, Jake?" she'd asked, knowing she deserved Jake's displeasure. But how could she explain her behavior when she didn't even understand it herself?

"Hell, I don't know. He's not a man to forget an insult, Lauren."

"Maybe if you just called him—"

"No, Lauren," Jake had said emphatically. "You call him. You messed it up; you fix it."

"But—"

"I'm telling you, Lauren. He won't come around with a silly bread-and-butter call from me. He'll want to hear an apology from you. And then maybe, just maybe..."

Lauren stared at the phone number jotted on the pad in front of her. Jake was right. She had created the problem. Now it was her place to fix it. Shivering, she picked up the phone.

After punching out the number, she waited through five rings. Six. Seven. Maybe he...

"Hello?"

She licked her lips while something curled through her stomach and whispered down her spine. His voice sounded deep and impatient and she could hear him breathing as though he was out of breath. She wondered what he'd been doing, something physical, surely. He was definitely a physical person.

"Hello!"

"Uh, hello, Mr. Braden. This is Lauren Holt."

Silence.

"Mr. Braden?"

"Yeah, I'm here." The impatience was replaced with a cool formality that bordered on rudeness. He was definitely entitled, she thought.

"Mr. Braden..." Suddenly, Lauren could find no way to express the reason for her call. What could she say? That she'd taken a dislike to him because he brought to mind feelings and events that had caused her pain a million years ago? That she was too cowardly to take a chance on dealing with a man who reminded her of a time when she was so naive that she'd been an easy victim? That he was too...

"You said that."

"What?" She frowned.

"'Mr. Braden,'" he said and a hint of the charm for which he was famous crept into his tone. "We've established who we both are, haven't we?"

"Yes." She took a deep breath. At least he hadn't hung up. "Mr. Braden—"

He chuckled softly.

"Please," she murmured, struggling against her reaction to that sound. "I'm trying to find the words and you aren't helping."

"Words for what, Mrs. Holt?"

Lauren stared at a photograph of a broadly grinning Justin, which was propped in front of her. "Words to apologize for my unforgivable rudeness to you this morning in Jake's office. Words to try and explain what came over me so that I behaved like some kind of arrogant bitch. Words to say how sorry I—"

"Whoa." Ryder's voice was low and laced with amusement. "Why not just say, 'I'm sorry'?"

It was Lauren's turn to be silenced.

"And be done with it."

Lauren found she was holding her breath. "Is that all it takes?"

"I'm a reasonable man."

"And a nice one, too," Lauren said and wondered at the sudden lift of her spirits. "I'm sorry."

"Are you sure this is the real Lauren Holt?"

"It is, although I certainly can't expect you to believe it. I do sincerely regret that we got off on the wrong foot. I'm still not sure what came over me, but it won't happen again. You have my word on it."

"Your last one, I hope."

She laughed. "My last one, I promise."

"Finally."

Lauren laughed again. "Did I interrupt anything? The phone rang several times. Am I keeping you from something important?"

"I'm not on a schedule lately," he replied. "No, you didn't interrupt anything important."

She took another deep breath. "Mr. Braden—"

"Ryder, please."

"Thank you. Ryder, I know this sounds presumptuous, and you have every right to tell me no and just hang up the phone. But we still need you as an expert witness. I would be extremely grateful if you would reconsider."

So polite and gracious, Ryder thought, standing in the old kitchen enjoying the sound of her voice and—he admitted it—having the upper hand. He had no difficulty bringing to mind an image of Lauren behind her desk, her long legs crossed with ladylike grace. He'd bet his next consultant fee she wasn't used to apologizing, but she'd certainly done it with all the warmth and sincerity he could have wished for. He'd give a few thousand dollars to know exactly why she had reacted to him in a way that required an apology in the first place.

"Are you there, Ryder?"

"I'm here, Mrs. Holt."

"Lauren, please call me Lauren."

He smiled. "Thank you."

"What about it, Ryder? Will you do it?"

"On one condition."

She hesitated. "Which is?"

"I'll need to familiarize myself with the disputed designs. Bring them out here tomorrow and I'll look them over. I'll give you my opinion just as soon as I can."

"Out there?" she said, sounding dismayed.

"Out here."

"But I don't know where your house is, Ryder. Wouldn't the plant be a better place? You may have technical questions, points that only our people in engineering are qualified to discuss."

"That's my condition, Lauren."

"Well, if you insist."

"I do. Now, do you need directions to this house?"

"No, Jake will be with me and he knows the way," she replied.

Ryder studied the look of his worn Nike running shoes. "Yeah, Jake knows the way," he said softly, hanging up the phone and wondering how he'd be able to think of anything but her for the next twenty-four hours.

LAUREN WAS MECHANICALLY navigating the rush-hour traffic on the beltline while her thoughts focused on Ryder Braden.

I can't believe I agreed to go to his house.

A strange dart of anticipation sliced through her. From the moment she'd hung up the phone, she'd been trying to understand how she'd let herself be so smoothly manipulated. Had he been serious? Would he have refused to reconsider if she hadn't agreed to come to him? Was it simply ego on his part? She inhaled deeply and turned off the main street and onto the curved, brick-paved driveway of her home, hoping that had not been his reason, but not quite willing to examine exactly what she hoped his real reason could be.

She pulled into the detached garage of the sprawling ranch house that she and Clay had bought about five years before. The neighborhood was fairly new, appealing mostly to newly established professionals, but she had never felt any special attachment to the house. Lauren had an appreciation for the history and tradition of old places. Both she and Clay had been reared in homes that were over seventy-five years old, but Clay barely knew the right end of a hammer to use, which made owning an old house impractical. One of these days she planned to find a little gem and restore it.

Justin would be her handyman, she thought, her expression softening as it always did when she thought of her son. He was as adept with his hands as he was at his computer. Smiling, she got out of her small Toyota and went into the house.

"I'm home!" Lauren laid her bag on the top of a Chippendale lowboy in the foyer and idly thumbed through a stack of mail.

"Lordy! Look who's home and it's only five-thirty in the afternoon."

"Hi, Hattie." Lauren smiled into the round ebony face of the woman waddling toward her. For thirty years Hattie Bell Brown had kept house and cooked for various Buchanans. Most of Lauren's childhood tears and fears had been soothed away on Hattie's expansive lap. When Justin was born, Hattie had announced to Pauline Buchanan, Lauren's mother, that her place was with Lauren and the baby, whereupon she'd packed her bags and moved over to the new house. Lauren knew how fortunate she was and couldn't bear to imagine life without Hattie Bell.

"I managed to get away at quitting time for once," Lauren explained, tossing the mail back onto the lowboy. She was used to Hattie's chiding criticism for the long hours she put in at her desk, and even though she'd like to spend more time at home, she simply didn't see how she could do so anytime soon. Maybe after the case was settled. "Where's Justin?"

Hattie smiled meaningfully. "Where do you think? If he isn't outside playing baseball or soccer, then he's going to be at that computer setup in his room. I tell you, Lauren, that boy is something else with all his energy. No telling what he'll grow up to be if he keeps on like this."

Lauren smiled. "Well, we have a few years yet to enjoy him, Hattie Bell." She turned her head at the sudden flurry of noise behind her.

"Hi, Mom!" Justin rounded the corner in the hall trailing a couple of yards of computer printout paper behind him. "Take a look at this. I had a heckuva time programming it." He pulled the paper around and stretched it out between his expanded arms.

Lauren leaned back to read an elaborate rendering of the words, All the Way, Bluejays! created with a million X's and O's. Besides his computer, Justin had two passions in life. One was baseball; the other was soccer. His Little League team, the Bluejays, were in contention for the championship in their division.

"Very impressive," she said, reaching out and fluffing his hair, ignoring his longsuffering look. Motherly kisses were strictly forbidden, to Lauren's keen disappointment, and a hug was tolerated only under the most exceptional circumstances. Most of the time Lauren regretted the speed with which Justin was growing up, but there were a few compensations, she'd decided, if once he had matured, he'd let her touch him again.

She gazed down at him and felt her heart swell with boundless love. His blond head, so like her own, and those amber eyes, also like hers, were a combination of little-boy beauty and male promise that no normal mother could look at without a burst of pride, she told herself. Every day she thanked God that Clay had persuaded her they needed a child.

"What's for dinner, Hattie Bell?" Justin asked, carefully folding the paper streamer.

"Smoked oysters, brussel sprouts and beets," Hattie said, her black eyes dancing.

"Aw, Hattie."

"Well, it's pretty late," Hattie began, "but I guess I could make some cream of cauliflower soup with a spinach salad 'cause I know how you love—"

"I don't love any of that!" Justin announced firmly. "And you know it. I need real food, Hattie. How'm I gonna keep up my batting average with oysters and cauliflower?"

Lauren smiled. "Especially if you won't eat them."

Hattie braced her hands on gigantic hips. "Well, how about fried chicken and corn on the cob?"

Justin's eyes lit up. "Yeah! Now, that's more like it."

Hattie started toward the kitchen chuckling. "I'll see what I can do, my man."

Lauren put her hands on her hips and eyed her son, her mouth twitching. "Justin, I believe you'd like it if we had fried chicken or pizza every night. Don't you ever want any variety?"

Justin had the paper streamer folded into a neat stack. "Sure," he said good-naturedly, "hamburgers and french fries would be okay."

"Go wash your hands," she said, shaking her head helplessly.

A soft smile tugged at her lips as Lauren watched him disappear down the hall. He was getting so tall! His eleventh birthday had barely passed and he was already into teen-sized jeans and still growing. Intellectually he was far ahead of most of his classmates.

A troubled look entered her eyes. A threat to the company wasn't just a threat to her and the employees. It was a threat to Justin and his birthright. A swift, fierce rush of maternal protectiveness arose in her. If the case should be resolved, she could devote the time to Justin that he deserved. And Ryder Braden's expertise would definitely help.

A picture of Braden as he'd appeared in Jake's office took shape clearly in her mind. Something about him appealed to her as no man had for a long time. The cool, practical streak that had governed her most of her adult life was strangely silent, while something else, something entirely unexpected had come to life. It was as though her senses had been awakened after a long sleep. A feeling of anticipation made her pulse quicken.

This was ridiculous! She would wake up tomorrow and be her old self again. This strange attraction she felt would probably be gone, changed to the uncomplicated feelings she had for...Jake, for instance. Or any of the hundreds of men who worked at the plant. Tomorrow, this strange, compelling awareness of the man would surely pass.

Or would it?

CHAPTER FOUR

"HERE WE ARE, just around this bend." Jake winced as the Mercedes's front end was jarred by a deep rut in the road.

"Great." Lauren gazed at the uncut, sun-parched grass along the roadside and tried unsuccessfully to ignore the fluttery sensation in her stomach. Being on Braden's territory made her feel distinctly uneasy. At this rate, she thought, by the time she saw the man, she would be as nervous as a teenager.

"I hope we're doing the right thing, Jake," she said, focusing on professional problems rather than personal ones. "Turning everything over to Braden seems so...so drastic."

"That unexpected contract you just landed from Hy-Tech in Pensacola will help hold you above water," Jake said with patience, "but it's only temporary, Lauren. With Ryder's help, we're going to get out of the woods permanently. Trust me on this, babe."

"If you say so." Lauren sighed and resumed her tense contemplation of the countryside. "But I can't stay long. Justin's game is at four and I can't miss it."

Jake swerved to avoid a pothole. "Fine. That's over two hours from now. And after you've talked with Ryder, if you decide you simply can't trust him, then you can take Clay's files with you."

Lauren didn't comment. What was the point? It was obvious Jake didn't have a single reservation about his old buddy.

"Ryder isn't interested in grabbing anything that belongs to you, Lauren."

"So you've said," she muttered. "Ten or twenty times."

He grinned at her, not without sympathy. "I'll grant you've got good reason to be distrustful of some people lately, but Ryder Braden isn't one of them."

She gave up and tried to relax. It was useless trying to argue with Jake. He was firmly in Braden's corner.

"I still think dragging us out here was uncalled for," Lauren grumbled, bracing herself with one hand on the dash as Jake took a hairpin curve. "Why did the man insist on it? It's hot and dusty. I didn't have time for lunch and I'm thirsty. Honestly, Jake..."

Her words trailed off as the Mercedes turned abruptly into a lane formed by a double row of ancient live oaks. At the end, looking like something created from her own imagination, was a house. It had the graceful look of an early Victorian, complete with wraparound porch and gingerbread trim.

"Oh, Jake..."

"Yeah," Jake said, smiling. "I'd almost forgotten how beautiful this old place is."

"How old is it?" Lauren asked, taking in the twin turrets and double front porches, one at ground level and another directly overhead on the second floor. Over the front door was a beautiful leaded glass fanlight. And those windows, she thought, marveling at the varied sizes and shapes. The place was a treasure!

"Sixty...seventy-five years, I'd guess." Jake brought the car to a stop. Resting his wrists on the steering wheel, he studied the familiar lines of the place.

"No wonder Braden wants to restore this," she murmured. "Has his family always lived here?"

Jake shook his head. "I'm not sure, although I never knew him to live any other place. He was always pretty self-contained when we were kids. His grandmother raised him."

Self-contained. And nothing's changed, Lauren thought. He wouldn't have become any mellower in the years he'd knocked about the world. Just the opposite, she guessed, recalling hard, closed features and the fathomless blue eyes that revealed nothing. It was not difficult to imagine a man like Braden living a solitary existence. But burying himself in an old house like this in coastal Alabama was something else altogether, she thought, intrigued in spite of herself.

She was pulled out of her thoughts when Jake suddenly opened his door. Gathering up the rolled plans and her briefcase, she got out of the car, bracing herself to meet Ryder Braden again, face to face.

The front door was equipped with an old-fashioned twist bell which Jake rang half a dozen times before it became obvious that no one was in the house. "I know he's expecting us," Jake said, surveying the grounds with a frown. "Must be out at the barn." He started down the steps, saying over his shoulder, "Wait here while I take a look."

Lauren nodded, feeling the heat after the abnormal coolness of Jake's Mercedes. She put her briefcase and papers on the seat of an old rocking chair and blotted moisture from her upper lip with two fingers of her hand. There was no quiet like the stillness of a hot Southern afternoon. Even birds and insects retreated to whatever cool shelter they could find. In the glare of the midday sun, Lauren stared out over Braden's land. The line of woods toward the back was darker and greener, lush with vegetation, making her think there must be a creek or bayou marking his boundary line. It was beautiful and somehow primitive. She left the porch and followed a narrow brick path by the side of the house, drawn by the promise of a cool stream.

It was then that she saw him.

He was naked from the waist up. In the full heat of the sun, sweat glistened on his body, collecting in the dark curls fanning out over his chest and running down the center of his hard, flat middle. Faded cutoffs rode impossibly low on his lean hips. As he bent to pick up something on a workbench beside him, she could see a flash of the white waistband on his underwear.

Her mouth went dry and for a few lost moments, Lauren simply stared, more than ever aware of the tightness that had been in her stomach all day. What was it about this man that made her feel this way? The question resurrected old defenses. Why was he flaunting himself like a teenage boy who'd just discovered his muscles? He was expecting her and Jake. Why didn't he have the courtesy to at least put on a shirt?

She watched him glance at a paper beside him, and then measure a piece of lumber with a metal tape. He marked the wood with a pencil and lifted an electric saw, flexing the muscles in his arms with the effort. Raising one foot to brace the board, he carefully positioned the blade. Just before cutting, he cleared sweat from his temple with an impatient swipe of his shoulder. Then the piercing shriek of the saw rent the hot stillness of the afternoon.

A piece of the board fell away and he set the saw aside, holding on to the longer section. Straightening, he looked up directly into Lauren's eyes.

Neither of them acknowledged the other for a few seconds. And then it dawned on Lauren just how odd she must appear, walking up unannounced in his backyard, gaping as though she'd never seen a man working without his shirt. She cleared her throat and came closer.

"We rang but no one answered," she said, waving a hand vaguely toward the front of the house.

He nodded once, unsmiling. Tossing the wood onto the workbench, he reached for his shirt and unhurriedly pulled it over his head. Like his cutoffs, the garment had seen better days. The sleeves had been cut and the bottom hiked up, baring a tanned section of his midriff. Ryder looked grubby and hot and distinctly masculine. Everything about him should have turned her off, Lauren told herself, but yet he provoked all kinds of confusing feelings in her. And not all of them were negative.

He glanced beyond her. "Did Jake come with you?"

"He's looking for you in those buildings we saw on the other side of the property."

He started toward her. "Sorry about that. The time got away from me."

She gestured toward the materials spread out on the workbench. "What are you building?"

A rueful look came into his eyes. "Would you believe a birdhouse?"

She smiled, surprised. "What kind?"

"Purple martin."

"Declaring war on mosquitoes, hmm?"

"They say one martin eats his weight in mosquitoes every day," he said, falling into step beside her as she turned back, retracing the path toward the front of the house.

Lauren glanced at him through her lashes. "There's no accounting for taste, I guess."

He laughed. "Right. Although I'm not stopping with a single family unit. I figure I'll need at least a high-rise hotel."

She made a face. "Pretty buggy out here, huh?"

He surveyed the neglected grounds, squinting in the sun. "No more than usual, at least for this part of the country, I suppose. Being away so long, you forget—"

"Hey, here you are!" They looked up as Jake appeared at the corner of the house.

"Good to see you, Jake." Ryder reached out to accept the lawyer's outstretched hand. "Come on into the house where it's cool," he said, waiting while his guests climbed the steps to the porch. Lauren collected the material she'd left on the chair, and when Ryder pushed the door open wide, she went inside.

"There's iced tea or beer," he said, ushering them into the spacious front room. "What'll you have?"

"Beer," said Jake without hesitation.

"Iced tea," said Lauren. "Please."

He disappeared through a swinging door, saying over his shoulder, "You can spread the plans out on the dining room table. I'll look them over now, then tonight I'll study them in detail."

He was back with their drinks before Lauren had the plans out of their tubes. He handed Jake a beer and set Lauren's iced tea down beside her. "I'm a mess," he said, making a face and pulling at the sweat-stained sweatshirt with his hands. "Give me two minutes to get decent and we'll get down to business."

As soon as Ryder left the room, Lauren looked at Jake. "Maybe I should withhold a few of the designs until we're certain."

Jake shrugged. "It's your funeral."

"Oh, all right!" The plans landed with a thump on the table. She'd managed to stretch most of them out, anchoring them with ashtrays and other articles in the room that had probably belonged to his grandmother by the time Ryder reappeared.

Instantly Lauren felt the now familiar, intense awareness. He'd obviously taken a quick shower. He smelled of
soap and warm maleness and nothing else. No after-shave,
no cologne. His hair, dark and wet, had received only a
quick swipe with a towel. It clung to the shape of his head,
curling around his ears and the nape of his neck. Had he
even bothered to dry off before pulling on his jeans? Was
that why they molded his muscled thighs and outlined his
maleness so faithfully? She cleared her throat and forced her
gaze to the jumble of numbers and mechanical symbols on
the plans and specifications before her. At least he wore a
shirt. It was white and fashionably loose, subtly flattering.
But wouldn't he look good in almost anything? Although
her assessment had taken no more than five or ten seconds,
his image was clearly imprinted in her mind. She bent over
the plans, determined to ignore the unsettling effect the man
seemed to have on her.

ALL OF RYDER'S ATTENTION was focused on the details
contained in the jumble of plans that littered the top of his
dining-room table. For the next half hour, as quickly as she
answered one question, he fired another at her. Jake was no
help. Lauren began to wonder why she'd insisted he come.
He sat behind them, a silent observer. In her efforts to concentrate on technicalities that were hazy at best to her, Lauren grew more and more tense. Finally, in response to one
of his questions, she pushed aside a schematic drawing in
exasperation.

"I can't answer that, Mr. Braden. If you recall, I suggested that we meet at the plant so that there would be
qualified people standing by who could answer your questions, but you—"

"Hey, hey..." He brought up both hands, palms out
front, his smile slanted and loaded with charm. "It's okay.

You did suggest that, Mrs. Holt, but I got so caught up in the designs that I forgot myself. I apologize. At any rate, you've answered most of my questions very respectably."

Jake stood up before the lively exchange between his two friends heated up any more. "'Mr.' Braden. 'Mrs.' Holt," he said with exaggerated patience. "Are you two back to formal address again?"

Ryder looked into Lauren's eyes. "Are we?"

Lauren's smile began slowly and then bloomed. Watching it, Ryder felt an answering heat spread through him like warm honey. "That would be pretty silly, wouldn't it?" she said.

Ryder grinned. "That it would, Lauren."

The moment stretched out, deep and silent. Jake, amused, cleared his throat deliberately.

"Well..." Lauren looked away and focused blindly on the scattered plans in front of her. "We should get on with this since I've got to leave in time to get to the ball field."

"Ball field?" Ryder frowned, unable to picture Lauren interested in sports.

"Little League," she explained. "I've got to be there at four o'clock sharp. I've been chastised too often for missing the first pitch."

Ryder very casually unrolled a set of plans. "Must be somebody important playing," he said, the criss-cross of lines and angles now meaningless.

"Yes," Lauren said softly. "My son."

Still bent over the plans, Ryder closed his eyes and inhaled deeply. Then he straightened and looked directly at Lauren. "Your son."

She nodded, unable to hide the pride and love in her tone. "Justin, eleven going on twenty-one, the Bluejays' star catcher."

"That good, is he?"

She laughed ruefully. "Maybe I should have said the Bluejays' only catcher. The team's not overmanned, I'm afraid."

Still holding her gaze, Ryder leaned against the table, crossing his ankles. "I can't see you as the mother of a jock, even an eleven-year-old jock."

"How about a computer whiz-kid?" Jake spoke up from behind them. "Justin's not exactly your average eleven-year-old. He's smart as a whip, but down to earth at the same time, a terrific kid." He glanced at his watch. "Lauren, we'd better get on with this if you want to stay in good with that terrific kid."

Looking thoughtful, Ryder bumped an empty cardboard tube against his thighs. At the first mention of the boy, his heart had actually jumped. Even though he knew it was a crazy idea, he wanted to see Justin. He swallowed painfully. *Justin.* Until this moment, he hadn't known his name. He told himself he hadn't wanted to know, but deep down, he knew better. Something inside him wouldn't be satisfied until he knew far more about the boy than just his name.

He looked at Jake Levinson. "Do you need to get back to your office, Jake?"

Jake glanced at Lauren. "Well, I—"

"I'd be happy to drive Lauren to the ball field." Ryder kept the expression on his face casual, sensing Lauren's wariness. "It's been a long time since I've seen a star catcher perform."

Jake grinned. "Say about twenty-five years?"

Lauren looked interested. "You were a catcher?"

"It's been a long time, but yes, I was once."

Jake turned to Lauren. "How about it, hon?" He swept a glance over the plans scattered on the table top. "It doesn't appear I'm making much of a contribution here. You have any objection if I head on back to my office?"

"I don't want to put you to any trouble," Lauren said to Ryder. "I—"

"It's no trouble," Ryder said quickly. "It'll be a nice break."

Still uncertain, her amber eyes searched his.

"Don't say no, Lauren."

He hadn't intended to say that. Or to sound like that. Feeling slightly embarrassed, he laughed softly and looked away, right into Jake's arrested gaze. He swore silently, imagining what the lawyer must be thinking. Not a week before, Jake had had to practically hog-tie him before he'd even consider Lauren's case and now here he was very nearly begging to take her to a kid's ballgame. Jake must be wondering whether he'd been out in the sun too long.

Two minutes later Lauren watched Jake turn the Mercedes around and then disappear down the oak-studded lane. Keenly aware of Ryder standing beside her, she raised her left arm and studied her watch. "If we're going to go through everything I brought with me and make the game on time," she said briskly, "then we'd better get on with it."

"Yes, ma'am."

Her eyes flew to his, tangling with a look so intensely blue that she had a ridiculous urge to fly down the front steps and call out to Jake before it was too late. Instead, she drew a calming breath and went back to the table. When Ryder didn't immediately follow her, she gave him a pointed look. Wearing an expression she didn't dare try to decipher, he pushed away from the door and joined her.

The man knew robotics. Even with her limited knowledge, Lauren recognized that. His experience was much broader and encompassed more than just the function of Clay's designs, she'd discovered. He talked with ease about product application and cost as well as prospective profits and markets. Provided the designs could be established as exclusive, she reminded herself grimly. Ryder, it appeared, could be every bit as valuable to the company and the lawsuit as Jake believed.

The next hour went quickly. She was startled when he began rolling up a set of prints.

"Time to wrap this up," he said, stacking everything neatly in the middle of the table and then turning to her. "What now, Lauren? Do you want to take all this back with you or will you leave it with me? It's up to you."

She looked up at him, searching his face as though something there would give her the assurance she needed to place the company's destiny—and hers and Justin's—in his hands. Again she felt the pull of attraction, the lure of his deep blue eyes, and something else that she couldn't name. Suddenly she had no desire to hold out against him. "I'll leave it all with you," she said.

He grinned and reached for her bag. "Then come on, lady. We can't be late for that ballgame."

RYDER GOT OUT of the Blazer at the ball field, emotion pounding through him so fiercely that for a moment he couldn't move. He had never allowed himself to even imagine this moment. He had always believed no reason could be good enough or strong enough to overcome the complications inherent in a meeting between him and this boy. But then he had never intended to let himself get close enough to actually meet Lauren, either. Fate, five years before, had fixed that. As he slammed the car door behind him, his anxiety fell away, and only the inevitability of the moment was left, clear and sharp, in his mind. From the day of his return to Mobile, he'd been caught up in something so intense and compelling that nothing he did, no effort to keep his distance, no attempts at cool rationale, no struggle to deny his emotions had mattered at all in the end.

"Coming?"

Lauren was standing at the front of the Blazer looking at him expectantly. Feeling his stomach tighten in anticipation, he nodded and fell into step beside her.

He was barely aware of the friendly greetings called out to her as they negotiated the grassy perimeter of the ball field on their way to the sidelines. The place was alive with kids of all sizes—boys and girls, some in uniforms, some not. Frowning, his gaze swept quickly over them, resting on various boys who appeared to be the right age and size.

"There he is."

Heart hammering, he looked where Lauren pointed to a knot of boys outfitted in blue and white. His teeth, he realized in amazement, were clenched with the same tension that knotted his stomach. He had once faced a street gang in Tokyo with less trepidation.

"Hey, Mom!" One of the boys suddenly raised an arm and grinned at Lauren. Peeling off a catcher's mask, he tossed it aside and then broke into a run, his eyes on his mother. In seconds he pelted to a stop beside her, breathing hard from the exertion and yet laughing at the same time. "You were almost late!"

Something in Ryder twisted and turned his heart inside out. Justin was tall for eleven and skinny, all knees and elbows. His hair was light, exactly like his mother's. His eyes were Lauren's, too—clear amber—bright and intelligent. But his chin, Ryder noted wryly, had a stubborn shape to it and resembled the one he, Ryder, shaved every morning.

Lauren put a hand on the boy's shoulder and smiled up at Ryder. "Justin, this is Mr. Braden. Jake brought him in to work on the lawsuit with us. Ryder, this is my son, Justin Holt."

Ryder couldn't help it. The moment Justin's eyes met his, he felt a surge of pride and sheer possessiveness that was so strong, he wondered that it couldn't be read all over his face. He put out his hand. "Hello, Justin."

Justin cocked his head and studied Ryder for a few seconds before slowly extending his hand. His expression was slightly curious as he shook hands politely.

Ryder looked the boy over intently. *For what?* he asked himself. Some common trait, some inherited characteristic that would link him in some elemental way that only Ryder could ever recognize? Why? For what purpose? Pride? Ego?

"I didn't see you drive up, Mom," Justin said, but his eyes were fixed on Ryder. No dissembling there, Ryder thought, accurately interpreting the look, one male to another. The boy wanted to know what the hell his mother was doing with some stranger. *Good for you, Justin.*

Lauren's hand still rested on the boy's shoulder. "We just got here, Justin."

Justin eyed the vehicles parked on the other side of the ball field. "I don't see the car."

"I rode with Mr. Braden."

Justin looked at Ryder again with new interest. "Why?"

"Oh, uh..." Lauren appeared flustered momentarily. "Well, Jake had to go back to his office and Mr.—"

"Mr. Levinson just ran off and left you?" Justin demanded, suddenly sounding older than his years.

Lauren glanced quickly from her son to Ryder. "Justin, you'd better get back to your team. They're up next. I think Scotty's looking for you."

Justin turned his head and made a motion to two Bluejays who were beckoning to him impatiently. "I guess Scotty's mom can give us a ride home," he said, a hint of suspicion in the look he gave Ryder.

Ryder met the boy's eyes squarely. "Your mother needs to pick up her car at her office, Justin. When the game's over, I'll drive you both over."

His tone was laced with authority. Justin heard him out in silence, and then turned to go.

Lauren and Ryder watched the boy head back to his teammates, his spine ramrod straight. At some sound from her, Ryder glanced down. "What?"

She shook her head. "I don't know what in the world—" She put her fingers to her temples and laughed self-consciously. "I've never seen Justin act so...so..."

"Possessive? Protective?"

She shrugged helplessly. "Was that what it was?"

Ryder's lazy smile appeared. "Either that or jealousy, I'd say." His gaze roamed over her face. "Or a combination of all the above."

"That's ridiculous!"

Ryder lifted a dark brow. "Is it?"

Without another word, Lauren turned and headed toward the stands. Smiling, Ryder fell into step beside her.

For the next two hours, his eyes were fixed on Justin. He watched him leap and yell and crouch and stretch, performing all the familiar moves that he himself had perfected playing the same position when he was about Justin's age. He squinted through the late-afternoon sun as a fast pitch zipped across the plate. The ball made a solid *thwack!* into Justin's glove. In one graceful motion, he surged up, cocked his arm back and threw to the frantic first baseman, who triumphantly tagged the runner. A double play. Ryder found himself on his feet. Pride and something else fierce and deep burned inside him. He eased back onto the bleachers beside Lauren, filled with a confused jumble of impressions and emotion.

He had never felt entirely comfortable with the concept of artificial insemination, but he honestly believed that he had come to accept his role as an anonymous donor years ago. Why then this intense emotional reaction to the boy?

Suddenly all his early doubts were back again. The impersonal contribution he'd made to secure Justin's birth didn't
feel impersonal at all, he discovered, shaken.

Justin's team headed for the benches in high spirits. Unless they totally fell apart or the other team miraculously
rebounded, the Bluejays were headed for victory. Ryder
watched Justin's affected nonchalance as his teammates
clustered around him. When Justin spotted someone walking across the turf and began waving enthusiastically, Ryder frowned. A tall man, slightly built with light hair and
sharp features returned the boy's greeting. Ryder wondered
who he was. Definitely a friend, he decided, watching the
quick, easy way Justin launched into conversation with him.

"Oh, there's Michael," Lauren said, lifting her arm in
greeting as Justin pointed toward his mother and Ryder in
the stands.

"The team's sponsor?" Ryder guessed. "Michael" didn't
look athletic enough to be a coach, but he kept that thought
to himself.

"Not exactly," Lauren answered. "The Holt Company
sponsors the team. No, that's Michael Armstead, general
manager at the plant." She smiled as Armstead's gaze
turned their way. In another moment, he left Justin and
started toward them.

Ryder could see both surprise and speculation in Armstead's eyes as Lauren made the introductions. From the
man's expression, Ryder assumed that Lauren wasn't usually accompanied at Justin's ballgames, at least by a male.
Being linked with her gave him an inexplicable sense of satisfaction.

Armstead took the seat next to Lauren without an invitation. "You must be new in town, Mr. Braden."

"Not really," Ryder said, his eyes on Justin.

"Ryder's career took him away from Mobile," Lauren explained. "Actually he's a robotics expert."

"Oh?" Interest sharpened in Michael's pale eyes. "What company did you say you worked for?"

"I didn't." Ryder surged to his feet suddenly. "Now, Justin, *run!*"

Startled, Lauren turned her attention to the playing field just in time to see Justin seize a chance to steal home. "Yea, Justin!" she shouted, sticking up both her thumbs when Justin looked up in her direction, flushed and grinning.

"Way to go, Justin!" Ryder yelled. He turned to Lauren. "Did you see that? I thought for sure he was going to get tagged by that kid at third, but he dodged him and took off like greased lightning!"

For a second Lauren was caught by something in Ryder's expression. He was flushed, and his grin was every bit as wide as Justin's. Who would have thought he'd get so excited by a Little League baseball game?

"Justin can usually be counted on to make a couple of daring plays," Armstead said. "Remember last week when he set up the triple play that won the game, Lauren?"

Michael spent the next few minutes reminding Lauren of some memorable moments in Justin's Little League career, pointedly excluding Ryder. Next he mentioned a few social events they'd both attended, giving Ryder the impression that he and Lauren shared more than a working relationship. As if reading his mind, Lauren glanced at Ryder, whose attention appeared to be fixed on Justin. There was nothing personal in her association with Michael and she found she didn't want Ryder to think there was. Lauren frowned, wondering why she cared what Ryder thought about her personal life. As for Michael he had been spending time with Justin. More and more, lately it seemed. And with her, as well, she realized with a little start. She was chewing her inside lip thoughtfully when suddenly the game was over.

"Okay, that's it! Ten to four, not bad." Ryder got to his feet and stood aside while Lauren stepped around him and started down the tiers of bleachers.

"I noticed your car still at the plant, Lauren." Michael fell into step beside her, away from Ryder. "You'll need to pick it up. Why don't we run by now? I've got time and—"

"The situation's under control, Armstead," Ryder broke in, using the same tone that had curbed Justin earlier. "I'll see Lauren home and take care of her car."

"Lauren?" Michael's expression when he looked at her was definitely possessive.

"Thanks anyway, Michael," she said, not wanting to encourage him. "But there's no need. I stranded myself by not taking my own car to Ryder's place this afternoon."

Michael looked alert suddenly.

"Jake and I had an appointment this afternoon with Ryder," Lauren explained. "At his place in the country. He's agreed to act as a consultant for us in the lawsuit."

"I could have sat in if I'd known, Lauren," Michael said, faint disapproval in his tone.

"Nothing was definite until this afternoon, Michael." Just then she caught Justin's eye and motioned him over. "However, now that Ryder has Clay's designs, he will probably need to spend some time with various sections. I'll let you know if we need you."

Armstead started to say something, but just then the beeper on his belt sounded. He shut it off, looking irritated.

"Duty calls?" Ryder said dryly.

Ignoring Ryder, Michael turned to Lauren. "I've got a late shift working on that Hy-Tech contract," he explained. "I'll have to check in, I'm afraid. Will you tell Justin? I promised I'd see him after the game."

"Of course." A tiny frown formed between Lauren's brows. "If there's a problem, call me at home, Michael."

"Don't worry, I'll take care of it." Again he hesitated, about to speak. But looking from Lauren to Ryder, he appeared to change his mind. With a curt "Good night" he walked off.

Ryder was silent as he watched Armstead's progress across the turf. The fellow wasn't happy. He glanced down at Lauren. "Another jealous male looking out for you," he observed softly.

Lauren turned startled eyes up to his. "Not really," she said. "He's just a friend, as well as a dedicated employee."

They stood facing each other, the sounds of the ball field all around. Kids yelled, cars started up and then accelerated, a horn blew, brakes squealed. A soft night breeze suddenly stirred, disturbing the neat coil of Lauren's hair. Smiling faintly, Ryder reached up and captured a pale strand that blew across her cheek. He rubbed its silken texture between his fingers before tucking it gently behind her ear. Her heart jumped at his touch.

"That makes three, so far. How many more, Lauren?"

She moistened her lips, transfixed. "Three?"

"Three men looking out for you. First Jake, then Justin, now Armstead. How many more?"

His hand was warm. She could feel the heat. She would only have to turn her face a tiny bit to nestle her cheek into his palm. For a moment, she was wildly, crazily tempted to do just that.

"Jake is my lawyer," she said, her voice husky. "He's just doing his job. And Michael is only a friend. Justin is my son and sees himself as the only man in my life."

"And is he?"

"Yes."

Background sounds of the ball field, movement, people, all receded and became distant and insubstantial. Standing there, her gaze clinging to his, it seemed to Lauren that the appearance of this man in her life seemed suddenly fated. The confused tangle of emotion he evoked was no longer tension and wariness, but breathlessness and sweet anticipation. And much more, she was only just beginning to realize. How and why and exactly what weren't clear. Maybe that would all come later. Maybe later she would decide that she had been momentarily bewitched. But for right now, feeling strangely lighthearted, she fell into step beside Ryder, and for once in her life she gave herself up to the moment. Together they went to meet Justin.

THE MAN HUNG UP the telephone. Rigid and still, he stared at his clenched hands, forcing himself to breathe slowly. Otherwise how could he contain his outrage? He had bargained for none of this. God in heaven! He was not a puppet to be jerked by his contact whenever she conceived yet another maneuver to harass Clay Holt's widow. What would they have him do next? Had he not furnished every technical secret they required? He was a highly specialized professional, not a tale-bearing old woman!

Muttering, he fumbled with a drawer and pulled out a thick telephone directory. His contacts wished to play on the widow's vulnerability to the press. Why must he be the one to leak information? Such tasks were best assigned to the coarse types with whom his contacts consorted after hours. The widow's business was in jeopardy. With patience and shrewdness it would fall into their hands. But no. His contact had a vicious streak. She wished the widow to learn of a new development before the eye of the camera.

Adjusting his bifocals, he focused on the small print in the Yellow Pages. News dealers...news magazines...news service...the finger stopped. Newspapers. He found the numbers and scribbled them on a memo pad. With a heavy sigh he began to dial.

CHAPTER FIVE

"MOM! DID YOU SEE ME steal third, huh?" Justin ran up, triumphant and grinning.

"Did I see you?" Lauren gave his cap a playful tug. "Didn't you hear me cheering?"

Justin straightened his cap and made a face. "Aw, Mom, you always cheer, even when I mess up."

She shrugged, still smiling. "Well, what are mothers for?"

"The team looked good out there, Justin," Ryder said, catching the boy's eye. "And so did you. You made some fine plays. Are the Bluejays in contention for the championship?"

Justin's enthusiasm cooled slightly, but his reply was polite. "Yeah, we can win our division, no sweat, if Curtis Wainwright gets back in time."

Ryder exchanged a look with Lauren.

"On vacation," she supplied helpfully.

Ryder nodded with understanding. "Curtis is indispensable, I assume?"

"He's our best pitcher," Justin declared. "What a time to go to Disneyworld!" He kicked at a dirt clod in disgust.

Lauren dropped a hand to his shoulder and urged him toward Ryder's Blazer. "It's only for a week, Justin. Besides, I thought Freddie Preston did a good job today."

Justin looked doubtful. "Yeah, well, I just hope he can do it again Thursday."

"He'll do it," Lauren said, sounding cheerfully confident. "Meantime, let's get a move on, slugger. We've got to pick up my car. We don't want to monopolize Mr. Braden's entire evening."

"I can still get Scotty's mom to drop us off," Justin offered quickly.

Ryder heard the suggestion and realized that while Justin was tolerating him for his mother's sake, the boy was wary. Ryder suspected it would take a while before Justin bestowed unconditional approval on any man who appeared suddenly in his mother's life.

As they approached the edge of the field, Ryder put his hand on the small of Lauren's back as she stepped over the low cable barricade at the street. They were only a few feet beyond it when he felt her spine tense beneath his palm. She gasped.

A camera flashed directly in front of them.

"Mom!" The cry was wrung from Justin.

It took a second or two for Ryder to realize what was happening. A reporter stood squarely in their path holding a tape recorder. At his elbow was a scruffy photographer. The camera's whirring sound was like a snake hissing before striking.

"Mrs. Holt, are you going to accept NuTekNiks's buyout offer or are you still determined to fight?"

Justin stepped in front of his mother, his chin set, his eyes flashing.

"Is this your son?" The reporter made a gesture to his cohort. "Get a shot of the kid, Marty."

Ryder felt a hot surge of outrage and without thinking, he reached for the camera. Stopping short of flinging it to the ground, he settled for shoving it hard against the startled photographer's chest. Turning back, he saw the reporter moving in. Impressions came and went on his brain like quick-stopped images on film: Justin's eyes bright with tears, but his expression determined; Lauren's face wearing a trapped look; the curious stares of Justin's teammates.

Quickly he took out his keys and gave them to Justin. "Take your mother to the car, Justin," he ordered, giving the boy a reassuring squeeze on his shoulder before pushing him on his way.

His eyes were sharp with fury as he turned on the reporter. "What the hell do you think you're doing?"

"My job, mister. The lady's news and I've got a deadline."

Ryder uttered an oath in a softly menacing tone and watched, satisfied, as the reporter took a step backward. "Is nothing off limits to you guys? Don't you ever rest?"

With a shrug, the tape recorder was pocketed. "Inquiring minds want to know the facts."

Ryder looked him over, not bothering to disguise his disgust. "Well, I'd better not see you back at this ball field, buddy. If you want a statement from Mrs. Holt in the future, call her office for an appointment. You got that?"

He watched both men stalk off before turning and heading for the Blazer. Still furious, he jerked the door open and got in behind the wheel. Ryder was aware of his two silent passengers, but for a moment, he didn't say a word. Emotions seethed inside him, and his thoughts were as tangled as the underbrush on his property. It seemed that ever since meeting Lauren, he'd been in a tailspin. He hadn't intended to get mixed up in her life. He hadn't counted on reacting so intensely upon meeting his son. What the hell had happened to his plan to keep his distance?

"Thank you."

Hearing her whispered words, he drew a deep breath and turned to look at Lauren. She was so beautiful. The breeze had ruffled her hair more now. It was loose at her temple, on her cheeks, her forehead. The effect softened the sculptured perfection of her features, enhancing her already considerable appeal. Again he had to forcibly remind himself of the deception that he was perpetrating just by getting to know her and Justin. It was one thing to work on the lawsuit with her, but he could not get emotionally involved. That would be crazy. Insane.

"Do you have to cope with that kind of thing often?" he asked, feeling renewed anger.

She touched her forehead with a shaky hand. "No, at least not until today. I couldn't believe it when that reporter appeared. I'm just glad you were there to hold them off until Justin and I could get away."

"We could have handled it, Mom."

Ryder glanced at Justin. The boy was positioned close to Lauren's shoulder, watching him. More emotion twisted through Ryder. Recalling the look on the boy's face when he'd stepped between the reporter and his mother, he was reminded of his own rebellious, scrappy adolescence. More than once he'd plunged recklessly into situations where he knew he didn't stand a chance. It would have been amusing if he hadn't totally lost his sense of humor.

"Is nothing private anymore?" Lauren cried as Ryder started the Blazer. "I thought I'd have a few days of peace after the court session Friday."

Ryder frowned. "What was that about a buy-out?"

Justin moved to the position between the two front seats. "That guy wanted to know if you'd decided to accept NuTekNiks's buy-out offer, Mom, or were you going to continue to fight," he said helpfully.

Ryder almost smiled. Justin was sharp as new nails. And spunky. As Jake said, a terrific kid.

Lauren looked at Ryder. "I haven't had an offer. I don't know what he's talking about."

Ryder down-shifted with renewed irritation. "That's just great. Now the media knows more about your business than you do."

Ryder wondered how the reporter had known she was at the ball field. And the information about the lawsuit was privileged. There were some things going on that needed looking into, he thought. Maybe he ought to have a few private words with Jake Levinson.

They were at the Holt plant within minutes. Seeing only one car in the parking area adjacent to the front offices, Ryder raised a questioning brow to Lauren. "Yours?"

She nodded and he pulled up beside it. Before he could get around to her side, she was out of the Blazer. Justin jumped out right behind her, jangling his mother's car keys. Smiling wryly, Ryder fell into step beside Lauren as Justin ran ahead of them, toward the car. "Now that it's summer, where does he stay while you're working?"

"At home with Hattie Bell," Lauren replied. "She spoils him rotten, but it could be worse. He's in his own neighborhood and Hattie Bell loves him almost as much as I do."

He smiled down at her. "Lucky kid."

She was silent a minute, watching Justin. "Truthfully we both spoil him, I suppose." Her voice took on a husky, loving tone as she added, "He's all I have. I worry about him."

"It works both ways, apparently."

She swung her eyes around to his. "What?"

"Justin feels the same sense of responsibility for you," Ryder said. "His reaction tonight when you walked up with a stranger and then again when that reporter approached you tells me that."

"He's just a little boy," she said, sounding distressed.

Ryder looked at her. "He's the man in charge, Lauren. That's the way he sees it."

"Mom, hurry up! Mosquitoes are everywhere."

"Well, get in the car, Justin," she told him, exasperated and amused at the same time. "You have the keys." She was smiling as her eyes met Ryder's. "You see? Fifteen minutes ago he was a tiger protecting me from pushy photographers and now he's whining about mosquitoes."

"As good an excuse as any to get you all to himself, again," Ryder murmured as they reached the car.

She glanced his way. "What?"

"Mom!"

Shaking her head, Lauren snatched Justin's cap off his head. Ignoring his indignant yelp, she gave him a playful whack on his rear and then pretended to cough and choke in the cloud of ball field dust that resulted. They were laughing together when she clamped the cap back on, turning the bill sideways. "Will you quit complaining and get in the car, Justin?"

"It's gonna be swarming with mosquitoes," he told her grumpily, his laughter fading as he met Ryder's dark gaze.

"Maybe we need to ask Mr. Braden to make us a birdhouse for the parking lot," Lauren suggested.

"You make birdhouses?" Justin asked.

"I'm working on one right now," Ryder said.

Justin studied him with his head tilted to one side. "You make birdhouses for a living?" His tone was filled with disdain.

"Justin!" Lauren put her hand on her son's shoulder, shocked at the boy's rudeness. "Mr. Braden is an engineer. He was building a birdhouse to put up on his property. Purple martins consume mosquitoes."

"I know all about purple martins, Mom," Justin said with longsuffering patience. "I just wondered about a man who spent his time building birdhouses, is all."

"I like to work with my hands," Ryder volunteered, feeling a mixture of fascination and delight with Justin. The boy was stopping short of outright hostility; his manners were too good for that. But he was still suspicious. And he refused to be intimidated. Ryder had to admire that kind of grit. Without conceit, he knew he could appear formidable. He had successfully vanquished men of power and position with a withering look. It pleased him to find that Justin could hold his own.

"Yeah, I like working with my hands, too," Justin said. "Maybe I'll build one myself."

"Justin—"

The boy waved away his mother's reaction. "I could do it in the garage."

"We don't even have a saw, Justin," Lauren pointed out.

"How would you like to check out the one I'm working on right now?" Ryder heard himself ask, seizing a chance to see more of Justin. He could set strict limits, he told himself, avoid getting too close or interfering in their lives.

"You could look over the plans," Ryder offered. "And then if you're still interested, you could try your hand at it. I've already worked up a material list."

"Ryder, I'm sure you don't—"

"Maybe you can't read a set of plans," Ryder said to Justin.

"I can read plans," the boy said firmly.

Ryder shrugged. "Then it's up to you."

Justin gave away nothing by the look in his eyes. "You mean go to your place?"

"Yeah, and since you don't have the tools, you could use mine."

Justin pursed his lips, thinking. "I don't know..."

"That is, if you decide you'd like to try it."

After another long, speculative look at Ryder, Justin nodded briefly. "I think I'll give it a shot."

Lauren made a strangled sound. "Wait just a minute, you two. I..." But her objection died as she eyed them both, Ryder, big and implacable, exuding confidence and male power. And Justin, exhibiting many of the same qualities tempered by his youth. Just now he looked inexplicably like the older man. She shook her head as if to banish the similarity.

"I'll pick you up tomorrow," Ryder told him. "How about eight o'clock? I like to get an early start...that is, if your mother has no objections." He looked at Lauren.

"No," she said faintly, then added, "if you're sure you have the time..."

"I have the time."

Ryder watched Justin get in the car on the driver's side and then shift over to the passenger seat. Holding the door for Lauren while she slid in behind the wheel, he waited until she looked up questioningly. "I want to study Clay's designs in more detail before making any recommendations," he said, adding when she nodded, "I'll take good care of Justin."

"Thank you," she said softly, her eyes meeting his.

They were both still as the moment stretched out. In the filtered glow from the streetlight, the delicate sculpture of her features was etched as if in moonglow. She was faintly smiling, her hair now hopelessly tangled by the wind, shining like spun silver. He wanted to touch her, Ryder realized. And more. To his chagrin, he felt his body stir and begin to ache. He straightened abruptly, tearing his gaze away. As she pulled out, he stood rooted to the spot until the taillights of her car disappeared into the night.

LAUREN WAS DRESSED and ready to go to work the next morning by seven-thirty, as usual, but she dawdled over her breakfast, took far more time over the newspaper than she ever did on a weekday morning and had three cups of coffee. Glancing at her watch for the third time in as many minutes, Lauren saw that it was finally eight o'clock. She got up then and, picking up the phone, called her office. She really had nothing pressing until ten.

She looked at her hand, still holding the receiver, and noticed the tiny tremor. Ryder would be here any minute. The uncomfortable feeling from yesterday had returned, stronger than ever. But this time she had no glib excuses. She knew the reason now—she was deeply attracted to Ryder Braden, and her time with him yesterday studying the designs, and later, at the ball field with Justin, had intensified that attraction. Replacing the telephone she began to pace the length of the room, admitting to herself that she was deliberately dragging out the time before going to work so that she could see Ryder. For the first time in her life she was waiting for a man.

She actually jumped when the doorbell rang.

Where was Justin? She'd counted on his presence to ease the subtle tension that seemed to hover like a palpable force whenever she was with Ryder. But Justin had been so excited that he had not brushed his teeth or made his bed, so she'd sent him back upstairs to do both.

The doorbell rang again.

"Mo—om! Will you please answer that!"

Lauren slid her hands down the sides of her skirt and opened the door. Standing in the sunshine with the fresh morning all around him, smiling that half smile of his, Ryder was more attractive than any man had a right to be.

"This is a surprise," he said, his expression unreadable as he looked her over. "I thought you'd be at work."

She stepped back so he could come in. "I would, ordinarily. I'm just a bit behind schedule this morning."

Dear heaven, now I've progressed to outright lying. It's a wonder lightning doesn't strike me where I stand.

As she closed the door behind him, Ryder made a quick inspection of the foyer and the stairs beyond. "Is Justin ready?"

"He will be in a few minutes. He's brushing his teeth and making his bed."

He lifted his eyebrows as though impressed.

She smiled. "Under duress."

For the first time since she opened the door, he smiled and Lauren felt suddenly breathless. "Would you like some coffee?"

He nodded. "Sounds good, if it's not too much trouble." Ryder followed Lauren as she led the way to the kitchen, accepting the cup she handed him. He looked out the double French doors that opened onto a patio and backyard while she turned to pour her own.

"Let's take this outside," she suggested, moving around him toward the French doors. "Justin shouldn't be too long."

"It's nice out here," he said, following her out into the clear, still-cool morning. He bent his head to avoid a hanging basket with bright pink bougainvillea cascading almost to the ground as they headed for a glass-topped table. Lauren took a seat, but Ryder refused a chair and leaned against a wrought iron support instead, crossing his ankles. "I used to like that first morning cup of coffee outside," he said.

"Was that when you lived with your grandmother?"

"Yeah, she'd always have biscuits or muffins for breakfast and they tasted even better outside." He focused on a carefully pruned wisteria alongside the patio. "There were flowers everywhere. And no gardener. I realize now how much work it must have been for her."

"Her garden was beautiful," Lauren said softly, recalling the old-fashioned flowers arranged in no particular order. "I fell in love with it—and the house, too." She studied him over the rim of her cup. "Were you born there?"

He smiled, cradling his cup between his palms. "I was born in a hospital."

"But did your parents live there?"

He looked down into his cup. "Not really."

She wanted to ask what that meant, but the look of him warned her off. "Did you have any brothers or sisters?"

His eyes lifted to hers again. "Uh-uh, there was just me. But I always wished I was part of a big family."

"Me, too," she said, letting her gaze drift beyond him to a bright red cardinal perched on Justin's bird feeder. "I always wanted brothers and sisters and aunts and uncles. I told myself when I had children, I would have half a dozen." Her tone became wistful. "Not only does Justin not have brothers and sisters, he doesn't even have any living grandparents."

"It's not too late," Ryder said, placing the empty cup on the table. "You're young; you can still have children."

Even as he spoke, Ryder rejected the thought outright. He moved beyond Lauren and stood looking out over the clipped and manicured perfection of her lawn, realizing that he hated the idea of Lauren having anyone else's children. The emotions clamoring inside him were strictly male, primitive and territorial. He was jealous. She made him feel possessive and protective and torn, as though she belonged to him. He closed his eyes. How on earth was he going to keep his distance if he was already thinking like that?

Justin's voice came suddenly from the upstairs window. "Mom, I can't find my baseball cap with Roll Tide on it!"

"It's down here, Justin," Lauren called back. Standing, she set her coffee cup down and moved toward shelves stacked high with Justin's personal junk. The cap was on the top, just out of her reach. Before Ryder could stop her, she stepped onto the bottom shelf. It boosted her a foot taller and she stretched an arm up to grab the cap. When she pulled it, several other articles were dislodged. Instinctively Lauren jerked back to avoid a baseball bat and lost her footing.

With a startled cry, she felt strong hands clamp around her waist and pull her backward. But it was not far enough. In one motion, Ryder turned her body into his as the avalanche of Justin's junk rained down around them.

The instant that his arms went around her, Ryder was aware of a host of sensations—the fresh, flowery scent of her, the soft, silky texture of her hair, the rapid-fire beat of her heart, her warm breasts pressed firmly to his chest, her thighs meshing with his. Her softness nestled snugly against him set up a throbbing ache that made him forget all the reasons he'd planned to avoid getting into just such a situation as this one.

Still he didn't let her go until he felt her stirring against him, bringing her hands to his chest. Another wave of her perfume filled his senses, and he inhaled deeply, his face buried in her hair. Instantly he was fully aroused. Lauren was soft and pliant and offered no resistance until she moved her leg and encountered the evidence of his desire.

A soft gasp came out of her and she looked up at him. He knew then that whatever the attraction was between them, she felt it, too. Her eyes were wide and startled. The clear amber of her eyes had darkened to a deep, smoky topaz. Ryder felt a mix of pleasure and pain. Her face was lifted to his, her lips, soft and moist, were slightly parted. The air between them seemed to throb with promise. He had never wanted to kiss a woman so badly in his entire life, he realized. With a soft groan he pushed her away from him, even as his instincts urged him to throw her down right here and now and satisfy the hunger that had plagued him from the moment he'd looked into her eyes in Jake's office. He was playing a dangerous game.

Moving quickly, Ryder went to the edge of the patio and stared across the bright green perfection of the lawn. His emotions were a chaotic jumble. The sensation was something utterly foreign to him.

Lauren's laugh, sounding soft and chagrined, came from behind him. He turned reluctantly. "I'm sorry about that," she said, indicating the chaos on the floor. "I've warned Justin a million times about throwing his stuff on those shelves." She picked up her coffee cup, not meeting his eyes.

"One of the hazards of living with an eleven-year-old boy, I guess," Ryder said, looking away uncomfortably when he saw the tremor in her hands.

They both turned in relief as Justin came through the French doors. He stopped short when he saw the mess. "What happened?"

"Justin, we have a guest," Lauren reminded him.

"Oh," Justin said, subdued. "Hello, Mr. Braden."

"'Morning, Justin." Ryder bent over and passed a battered baseball glove over. "If that look in your mom's eye means what I think it means, we're probably going to have to pick this stuff up before she gives us permission to leave."

"You are absolutely right about that," Lauren said, collecting Ryder's coffee cup and heading for the patio door. "I was almost maimed by that dumb baseball bat, Justin. Before you go to bed tonight, young man, I want those shelves as tidy and organized as Hattie Bell's pantry."

Justin glanced quickly at Ryder. He was in for a lecture and he didn't like having a witness. But when he encountered only shared male sympathy in Ryder's expression, he relaxed. Scrambling around, he loaded up his arms. "I've been meaning to clean out these shelves, Mom, but you know how busy I am."

"Spare me, Justin."

"Honest, Mom, I was gonna do it Sunday afternoon."

"I know, you promised on your word of honor," she reminded him.

"Scotty and Mike came by and interrupted me, remember?"

"So what happened Monday?"

"My computer—"

"Okay, that ought to take care of it," Ryder said, breaking in smoothly. He took the remaining articles from Justin and placed them on the top shelf. The boy's attitude was familiar. At the same age he had perfected every delaying tactic known to man with his grandmother. Mama Jane, however, had been as canny and determined as he. Unlike Lauren, who was too indulgent, too permissive. In another year or two, Justin would be rolling over her like a tank.

It was not his concern.

Lauren couldn't believe she was standing there bickering with Justin. Ryder was going to think her a complete failure as a disciplinarian. She turned abruptly and went inside, still a little shaken by that clumsy encounter with Justin's things. She hardly slowed down to drop the two cups into the sink with a clatter before heading for the foyer. What had caused her to melt like a besotted teenager the instant their bodies touched? The irony was, she thought as she shrugged into a raw-silk blazer, she'd never felt this way, even as a teenager.

Following silently, Ryder was behind her when she reached the front door. Before she had a chance to do it herself, his hand was on the doorknob, opening it for her. Justin darted around them and down the steps, making a beeline for the Blazer. Wordlessly Ryder waited for Lauren and then followed her outside, pulling the door closed behind him.

"Thank you," she said quietly, using her key to turn the lock. "I didn't think to ask last night, but will it be okay to pick Justin up around noon? I can take a few minutes at lunchtime."

Ryder gestured for her to go down the steps in front of him. "It's not necessary. I'll drive him home sometime this afternoon," he said quietly. "Hattie Bell will be here, won't she?"

"Well, yes, but I don't want to put you to any trouble. It's enough that you've taken the time to give him this treat."

"It's no trouble," he told her, walking beside Lauren to her car and waiting while she unlocked it. He opened the door and she brushed by him and got in. Just that brief contact sent a quick tingle through her and she felt breathless again. He waited, while she smoothed her skirt over her knees and put her key in the ignition, before closing the door.

As Lauren looked up at him, she suddenly wished she had the nerve to do what she felt like doing at that moment. Ryder Braden was the most attractive man she'd ever met. What would he do if she just reached out a hand and touched that seductive mouth? Her fingers itched to trace the bold line of his eyebrow. She could almost feel the hard, uncompromising shape of his jaw against her palm. Oh, to just forget appearances and propriety. Oh, to be more like Clancy...

But she wasn't impetuous. She wasn't a risk taker. She would probably never feel Ryder's hands caressing her, his mouth tasting her. She would probably never hear him say things to her, sweet things, intimate things, things she couldn't even imagine because no man had ever spoken them to her.

"Take care," he said.

Her eyes clung to his for another timeless moment. And then, with a final soft tap on the roof of her car, he stepped back and she started her car and drove away.

Numbly, Lauren guided her car through her neighborhood and eventually out onto Spring Hill Avenue, which would take her to the Holt Company. For once her thoughts were not remotely concerned with work or its problems or her responsibilities. At a red light, she caught a look at her dazed expression and simply leaned back, closing her eyes.

What's happening to me?

How could she be so enthralled with a man she'd known only a few days? It was as though she'd been given a taste of something so intense and compelling that she had abandoned her innate caution, thrown it to the winds. It was as though a stranger had been lurking deep inside her, waiting to emerge after a twist of fate brought Ryder into her life. It was as though she was finally alive after... after what?

Lauren had spent years in a marriage with Clay Holt without feeling intense emotion. Clay had not been very passionate. The bond they shared was based on friendship, their backgrounds, similar interests. They'd married for all the right reasons, or so she'd always believed—compatibility, mutual respect, genuine affection. But not passion. There had been no breathless, intense *need* between them.

Only during her pregnancy had Lauren felt anything that came close to her feelings now. But something about the way she was feeling today brought back the emotional turmoil of those months. The sensual side of her nature had been carefully restrained most of her life. And her marriage to Clay was no exception. But when she'd carried Justin, there had been moments when she'd known there was more. Something, some element had been missing in her life.

Clay had been a scientist, a thinker. Logic and pragmatic action had been his way. When he discovered soon after their marriage that he was sterile, he immediately went about seeking a method to ensure that Lauren would not be denied the ultimate experience of childbirth. In expectation of the long life they would have together, he wanted her to have a baby and, he'd pointed out with a scientist's direct reasoning, modern techniques made childbearing possible through artificial insemination.

Lauren didn't think about her pregnancy often. It was just that somehow Ryder Braden brought back all those feelings. Why that should be so was as much a mystery as the medical miracle that had filled the void of a passionless marriage with the gift of Justin's birth. There was no connection surely, and yet... Lauren sat still, staring into space, knowing only that in her heart there was a very compelling connection.

CHAPTER SIX

RYDER DROVE THROUGH the mid-afternoon traffic, heading for the Holt Company. He was on his way to return Lauren's designs. As usual of late he was soul-searching, something he'd done more of the past few days than in all the rest of his life. After a day spent watching Justin, teaching him, enjoying him, Ryder was hooked. He'd been totally off the mark to think he could keep Justin at arm's length, spend a few casual hours with him here and there and then simply walk away. There was a link between him and the boy that could not be ignored. Walking away from Justin appealed to him no more than walking away from Lauren.

First the mother and now the son. A faint smile laced with a dash of self-directed mockery played at his mouth. For a man who didn't intend to get involved, his behavior was more than a little strange.

He pulled into the parking lot just as Jake Levinson was getting out of his car. Good, Ryder thought, he wanted to talk to Jake. The unexpected appearance of that reporter at the ball field still bothered him, plus the fact that the questions he'd fired at Lauren had been based on inside information. Maybe Jake could shed some light on the situation, otherwise . . . otherwise, he'd take care of it himself.

Ryder lifted a hand in greeting as he got out of his Blazer. When Jake spotted him, he waited, and Ryder fell into step beside him as they headed for the entrance to the business offices of Lauren's plant. Jake glanced down at the tubes under Ryder's arm that held the rolled-up designs.

"Did you get a chance to look them over?" the lawyer asked.

"Yeah."

"What do you think?" Jake reached for the door and waited for Ryder to precede him.

Ryder shrugged. "It's like everybody says—Clay Holt was a genius. The designs prove it." Using one of the tubes, he halted Jake before they reached the receptionist's desk. "And they're original, Jake. I'd stake my soul on it."

Nodding slowly, Jake smiled. "I'm relieved to hear it, especially from you." He studied Ryder for a moment. "And you're definitely going to help us?"

"Yeah, I'm in." Lauren's troubles concerned him in some elemental way; there was no use trying to deny the feeling.

Jake's smile widened. "Good, good."

"Jake—" Ryder hadn't moved. He looked past the lawyer down the hall where he assumed Lauren was waiting. His expression was troubled. "The designs are a gold mine, Jake."

Jake looked slightly confused. "That's what the lawsuit's about, Ryder."

"Except for one thing."

Jake stared at him, waiting.

The receptionist was watching them curiously and Ryder took Jake's arm and turned slightly, keeping his voice low. "Some of the designs are incomplete," he said. "Did you know that?"

Jake shook his head. "No. Are you sure?"

"The ones that were pirated by NuTekNiks are noted on the plans and they appear to be complete, workable designs. Others lack a couple of vital elements here and there, but the gaps are enough to make them unusable." He looked at Jake directly. "Did Lauren bring me everything, or are the originals in a vault somewhere?"

Jake was silent, thinking. "You're saying she purposely withheld the complete designs?"

"It looks like it."

Jake shook his head. "I don't think so, but there's one way to find out." Again, he attempted to walk.

Ryder put out a hand. "There's one more thing. Has she received an offer for the business?"

There was an immediate change in Jake. "Where did you get an idea like that?"

"Is that a yes?"

"You know that's privileged information, Ryder."

"Then maybe if I flashed a press badge, I could have the details," Ryder said, sarcasm in his tone.

"What the hell are you suggesting?"

Ryder studied the lawyer in silence and then made an impatient gesture with one hand, muttering something resembling an apology. He hadn't suspected Jake, not really, but years of corporate intrigue had made him a cynic. "Last night, a reporter just happened to find Lauren at the ball field," he explained. "One of the things he wanted to know was whether she was accepting NuTekNiks's buy-out offer. And since she knew nothing about a buy-out, I'm wondering how that reporter knew. Also," his tone took on a hard edge, "I'm wondering how he knew where she was."

Jake swore. "For the reporter, I can't say," he told Ryder. "As for the buy-out, that's what I'm here for now. I think she'll turn it down flat but they've made her an offer. I didn't receive it until late yesterday and I don't have any idea who leaked it."

"It would have to be damn generous to even come close to the value of those designs," Ryder said.

Jake met his gaze squarely. "That's for Lauren to decide," he said, then added in response to Ryder's skeptical look, "She knows the value of the business, man. She's not going to be suckered in by the sleazes at NuTekNiks."

"Damn right."

Jake's eyebrows rose. No two ways about it, that statement had a protective ring to it. Intrigued, Jake watched as Ryder's gaze strayed in the direction of Lauren's office. Unless he was very much mistaken, Ryder had the possessive look of a man with Lauren's welfare at heart. Very interesting, he decided suddenly, when not five days before, he'd had to practically beg to get the two of them together.

"How was the ballgame?" Jake asked. He'd wondered what could possibly interest a man like Ryder in a Little League game. Now it was coming to him. Lauren was a beautiful woman.

Ryder dragged his gaze from the hall back to Jake. "Uh, okay. You were right, Justin's a terrific kid."

"Uh-huh."

"His interests are at stake here, too," Ryder said after a moment.

Feeling better suddenly about Lauren's predicament than he had in a long time, Jake grunted and shifted the weight of his briefcase. Motioning Ryder ahead of him, he said, "So let's go hear what the lady has to say."

She said no.

Lauren offered them both scotch and they drank it while watching her pace the length of her office reeling off all the reasons why she wasn't amenable to a buy-out. Ryder was silent, savoring his drink and the sight of her. Each time he saw her she became more beautiful, he thought, roaming the shape of her cheekbones and the delicate strength of her chin with admiring eyes. Without hearing the words, he watched her mouth as she told Jake exactly what he could report back to NuTekNiks. She moved her arms to emphasize the message and he caught a glimpse of the soft, white swell of her cleavage where her blouse came together. His body tightened involuntarily.

Jake tossed off the last of his drink. They'd already covered the matter of the incomplete designs and unless Ryder had totally lost his touch in judging when a person was lying or telling the truth, Lauren was as surprised as Jake had been.

With his hand on the doorknob, Jake turned, dividing a look between Ryder and Lauren. "Now that we've turned down NuTekNiks's offer, I expect them to try some other delaying tactic," he said. "The thing that would really clinch our case is to come up with something to prove outright theft of the designs."

Ryder nodded, acknowledging the message. After months of futile effort, it was obvious that Lauren and her present staff weren't going to be able to prove any such thing. From Jake's expression he appeared to believe Ryder might manage it. When the door closed behind the lawyer, Ryder raked a hand against the back of his neck and drew in a deep, resigned breath and accepted the inevitable. He was up to his neck in Lauren's troubles whether he'd wanted to be or not.

"I don't know what else we can do," Lauren said, sounding discouraged. "With so little documentation, it seems impossible to prove anything."

"Don't worry, the proof's around here; it's got to be." Ryder glanced around the office. "It's just a question of finding it."

Lauren heard the confidence in his voice and took heart. "I don't suppose it bothers you that everyone's been looking for that proof for almost a year and getting nowhere," she said.

"Not really." He folded his arms across his chest. "But now, it's time we got really serious."

She cleared her throat awkwardly. "You know, you don't really have to do this, Ryder."

"I need to see the complete designs, Lauren. The only way to do that is to turn this place upside down for the missing elements. Without them, any expert opinion is worthless." He smiled. "So, you see, I do have to do this."

In spite of the fact that she had Jake as her lawyer, and she'd never doubted his ability, Lauren had always privately feared that everything was slipping away from her— Clay's life work, the company he'd entrusted to her, Justin's inheritance—everything. She didn't know what it was about having Ryder in her corner that dramatically lessened her doubt and fear about her legal battle. But it did. Smiling at him, she found herself wondering suddenly how he and Justin had made out together. If her son had found him half as appealing as she did, then they'd gotten along like a house afire.

She studied him in silence for a moment and then nodded. "Okay, but will we recognize them if we do stumble on them?"

"I can read a set of specs, Lauren," he said dryly, then added, "and so can Justin, by the way."

"Oh?" Her pulse quickened with interest. "How did it go today?"

"Put your mind at ease," he said, smiling. "He hammered and sawed like a pro. If he chooses, he can be a carpenter some day."

"Really?" Lauren felt a little surge of pride that Justin had acquitted himself well in Ryder's eyes.

"Really. But from the way he talked, I'd say he's leaning more toward sports or computers."

"Tell me about it," she said with feeling. "Between Little League and soccer and that computer in his room, it's all I can do to get him to do his homework."

Ryder opened his mouth to tell her she was too easy on Justin, but with a quick shake of his head, left the words unspoken. The thought had come quickly and naturally, as though parental responsibility was something they shared. He looked at Lauren, thinking of the awesome bond they did share. Maybe he should tell her now. Maybe, before he got in any deeper, he should lay it all out before her. He didn't know what to do. Ryder raked a hand through his hair and tried to fix his mind on robotics and the missing designs.

His eyes fell on the computer terminal behind her desk. "What about the material stored in the computer?" he asked, walking around to examine it. "From everything I've learned about your late husband, he seems the type to fully utilize a PC." He turned and lifted a questioning brow. "Has everything that he stored in them been accessed?"

"Yes, Michael checked all that." Lauren came to stand beside him, smiling as she touched the keys. "You're right, of course; Clay loved computers. And he passed his fascination right on to Justin. As soon as he was old enough to comprehend the concept, Clay bought him a PC. Just like Clay, Justin took to it like a duck to water."

"We need to find the missing designs, Lauren," Ryder said abruptly. She glanced up quickly, looking puzzled at his tone, but he went on impatiently, "Clay must have stored them somewhere. Was this his office?"

"Before I inherited it, yes," Lauren said, wondering what had annoyed him. Had he underestimated her problems and was Ryder now wishing he was elsewhere?

"No vault or wall safe?" She shook her head. "Which areas of the plant are secure?" he asked. "Besides Research and Development, I mean."

Looking more and more dismayed, she told him none. Access to Research and Development was controlled with strict security, but there was nothing there that hadn't been scrutinized over and over again.

Frowning, he examined the interior of the office again. "What's behind those two doors?"

Lauren walked over and opened the first one, revealing a private bathroom. "The other one is an old storage room," she told him. "I never use it and neither did Clay."

He tried the knob and found it locked. "Let's take a look anyway," he suggested.

Lauren scooped up her keys and went to the door. She unlocked it and then, before going inside, flipped the light switch which was on the outside wall. Ryder followed, but failed to catch the door which swung shut behind them. When he tried the knob, it was locked.

"Don't worry," Lauren said, dangling the keys in front of him. "We're not locked in."

"I'm happy to hear that," he said, casting a quick look around the long, narrow room. There was no window and a fine film of dust lay over everything. There didn't appear to be any particular order to the stacks of boxes and documents. Some weren't even labeled.

"I'm afraid it may be difficult to find anything in here," Lauren said, echoing his thought. She began opening cabinet doors which appeared to be the only logical location in the room for anything valuable.

Ryder made his way down the middle of the room. Bending to examine a few of the boxes, he discovered the dates marked on them were too old to be useful. Looking around with a frown, he picked up a set of obviously old specifi-

cations and slapped them against his thigh, making a face
when the dust flew. "Hope you're not allergic to dust," he
said.

"Not dust or anything else that I know of," she said,
closing the cabinet with a soft bang. "Are you?"

"No, only shrimp."

"Oh." She glanced up, smiling. "So is Justin. Isn't
that—"

"No offense," he said, "but this place is a mess." He
tossed the specs back where he found them.

The brusque note was back in his voice. Hearing it, Lauren
was mystified. She looked around at the evidence of
Clay's untidiness and smiled ruefully. "Looks like Justin
inherited more from Clay than a propensity for computers.
This place looks a lot like Justin's junk shelves on the patio."

When he didn't reply, she turned to look at him.

Somewhere in Ryder's mind, he registered the curious,
arrested look on Lauren's face, but he didn't acknowledge
it. He was too busy coping with the raw, frustrating effect
of her words. *How could Justin inherit anything from Clay!*
he wanted to shout at her. Maybe Clay had taught Justin,
nurtured him, offered the fatherly guidance that had gone
a long way toward molding Justin into the person he was
today. But the boy didn't inherit anything from him.

"Ryder—" Suddenly, the lights went out, plunging the
room into total, inky darkness.

Ryder froze. Calming his thoughts about being alone with
Lauren in a dark room, he struggled to recall the layout of
the storage area. The floor, he remembered, was an obstacle
course. The walls were lined with boxes and junk, some
of it stacked high and balanced precariously. Moving
around blindly, they could dislodge something and it would
all come tumbling down on their heads. On Lauren's head.

"Stay where you are, Lauren," he told her, instinctively moving toward the soft sound she made. "Where's the light?"

"It's outside on the office wall," she said, sounding disgusted instead of concerned.

"Great. Terrific," he muttered. He stepped around something in his path and stubbed his toe painfully on something else. "Ow!" He swore viciously.

"Wait," Lauren said, "I think I—" She gave a little cry when her elbow connected with a cabinet door that she'd left hanging open.

"Damn it! Just stay there, Lauren." Disregarding the debris littering the floor, Ryder plowed through the pitch blackness, homing in on the sound of her little moans. He reached her just as she straightened up and the top of her head connected with his chin.

"Ouch!"

"Ow!"

Swearing again, Ryder reached out blindly and hauled her into his arms. For a second, he couldn't tell much about what he was holding on to. In the total darkness that enclosed them, she could be backwards or upside down in his arms, he thought, just before he was swamped with sensation. Then there was only the sweet scent of her and the silky brush of her hair, and then her temple, against his mouth. In a sudden rush of heat and hunger, the softness of her and the womanly shape of her body were revealed to him. There was nothing blind or awkward in the way she fit. Her head was nestled in a spot perfect for her under his jaw. His hands curled naturally around the shape of her and everything in him urged him to pull her closer, tighter.

"Are you hurt?" he whispered thickly in her ear, his heart hammering so hard and loud in his chest that he could barely hear the sound of his own voice.

She must have whispered, "No," because he felt the small, negative toss of her head. He sucked in a deep, unsteady breath, flooding his senses with the intoxicating scent of her. Independent of his will, his hands moved over her back and the sweet curve of her spine, and then lowered to caress the soft, beguiling shape of her hips. His mouth skimmed her temple, her cheek, the corner of her mouth. A wave of longing washed over him, so deep and so compelling, that it was almost painful. Resisting that need was suddenly beyond him. Moving like a man in a dream, he breathed in deeply and covered her mouth with his.

It was nothing like a first kiss. They both fell into it headlong as though each was starved for the taste of the other. Lauren's lips opened under Ryder's and her body went soft against him. Her hands played over his back, then crept up until her fingers sank into his hair and held on as their tongues met. He groaned, muttering something, and tightened his arms so that she was crushed to him.

But one taste of her wasn't enough for Ryder. He craved more and more. Breaking the kiss, he turned his head to the curve of her neck and shoulder, grazing and nipping the sweet-smelling flesh. He stopped at the V of her blouse and with fingers that were unsteady, began to unbutton it. He found one breast and freed it, taking the weight in his palm, probing the nipple with his thumb.

"This is what I wanted to do this morning," he told her, in a voice rough with passion. She moaned and he raised his head to kiss her again, hotly, endlessly, fired by wild, hungry need that blotted out everything except how good she felt in his arms. How right...

Ryder came to himself with that thought and tore his mouth from hers, pulling away so abruptly that he castigated himself when he heard the soft, bewildered sound she made.

"Hell, I'm sorry, Lauren." His breath was heavy and labored. Desire still clawed at him, burned in him like a hot flame. He turned from her, sensing that she was still aroused, still willing. More than he'd ever wanted anything, he wanted to drag her back into his arms.

"This shouldn't have happened," he said in a low tone.

She was silent, but he heard the soft, rustling sounds as she adjusted her clothes.

"It won't happen again, Lauren," he promised. He knew she was feeling confused, and he squeezed his eyes shut, wishing he was somewhere else, anywhere else. She was probably cursing the day she'd ever laid eyes on him. He knew he was. He felt as though he'd been run over by a train—a part of him rejoicing the sweetly uninhibited way she'd responded and another part of him guilt-stricken for failing to exercise some control.

In the dark, Lauren's fingers fumbled with buttons. She was still reeling, not only from the explosion of passion between them, but also from the unexpected way Ryder had suddenly stopped. Lauren tucked the tail of her blouse back where it belonged and took in a long, unsteady breath. She was not a stranger to physical desire, but no kiss had ever, ever affected her this way. Surely he'd felt it, too?

"Lauren?" Ryder's tone was soft, husky with concern.

"It's okay," she said, backing away from him cautiously. He was easy to locate, even in the dark. She could feel the heat emanating from him, smell his musky maleness. "Stay where you are," she told him, keeping her voice steady with an effort, "and let me get the door. I've got the keys."

"No." The word was abrupt and she was startled. He must have sensed it because his next words sounded gentler, coaxing. "Please, just . . . just stay there and let me," he said his hand finding hers unerringly in the dark. He ignored it when she jumped as though jolted by a live wire. "Give me the keys."

She was reaching into her pocket when light suddenly flooded the storeroom making them flinch and blink, both temporarily blind.

"Lauren, are you in there?" It was Michael Armstead. He pushed open the door further and frowned as he took in the sight of Lauren and Ryder standing side by side in the litter of the storeroom. "What in the world are you doing here?"

"Michael." Lauren's mind went blank. Ryder touched her arm, urging her in front of him, and she moved forward into her office.

"How did you know anyone was in the storeroom?" Ryder asked, deflecting Michael's curiosity.

Michael pulled his gaze from Lauren to give Ryder a hard look. "I knew she hadn't left for the day. I came to her office looking for her and heard voices in the storeroom." He turned to Lauren again. "What's going on, Lauren?"

"I . . . we . . ."

"It has to do with the lawsuit," Ryder said smoothly, his tone discouraging more questions.

Michael's frustration was almost tangible as he turned back to Lauren. "Lauren?"

In truth she had almost forgotten the reason she and Ryder had originally been closeted together. She was still reeling from the kiss.

Michael studied the flush on her cheeks. "Is something wrong, Lauren? Are you sure you're okay?"

"I'm fine, Michael. Really."

Armstead hesitated, glancing at Ryder with cold suspicion before turning back to Lauren. "I don't have to remind you that I'm here anytime you need help, do I,

Lauren?'' When she merely gave him a brief, albeit polite smile, he added, "You know that, don't you? All you have to do is ask."

"I know, Michael," she said. "And I appreciate that. But you can help me best by doing exactly what you've been doing—staying on top of things here at the plant while Jake and I and—" she glanced at Ryder, not quite meeting his eyes "—Mr. Braden here, concentrate on our court case."

"If you're absolutely certain," Michael said, still reluctant. "But call me if you need me, will you promise me that?"

"I promise. And thanks, Michael."

"I think you hurt his feelings," Ryder said as the door closed behind Armstead.

Lauren didn't respond. She would have to be deaf, dumb and blind not to sense the male hostility that thrummed in the atmosphere whenever Ryder and Michael were in the same room together. A part of her was dismayed by it, while another part of her was pleased. But that brought her thoughts back to the few precious, magical moments in Ryder's arms. Had she only imagined the fierce, tender hunger in Ryder as he'd kissed and caressed her? Then why had he stopped?

"Lauren?" Something in his voice drew her eyes to his. "I'm sorry about what happened—grabbing you like that."

Lauren's gaze fell.

"I meant it when I said it won't happen again."

Lauren was amazed at her thoughts, amazed to discover how much she did want it to happen again. But she nodded mutely, her face turned from his. "There's no need to apologize," she said quietly. "It's forgotten."

With another long look at her, Ryder nodded once and then left.

"MAYBE HE'S MARRIED."

Startled, Lauren turned quickly to look at Clancy, who shrugged and leaned over, placing her wineglass on the low coffee table in front of the sofa. "It's been known to happen, sweetie."

Lauren gazed into pale gold Chablis and considered the possibility that Ryder was a married man. It was one logical explanation for the way he seemed to react to the growing attraction between them. It would also explain his promise not to touch her again. But somehow... She brought the wine to her lips slowly. "I don't think so, Clancy."

"What do you think?"

"I don't know." She leaned back against the cushion and recalled the rush of sensation that had flooded her body as Ryder's hands and mouth had worked their magic. "Whatever his reason, he forgot it in the heat of the moment and then when he remembered, he stopped cold. I don't think you forget a wife like that."

"Hmm," was Clancy's response.

"I want him, Clancy."

This time it was Clancy who was startled. She laughed. "I don't believe you said that. Is this the terribly proper, inhibited Lauren I know, lusting after a man and admitting it?" Clancy reached for the wine bottle and checked the contents. But it was still half full. "How much have you had to drink?"

"You see, Clancy!" Lauren came up off the sofa and began to pace the room. "If you'd said to me that you wanted a man, I wouldn't have batted an eye. You're honest and candid about your feelings, and you have been from the moment you first put on a training bra."

"I never owned a training bra," Clancy said.

Lauren whirled around. "That's just what I mean! I wore a training bra before I even needed one. My mother insisted."

"She meant well," Clancy offered.

"She was a tyrant."

"Steel magnolia is the term, I believe," Clancy murmured, sipping Chablis.

"I've been a good little girl all my life," Lauren said. "I've always obeyed rules, meekly followed directions, done all the things expected of me as a proper Southern woman. I've never taken chances, Clancy."

"You've never had to, Lauren."

"No. I've always chosen the easy way. Even when I married Clay, I did it because I knew it would be a comfortable marriage. There was no passion, but I overlooked that. I knew he loved me and would never hurt me."

Clancy watched her intently. "Ryder might hurt you, Lauren."

Lauren nodded. "He might, but I'm willing to risk it. I've been too inhibited all my life and too ready to place my destiny in the hands of other people. I need to be more assertive. I need to break the habit of relying on someone else to solve my problems. I know it won't be easy to change. But I'm going to."

"I think you're being too hard on yourself," Clancy said, her wine forgotten. "You could hardly handle your legal problems without a lawyer and you certainly needed help to run the plant. Why this soul-searching, all of a sudden?"

"It's a little complicated," Lauren said, frowning. "I like Ryder and I want him. But, true to form, here I am waiting for him to take the lead, to do all the running after me even though a relationship with him would make a major impact on my life."

"And your emotions," Clancy added.

"Exactly." Lauren stopped and looked at her friend. "You wouldn't hesitate to let the man you wanted see how you felt, would you?"

"Well—"

"You wouldn't, Clancy." Lauren's expression revealed her insecurity, but her chin was set, her mouth firm. "It might backfire on me. Instead of capturing his interest, he may be turned off.'"

Clancy smiled. "Or flattered all to hell and back."

"I mean it, Clancy."

"Hey, fine. All right. So... here's my advice." Clancy lifted her wineglass high. "Go for it!"

Lauren's smile was a little strained, but she finished off her wine, and then with a flourish sent her wineglass sailing across the room toward the brick fireplace. Clancy's mouth fell open as the crystal splintered in a shower of tiny fragments.

"I can't believe this," she said, studying Lauren as though she had sprouted a third eye. Suddenly she grinned. "This is a new twist. Usually it's you urging caution and me about to embark on some reckless venture."

Lauren nodded. "True, and look how interesting your life has been."

Clancy was shaking her head. "This really is too much. Here I am trying for a little stability, getting ready to settle down and counting on you to show me the way."

Lauren eyed her shrewdly. "For Jake's sake?"

Clancy sighed. "Is it that obvious?"

"Yes," Lauren said flatly.

Clancy groaned and then with a return of her natural optimism, she giggled. Copying Lauren, she lifted her wineglass. "Then I repeat, let's go for it!"

UNFORTUNATELY WHILE LAUREN had resolved to go for it, the object of her obsession had decided to do just the opposite. Ryder wasn't going to renege on his promise to appear as the expert witness in Lauren's court case, but he wasn't going to get involved in her personal life any more than he already had. Since he couldn't keep his hands off her, he resolved simply to avoid her. And for two weeks, he managed to do just that.

He was amazed how hard that was to do. Ryder thought of a dozen reasons to go back to her company. Or her house. He came up with so many creative ideas to spend time with Justin that he surprised even himself. But he didn't act on any of them. Instead he confined himself to a single visit to Jake Levinson in order to discuss the possibility of someone inside Lauren's company feeding secrets to NuTek-Niks.

As it turned out, Jake suspected the same thing, he told Ryder, but flushing the informer out had proved impossible.

"Any idea who it could be?"

Jake shook his head. "Not a clue." He looked at Ryder. "You got any ideas?"

Ryder knew who he wanted it to be, who it might be. Michael Armstead was in a position to leak vital technical information. Lauren trusted him completely. But he was so visible that he made an almost too-perfect suspect. Just because Ryder had taken an instant dislike to the man didn't mean he was guilty of industrial espionage.

"What do you know about Armstead?"

Jake nodded slowly. "You, too, eh? I don't know, Ryder. It appears he's just exactly what he seems—a damn good salesman who worked his way all the way up to the top job. I've done some discreet background inquiries—without Lauren's knowledge, you understand—and turned up nothing." He looked squarely at Ryder. "He's got his eye on Lauren, of course."

"He seems to manage time with Justin, too," Ryder said as he got up and went to the window. "Justin's a kid; it's easy to fool a kid."

"I wouldn't say that," Jake murmured, "especially about Justin."

Ryder laughed then. "Yeah, he's something else. I noticed it, myself."

Speculation sent one of Jake's eyebrows upward. "Been spending some time with him, yourself, have you?"

"A little." *But not nearly enough.*

"Uh-huh."

Silence in the room stretched out while each man was occupied with his own thoughts. Then Jake sat back in his chair.

"I've got an idea, Ryder."

Ryder's expression was impassive while he studied the lawyer. He knew that look. He had seen it on Jake's face before, but it had been years ago. He said as much and watched a wry smile spread over Jake's face.

"That was a long time ago, buddy," the lawyer said. "We were just kids then—high school kids pulling juvenile pranks. Besides, you always managed to pull everything together before the stuff hit the fan." He dismissed Ryder's objection before it could be spoken and leaned forward suddenly. "You know what Lauren really needs, Ryder?"

Ryder grunted. "You're gonna tell me, right?"

"She needs somebody on the inside looking out for her interests."

"She's got Armstead."

"Yeah."

"You think I ought to go to work at the plant?"

"You picked up on my idea so fast it makes me wonder whether you've already thought of it."

"I know you too well," Ryder said.

"You would be perfect, Ryder," Jake coaxed. "Lauren could hire you as . . . as . . ."

"Production manager," Ryder supplied, leaving the window to begin pacing. "Not too elevated in the management hierarchy so that I'd be alienated from the majority of her employees and not so low that I couldn't have access to sensitive data."

Jake's eyes lit up. "Just enough authority to stick your nose into everything."

"Uh-huh."

"I see you have been thinking."

Ryder met his gaze with a bland look. "It'll screw up the expert witness thing," he reminded Jake. "No Holt employee would be acceptable to the court."

Jake shrugged. "So, we'll go with one of the other three men on your list."

Ryder went back to the window. "What if Lauren doesn't agree?"

Jake didn't even dignify that with a reply. Instead, he laughed. "You want to tell her or shall I?"

"You do it."

DRAWING A DEEP BREATH the man shifted in his chair, impatient for everyone to clear out. He stared at his watch, waiting. This time what she wanted was more difficult. He had tried to reason with her, but she was a hard woman. She never let up. Her promises meant nothing. Always it would be the last time, she said. A chill crept over him. What if all her promises were lies? What if everything he'd done was for nothing? Despair rose, almost choking him. No, he couldn't, wouldn't think like that. It could never be for nothing. The purpose he had was everything. His goal was as pure and perfect as his love.

He stood suddenly, realizing the plant was empty. In his hand was a plastic card. Getting inside the restricted area after hours was the biggest obstacle. He had to wait until he was certain everyone was gone. Once inside he knew his way around well and could take care of her latest demand. He made his way down the corridor. It would have been better if he could have stayed late. But he had to be seen leaving, just in case.

He could not afford to make any mistakes at this point. He was close. So close. It would only be a little while now and he would be happy again. What he was doing was dangerous, but the risk was worth the taking. He would do anything, dare everything, risk all for his Anna.

Looking once over his shoulder, he inserted the card, punched out the security code and waited. The door buzzed. He pushed it open and stepped inside.

CHAPTER SEVEN

"I DON'T KNOW WHAT to say, Jake." Lauren leaned back, her lunch forgotten. She hadn't seen or heard from Ryder for over two weeks and now suddenly he was applying for a job as her production manager. Delight and hope blossomed in her. "Are you sure you didn't misunderstand?"

"I didn't misunderstand, Lauren." Jake grimaced as he inspected the insides of the ham and swiss sandwich he'd bought from the snack bar's vending machine. .

"I thought Ryder was going to be our expert witness. He can't do that if he's on the payroll."

Jake gestured with the sandwich. "No problem, he's already contacted a friend of his who's agreed to serve as our expert."

Lauren stared at him. "Why is he doing this, Jake?"

Jake pushed the sandwich away untouched. "He believes... We both believe that someone right here in your plant is feeding Clay's designs to NuTekNiks. As production manager, Ryder will be free to circulate. He'll get to know the employees, hear the scuttlebutt on the floor, be everywhere."

"I'm not arguing that," she said. "It's just that—"

"You're free to refuse, of course, but I've got to say I think it's the perfect opportunity to discover who's selling you out, hon."

She searched his face intently. "You didn't answer my question, Jake. Why is he doing this?"

She was never to know. Jake was distracted by a small flurry of activity across the room. He glanced past her shoulder with a startled look and then his expression was suddenly blank.

"Hi, Mom!" Justin called out. In jeans and sneakers with untied laces flying, he ran ahead of Clancy St. James, who was negotiating the crowded lunch tables with the help of her exotic cane. Shaking her head, Lauren watched her son twist through the tables at his usual breakneck pace. When he skidded to a stop beside her, she tweaked the bill of his treasured 'Bama baseball hat. "Hi, kid."

"No, no, don't get up." Clancy waved a hand as Jake politely started to rise, seemingly unaware of the guarded look in his gray eyes. With her cane, she hooked the leg of a chair and deftly pulled it around. Eyeing Lauren's yogurt and Jake's sandwich, she wrinkled her nose. "Wow, a gourmet lunch. You guys really know how to live it up," she said, sinking into the chair.

"Hi, Clancy." Lauren smiled and then glanced at her watch. "You two are forty-five minutes early, you know that?"

"Yeah, I know it and you know it," Clancy said, and playfully whacked Justin across the kneecaps with her cane. "But your firstborn here apparently wants to get an early start. I'm lucky I managed to hold him off till now."

Justin grinned and dodged just out of reach. "I didn't want to be late," he said, wide-eyed. "All that traffic and maybe a couple of accidents could have messed us up for hours."

"Give me a break!" Laughing, Clancy threw up her hands.

"Well, it's true!" Justin insisted. "Army Surplus could be closed by then."

"Army Surplus?" Jake repeated, looking at Lauren.

Shaking her head, Lauren waved Justin in the direction of the door with both hands. "The new hamburg-flipping robot is being tested in Research and Development, honey. Go check it out. I'll be finished here in a jiffy." Her smile lingered as she watched him dash off. She turned back to Jake. "In a couple of weeks, Justin's Boy Scout troop is camping out overnight and we're shopping this afternoon for his gear. He insisted on 'authentic' military stuff, hence Army Surplus." She smiled at Clancy. "Having camped out in some of the world's most desolate places, Clancy volunteered her services."

"For the shopping and the camping," Clancy put in. "I'm feeling magnanimous."

"And I really appreciate it. I'd probably embarrass Justin beyond words with the extent of my ignorance."

"No problem, sweetie." Clancy generously dismissed Lauren's inexperience. "Between Justin and me, we'll have you whipped into shape in no time."

"Don't they have men for that kind of thing?" Jake asked tightly.

"For what, whipping her into shape?" Clancy asked facetiously.

"For roughing it outdoors with a bunch of kids," Jake said evenly.

"You volunteering?" Clancy's blue eyes dared him.

Lauren cleared her throat hastily. "Clancy, have you had lunch? The ham and swiss is . . . interesting, right, Jake?"

Jake grunted and wordlessly passed his sandwich to Clancy.

Clancy just as coolly nudged it back to him before arching an eyebrow and dividing a look between her friend and her ex-fiancé. "So...you two still working on a strategy for flushing out the resident bad guy here at the plant?"

Jake's eyes narrowed, and for the first time he spoke directly to Clancy. "What's that supposed to mean?"

She shrugged innocently. "What? Wasn't I explicit enough?"

Jake looked at Lauren. "The less people who know about our suspicions, Lauren, the better our chances are of getting to the bottom of this," he said.

"Oh, for Pete's sake, Jake, stop sounding like a tight-assed lawyer!" Clancy said, exasperated. "Lauren didn't tell me anything. I'm reasonably intelligent *and* a journalist. Look into my baby-blues, man. I'm not blind. Anybody who can see beyond here—" she tapped the end of her freckled nose with her index finger "—can figure it out. Lauren's secrets are being pirated by a greedy-gus right here on her own turf."

She leaned back, eyeing them both speculatively. "So what do you plan to do about it?"

"It's none of your damned business what we plan to do about it," Jake told her through his teeth.

Lauren could count the times on one hand that she'd seen her unflappable lawyer ruffled, but at this moment, there was no mistaking the signs that Jake was tightly furious. All his attention was focused on the impudent redhead taunting him. Lauren might be his client, but he'd obviously forgotten her existence. It was just as well, Lauren thought. She had no desire to get caught in the crossfire between these two.

"I happen to consider it my concern if my best friend's business is being sold down the river," Clancy informed him.

The plastic spoon Jake held snapped in half. "Yeah, well, your concern's duly noted. We'll try to remember to send you a thank you note when you ride off into the sunset as soon as you can stand on that." He jerked his head toward her wounded knee.

"I'm not going anywhere," Clancy said.

Jake snorted. "I've heard that before."

"Well, you can believe it this time." Deliberately she turned to Lauren. "What happened with Braden?" Her eyes widened. "Don't tell me! Your new image must be work—"

"It's nothing like that," Lauren started to say.

Clancy was confused. "Well, what then? Isn't your super-duper lawyer here managing everything?"

"Well..." Lauren glanced at Jake and shrugged helplessly. "Ryder isn't the witness anymore; he's coming to work for me instead."

Clancy blinked. "Say, what?"

"Lauren, for Pete's sake!" Jake shoved his chair back but Lauren stopped him from rising with a soft touch on his arm.

"Jake, Clancy is my friend. I trust her."

"Thanks, sweetie." For a second the usual brashness in Clancy's blue eyes softened. "I thought this guy was a world-class executive. Why's he coming to work here?"

"I was just asking Jake that very question," Lauren said.

"And I was just trying to get a moment of privacy with my client to explain," Jake snapped.

"We need someone right here on the premises to expose whoever's stealing Clay's designs," Lauren said quietly.

"A plant in the plant!" Clancy looked delighted. "Great idea. Braden has volunteered?"

Lauren nodded. "Apparently."

"And you're going for it?"

Lauren hesitated and then nodded again. "I think so."

"Whose idea was it?"

That was something Lauren wondered about herself. She glanced at Jake. "Yours, Jake? Or Ryder's?"

"Both," Jake said shortly.

Clancy leaned back, looking pleased. "Well, frankly I can't wait to meet Mr. Wonderful. He sounds like my kind of guy, managing to shake you up, Lauren, and wringing a somewhat daring idea out of Jake, for a change." She shook her head and put her hand over her breast. "It's almost too much. Be still my heart."

"Clancy!" Lauren laughed helplessly.

"Look out, woman." Jake's tone was softly menacing. "You think you know me, but I just may decide to prove that you don't."

Clancy eyed him from beneath tawny lashes. "Promises, promises..."

Jake made a choking sound and Lauren quickly dipped into her yogurt. These two might come to blows before lunch, such as it was, was over!

"I've got an idea, Lauren." Looking thoughtful, Clancy tapped a forefinger against her lips. "One that goes hand in hand with your plan to put a spy in the plant."

"Leave Lauren out of your schemes," Jake told her flatly, "whatever they are. If I know you, it'll be some harebrained, reckless idea with no chance of success and every chance of somebody getting hurt." He glanced pointedly at her knee.

"I got this when a car bomb blew up in front of a sidewalk café in Paris," Clancy shot back. "I was drinking coffee and reading the morning paper."

Jake's hand shook slightly as he crushed sandwich wrapping and a paper plate in one hand. "This doesn't concern you, Clancy."

"Look, isn't Lauren capable of deciding for herself if she wants to hear my plan?" Clancy demanded. "You're her lawyer, Jake, not her daddy."

"I'm warning you, Clancy—"

Lauren put a hand on Jake's wrist. "Just a minute, Jake. What do you have in mind, Clancy?"

Clancy hitched her chair closer to the table. "Look, we know somebody over at NuTekNiks is getting Holt designs; we're all agreed on that. You've already got Braden looking from this end. But what about from that end? If we cover the situation from both sides, we double our chance of success."

"How would we cover the goings-on at NuTekNiks?" Lauren asked. "We can't put a spy over there."

"I can't wait to hear this," Jake muttered.

"I thought maybe a little undercover work," Clancy said, ignoring Jake. "Have a couple of hangouts near NuTekNiks's plant under observation, see what we can pick up. After hours, of course. Guys talk about their work over a few beers." She sent Jake a sly look. "It's sort of a variation on the pillow-talk theme."

"Hmm." Lauren frowned, thinking it over. "You might have something there, Clancy. But how—"

"Nothing to it," Clancy said with a negligent lift of one shoulder. "Hang out a few nights, have a few beers, just like the guys. No telling what we'll pick up."

Jake's palm hit the table with a crash. "Absolutely not!" he roared. "I forbid it, damn it!"

Clancy glared at him. "I meant me, Jake, not Lauren. I'll go undercover. I've done it before. We're not going to harm a hair on the head of your client. Look, there's this place called the Blue Marlin. It's frequented by the guys at NuTekNiks; I've already checked it out. I'm bound to—"

"You're bound to get more than you bargain for at the Blue Marlin, you little fool," Jake said heatedly. "Be reasonable for once in your life, Clancy."

"There is nothing unreasonable or reckless about the idea, Jake," Clancy said. "It's just as rational as your own plan to put Ryder Braden in the Holt plant. In fact, there's absolutely no difference except in your head. You've got a man spying here at Holt. Why not have a woman at the other end spying on NuTekNiks? Or is your thinking so antiquated and chauvinistic that a woman simply mustn't be allowed to do that?"

"Looks like you're about to find yourself in deep water, my friend," Ryder said, coming up behind Jake. His slow smile included both Lauren and Clancy. "Lawyers—" he shook his head "—always ready to argue."

Jake laughed shortly. "Glad to see you, too, buddy. Take a seat and help me try to talk some sense into these two."

At the first sound of Ryder's deep voice, Lauren's heart had leaped wildly. It was the first time she'd seen him in anything except jeans. Even though he was outfitted exactly like a thousand other businessmen in town, as well as half a dozen of her own employees right here in the plant, no other man brought her senses alive or made her body burn with just one look. No other man very nearly took her breath away.

"Mr. Wonderful, I presume," Clancy said, her eyes dancing.

With a start, Lauren gathered herself and quickly introduced Clancy, who studied Ryder frankly, her head to one side. "I guess you know these two think you're a cross between James Bond and The Equalizer." She grinned when Ryder winced. "Frankly, it's about time somebody decided to actually do something to flush out the traitor in our midst."

Ryder glanced quickly at Lauren. "Jake told you what we discussed?" When she nodded, he continued, "What do you think?"

She looked uncertain. "I don't know what to think."

There was a moment of odd tension as Ryder studied her. "It was just a suggestion," he said, his eyes suddenly shuttered. There was an edge to his voice when he said, "You have more than enough help as it is."

"Maybe so," Lauren agreed. "But Clay's designs are still being compromised. If you're willing to pretend to be the production manager for the Holt Company, then the job and all its dubious benefits is yours."

Ryder hesitated for a heartbeat before the corners of his mouth lifted in a smile. "You've got yourself a production manager, lady." He reached for her hand and pulled her to her feet. "Now, come and break the news to my boss, whoever he is."

Before she could protest, Ryder's hand was at Lauren's waist gently but firmly nudging her along. "Clancy," she called hastily over her shoulder, trying to keep pace with his long strides. "If Justin shows up here before I run into him in the plant, tell him that something came up and I'll be back as quickly as I can."

"No problem," Clancy said, looking amused.

"Justin's here?" Ryder asked, slowing down once they were out of the snack bar. He liked watching her, listening to her, being with her. Now that he had Lauren to himself, he intended to prolong their time together, to savor her company. He had a legitimate excuse, he told himself.

"Hmm? Oh, yes. He's somewhere in the plant." She frowned slightly. "I don't know where Michael is at the moment," she murmured.

"He spends a lot of time at the plant?"

She gave him a startled look. "What kind of question is that? He's general manager, Ryder. It'll be understandable if he's a bit disgruntled to find out I've already hired someone without consulting him."

"I'm talking about Justin, Lauren, not Armstead."

"Oh." It was obvious that Ryder wasn't concerned about Michael's reaction, or anyone else in the plant for that matter. "Clancy and I are taking Justin to get outfitted for a camping trip as soon as I can break away," she explained. "He's probably entertaining himself just now at the expense of some poor engineer."

"Asks a million questions, does he?" Ryder pushed at a door and waited for her to precede him.

"And then some. I admit I feel slightly overwhelmed sometimes."

"Who's taking him camping?"

She laughed wryly. "Would you believe, me? And Clancy, thank goodness."

Ryder arched one eyebrow. "With an injured knee?"

"She swore to me it would be healed in two weeks." Lauren looked up into his face and laughed. "When you're desperate, you tend to overlook niggling details."

Her smile hit Ryder with the force of a doubled fist. He stared at her, feeling desire curl through him and settle in, heavy and deep. Two weeks away from her and he'd forgotten the immediate, intense reaction she triggered in him. How could he keep his hands off her if he saw her every day? But damn it, she needed him. And he needed to do this for her. And Justin.

As they toured the plant, Ryder kept a low profile, preferring at first just to observe. They weren't half through before he began to revise his thinking about what he'd stepped into. He had planned to make a mental list of employees who might be suspect, but after an hour it seemed nearly everyone Lauren introduced fell into that category. The company still operated with the close-knit harmony of a family owned and operated business. Security was a joke.

"This is our think tank." Lauren pushed a plastic card into a slot and punched out a security code. Ryder grunted, thinking that at least there'd been one area Clay Holt had felt compelled to safeguard. He followed as Lauren entered an all-white room where half a dozen technicians were bent over drawing boards.

"Clay, of course, was the driving force here. Fortunately his undeveloped ideas weren't lost. He recognized talent and creativity in others and encouraged the participation of his 'crew,' as he called them, in his experiments. We've almost perfected a robot designed to help a handicapped person. It isn't operated manually, but responds instead to voice commands. There are still a few bugs in it."

Ryder listened to Lauren's detailed explanation of the problem and found himself revising his assessment of her as well. She must have put in countless hours after her husband died in order to familiarize herself with reams of technical material as well as the functional and administrative details of the company. According to Jake, her original career had been in marketing and public relations. Just holding the company together would have been a major feat, but she'd gone far beyond that, he thought, watching her use her hands to help explain a particularly complicated concept.

There was an air of vulnerability about her that he found almost irresistible. But she had shown remarkable strength and resourcefulness as a businesswoman. He wondered what other surprises were hidden beneath her cool exterior. It would be a delight to unveil her secrets slowly, one at a time. With just one kiss, she had turned to flame in his arms. He had been haunted ever since by thoughts of what it would be like to take her to bed.

The idea was so tantalizing that for a moment he was lost in the sheer pleasure of imagining himself entangled with those long, long legs, of losing himself in the sweet, warm depths of her body. Already he knew that loving Lauren would demand more of him than the quick, unemotional coupling of past sexual encounters. She would be—

"Here's Michael now," Lauren said, and Ryder felt the tension that rippled through her as she looked beyond him to Armstead approaching them. "Good, it'll give me a chance to fill him in on what I've done."

Ryder wanted to shake her. "You sound like you've done something wrong, Lauren. The company belongs to you, not Armstead. You don't have to have his approval to make a management decision."

"He may see it differently," she murmured, moving a little closer to Ryder. "Michael, ah . . . I've just been showing Ryder around the plant."

Armstead looked at Ryder before silently lifting his eyebrows. *A classic tactic,* Ryder thought and wondered if the man often resorted to intimidation in his dealings with Lauren. He felt a surge of anger and barely resisted an urge to protectively place his hand on her waist.

"I've just been added to the payroll, Armstead," he said, issuing the statement flat out with a feeling of satisfaction.

"He's our new production manager, Michael."

Armstead's eyes narrowed. "I wasn't aware you were interviewing for that position, Lauren. Or any position, for that matter."

Lauren shrugged. "Well, Ryder is extremely qualified, Michael, and when I learned he was available, I knew we'd be lucky to have him." She appeared not to notice Armstead's lack of enthusiasm. "Production is scrambling to meet the terms of that new contract from Hy-Tech in Pensacola. Wasn't that what you said this morning? I assumed you'd appreciate all the help you can get."

"Of course." After a deliberate glance at Ryder, Armstead drew a deep breath. "The shipping department is having some difficulty." He turned to Ryder. "You can start down there tomorrow, Braden."

Ryder almost laughed. He had no doubt that Armstead would dearly love to bury him in the shipping department.

Lauren spoke up quickly. "To tell the truth, Michael, I've decided not to confine Ryder to one area. To begin with, I think it's best for him to be a free agent and sort of float around. His experience is broad based, and heaven knows, we can use all the help we can get." She gave Ryder a look of approval. "I thought we'd let him use his own judgment."

Ryder watched Armstead's jaw clench. He was beginning to understand Lauren's hesitation in going over his head. This was a man who did not cotton to any intrusion into his territory.

"Come into my office, Lauren. We can't talk here in the hall." Confidently Armstead stepped back to allow her to precede him.

"I'm afraid I don't have a minute right now, Michael," Lauren said politely. "Tomorrow morning at nine you can brief Ryder in my office on those areas where we're in trouble."

"I can see your mind is made up," Armstead said tightly, making a visible attempt to rein in his temper.

Lauren looked at Ryder, who gave her a slow, conspiratorial wink unseen by the other man. Her mouth twitched with an urge to smile, but she conquered it. "Yes," she told Michael softly, "my mind is made up."

He gave her a curt nod. "Then I'll see you both tomorrow."

Ryder felt Lauren wince when Armstead went inside his office and closed the door with a restrained snap. "A peach of a guy," he said dryly.

Lauren sighed. "Really, he is." When Ryder snorted, she felt compelled to defend Michael. "It's perfectly natural for him to be resentful. I hired you without consulting him and he's supposed to be the plant manager. How would you feel in his place?"

Ryder looked down at her. "The truth?" She nodded. "I would have been furious, too, but I wouldn't have stopped with a few mealy-mouthed objections. I'd have hauled you off to your office alone and given you an ultimatum."

"And I would have fired you."

He shrugged. "Maybe."

She stared at him. "Then why—"

"The fact that he didn't push you a little harder makes me more suspicious."

"It's because he's more than an employee, Ryder. He cares about the Holt Company and he cares about me."

He grunted and closed his fingers around her arm and guided her away from Armstead's office. The last thing he wanted to think about was Lauren's relationship with another man. "I think I've taken enough of your time today. Why don't you head on out?" he suggested. "Clancy and Justin are probably waiting. I'll cover the rest of the plant on my own and we'll talk again when you get back." He had another thought. "Better yet, why don't you do Justin's shopping and go home? I'll come by when I've had a good look around. Then we'll talk."

"Well..." It was tempting to turn everything over to him, Lauren discovered. There was something about him that awakened a feminine instinct to lean on his strength. But that was hardly in keeping with her new resolve to take charge of her own life. She hesitated, looking beyond him. "Oh, here's Justin now."

"Hi, Mom." Justin greeted his mother and looked curiously at Ryder.

"Hello, Justin," Ryder said with an easy smile. It still amazed him how much pleasure he got out of just looking at the boy. "How's your birdhouse project coming?"

"I finished painting it yesterday," Justin said proudly. "I'm going to mount it on a tall pole when it's good and dry."

"You need any help with that?" Ryder asked.

"Me and Mom can do it. I looked up in a book how you're supposed to anchor the pole in cement."

Lauren blanched. "Justin—"

His look stilled her protest. "We can do it, Mom."

Territorial rights again, Ryder thought. He breathed in deeply and replied patiently, "You'll want to be sure it's nice and sturdy..."

"I know that," Justin said.

"...because in a high wind, it could topple over."

"Well, sure..." The boy screwed up his face and considered that unthought-of possibility.

"There might be baby birds inside by then," Ryder reminded him.

Justin stared at Ryder. "Aren't the directions on those bags of dry cement you buy to do it yourself?"

Ryder nodded. "Uh-huh, all spelled out for you step by step. You're right, Justin. If you're careful, you can handle it." He glanced at Lauren, making a point to study her slender arms and smooth hands. "With your mother to pitch in and help hoist it, it'll probably be okay."

Following Ryder's example, Justin glanced at his mother as though considering for the first time her size and strength.

Inhaling, he shifted his gaze back to Ryder. "I guess you've mounted plenty of birdhouses, huh?"

Ryder kept his expression neutral. "A few. I've had even more experience with dry cement."

"That stuff weighs a ton," Justin said, making a face.

"You're right there."

"How I know is I checked it out at the building supply place."

Ryder nodded. "You seem to have covered all the bases."

Justin chewed thoughtfully on the tender underside of his lip. "You could come over and check me out," he offered casually. "I mean if I start to do something really off the wall, you could stop me. I've noticed you're pretty good at showing how something's done."

Ryder savored the words, feeling a sweet satisfaction in earning a bit of respect from this boy. He was just beginning to realize how much more he wanted. "This afternoon okay?" he suggested. "After you get your camping gear, that is."

New interest quickened in Justin's amber eyes. Cocking his head to one side, he studied Ryder. "You probably know a lot about camping out, too."

Ryder hid a smile. "I've slept under the stars a time or two," he acknowledged.

"We've got two weeks before the trip," Justin said, favoring his mother with a tolerant glance. "Maybe you could give Mom a quick crash course. She's got guts but she's pretty much an indoor person so far." He turned to his mother. "Are you about ready to go to Army Surplus, Mom?"

"Justin—" Lauren sputtered.

"She'll meet you in a few minutes," Ryder told the boy, laughing at Lauren's outraged look.

With her hands on her hips, Lauren watched Justin dash off toward the snack bar, exasperation and amusement mingling on her face. Between the two, she was beginning to feel—

"Ah...Mrs. Holt..."

She turned, distracted. "Oh, Malcolm..."

A man, balding and permanently stooped, made his way out of a cluttered office toward Lauren. His threadbare lab coat was dingy and buttoned up wrong. Ryder judged him to be about sixty, easily the oldest employee he had met today.

"Did you...have you looked at my proposal?"

Lauren's expression showed regret and a touch of genuine apology. "I'm so sorry, Malcolm, I just haven't been able to manage it yet."

The man pushed at a pair of outdated spectacles. "I know you're busy, ma'am, but Armstead tells me you're the only one who can authorize more testing." The request was worded with respect, even a hint of subservience, but it was his fixed, intense gaze that made Ryder frown.

Lauren turned to Ryder. "Malcolm, this is Ryder Braden, our new production manager. Ryder, Malcolm Stern, an engineer who's been with the company since day one. Malcolm worked very closely with Clay."

Stern merely grunted in Ryder's direction before turning back to Lauren. "I've got Armstead's approval, Mrs. Holt. You talk to him; he'll tell you we should go on this one."

"Yes, all right, Malcolm." Lauren touched her temple with two fingers and closed her eyes briefly. "I'll try and look it over tonight, I promise."

The old man grunted again as though debating whether to push the issue. He muttered something, definitely nothing polite, and turned to leave. Ryder felt Lauren's distress as she watched Stern make his way back in the same direction he'd come.

"The resident absentminded professor, I assume," he said dryly, closing the door firmly on Stern and the slightly ratty work area he inhabited.

Lauren's laugh was forced. "Yes, actually. He was the first engineer Clay hired. I know he feels the company is going to wrack and ruin in my hands."

"Enough so that he would sell out to NuTekNiks?"

Lauren looked up, startled. "No! Absolutely not. It's true Malcolm resents me. I'm a woman and I'm not technically qualified to his way of thinking. But he's intensely loyal to the company and to Clay's memory."

"Yeah, maybe," Ryder said, but he was reserving judgment. So far Stern was the first person who didn't fawn all over her. Instead of feeling relieved, it made him slightly uneasy. Clearly the man had little patience in dealing with a woman, especially if she wasn't moving quickly enough on his pet project. Ryder had met Stern's type before. Eccentric, brilliant, single-minded. He glanced at Lauren and found her watching him. "What?" he asked.

"Nothing, just . . . did I remember to thank you?"

He shrugged. "Forget it."

Giving in to temptation, he curled his fingers around her arm. She was soft and warm, delicately feminine. He swore silently. Seeing her every day would be a little bit of heaven and a little bit of hell.

"I'm not going to forget it," Lauren said softly. "Thank you."

They stopped at the door to the snack bar. Ryder's smile as he looked down at her was wry. "The pleasure's all mine."

CHAPTER EIGHT

HOURS LATER RYDER was on his way out of the plant when he noticed the light beneath the door of Lauren's office. He stopped short, aware of conflicting urges—the first being to demand why she was back here working when she was already exhausted. But he was willing to ignore the first to indulge the second—the chance to see her alone, to be with her without the distraction of her friends, her lawyer, her employees, without any of the dozens of people who had claims on her time. He bent his head, shaking it slowly, feeling like a man going down for the third time, and pushed the door open.

"Why the hell aren't you at home, lady?"

Startled, Lauren glanced up into the midnight-blue eyes and tough, too-strong features that were growing ever more fascinating to her. He had discarded his coat and tie and rolled up the sleeves of his shirt. He looked big and slightly rumpled, incredibly sexy. "Ryder..." Even to her own ears, her voice sounded breathless. What happened to the poised professional woman she used to be?

He covered the space between them in a few lazy strides and glanced down at the papers that covered the surface of her desk. "What's so urgent that you had to rush back after promising me you'd go home with Justin and stay there?"

Lauren tossed her pen aside and pushed back in her chair. Sighing, she rolled her shoulders a couple of turns to relieve muscles that had tensed up. "I didn't *promise* to go home," she told him, sounding weary. "This is Malcolm Stern's proposal. I knew I wouldn't have a chance to study it tomorrow, so..." She shrugged. "It was either now or put him off again."

On impulse, Ryder moved behind her chair and put his hands on her shoulders. She tensed up instantly. "Relax," he murmured, finding the knobby bones of her spine with his thumbs while his fingers pressed into the strained muscles of her neck. She responded with a faint whisper. "Oh, Ryder, that feels wonderful."

Lauren was suddenly pliant and yielding under his hands. Her head fell forward as though too heavy to support her neck. Caught in a snare of his own making, Ryder's senses reacted to the sight of her, relaxed and luxuriating in his touch, with a rush of unbridled desire. He stared at the silky, baby-fine hair at her nape and felt the shudder that rippled through her. He closed his eyes and imagined how it would feel to have her body beneath his while she was overtaken by another kind of trembling.

This was a mistake. Even if the slight, delicate feel of her bones and the warm satin of her skin was like no other woman's, this was crazy. Next he'd be wanting to touch more, and then he'd want to taste... He felt his body tighten, his manhood thicken. Fighting frustration and need, he inhaled and took his hands away.

Ryder swore and pulled the plans around. Somehow he managed to focus on them. Holding his rioting senses under some kind of control, he studied the papers. "Does this thing work?" he asked. A part of him wanted to take her to task for letting a thoughtless old man impose on her while another part of him wanted to take on all the excesses she was burdened with.

Still utterly relaxed from Ryder's skillful massage, she glanced up and gave him a dreamy smile. "Would you believe, yes, it does?"

He tore his gaze away and frowned over a detailed schematic. "How do you know?"

"Before I dug into the proposal, I went to Malcolm and he gave me a personal demonstration in the lab."

"This would be a godsend to a paraplegic."

"I know," she said softly. "A robot that will answer the doorbell, the phone, turn on a stove and the TV, to name just a few of the tasks it can perform. And all commands are voice activated. It can even transfer a person from bed to a wheelchair."

"True state-of-the-art robotics," Ryder murmured, squinting at the penciled notes made in Stern's wavering script.

"You want to see it work?" Lauren stood up.

"You think Stern's still on the premises?"

"It doesn't matter. I can show you what he's programmed it to do, so far." Lauren skirted around her desk, looking adorably flustered when she had to brush against him to get by.

His jaw clenched. "Lead the way."

"It looks like no one's here," Lauren said, hesitating when they reached the door of the Research and Development area. She reached for a switch on the wall and flooded the place with additional light before making her way toward the rear. Ryder followed. He had toured the area earlier, making a mental note to examine the half-dozen models in various stages of completion later in detail. Lauren passed them all and stopped finally before a unit that Ryder recognized from Stern's plans.

She swept out an arm. "Meet Hercules."

Ryder's eyebrow went up. "I could see Stern's interest in his pet project went beyond the norm, but ... 'Hercules'?"

Lauren shrugged, smiling. "You know how proud parents can be."

Did he ever. Ryder watched Lauren walk to the control board and touch a button. With a whirr and a few beeps the robot immediately came alive. "Malcolm put it through a few simple procedures," she murmured, frowning in concentration as she punched out a series of numbers. "I think I can recall a few, just to give you an idea of what ol' Herky can do."

"Be careful," Ryder cautioned, glancing at the long steel arm poised over her head. According to Stern's claims, the robot could perform a task as delicate as moving a chess piece or as impressive as lifting an occupied wheelchair. That kind of strength could be potentially dangerous. "Remember, when you give it a command, it's going to do whatever's programmed," he cautioned.

"Don't worry," Lauren said, still concentrating on the control panel. "It's only going to pick up that telephone." She waved vaguely at a telephone which had obviously been set up as a testing device.

Ryder grunted and moved to stand beside her. "Maybe, but let's not take any chances. Let me just check it out first."

"It's not necessary, really." She bent slightly. "Answer the phone, Hercules," she intoned, speaking into the built-in microphone on the control board.

It happened so fast that both were caught off guard. Instead of answering the phone, the robot's arm came around in a wide arc in the opposite direction. Lauren gave a startled cry as the steel bar connected with her waist and swept her inexorably backward toward the wall behind her. Frantically she tried to stay on her feet. It would crush her!

Horror and fear rose in her throat as she felt the force of the cool steel pressing hard into her stomach.

With a harsh oath, Ryder lunged toward the control panel. His face wild, his hands flew over the instruments, pushing buttons, furiously punching out numbers. He swore savagely when the rote movements of the robot could not be interrupted.

"Don't fight it, Lauren!" he told her urgently. "Just be still until I find the code to cancel!"

Somewhere in her panic, Lauren heard him and stopped struggling. Desperately her eyes clung to Ryder's as though to a lifeline. The oxygen was being slowly squeezed from her lungs by the excruciating pressure tightening on her middle. Blackness dotted with tiny flashes of light swirled in her brain. She tried to call out Ryder's name but no sound came. Her hands lifted weakly in supplication only to fall back as she felt herself losing consciousness.

Ryder had never been so terrified in his life. If something happened to Lauren... He fought rising panic. There *had* to be a way to abort the command. He was aware of a slight sound and movement near the door. "Hey!" he yelled, glancing in that direction. "We need some help in here!"

There was no response. In a burst of fury and fear, he slammed a fist into the control panel. Short-circuited wiring popped and crackled and then the lights went out. Without power, the robot was suddenly lifeless.

"Lauren?" Ryder's harsh voice cut through the silence. The room was windowless and black as pitch. Cursing again, he kicked aside something obstructing his path and feeling his way, he started toward her.

"Hold on, sweetheart," he managed to say in a ragged voice. "I'm headed over there. Everything's fine." He thought she made a slight sound, but he couldn't be sure.

Please God, let her be all right, please just let her be all right.

"Just hold on, love." He reached for her.

"Ryder..." Lauren made a soft, whimpering noise and his knees almost gave way in relief. Instantly he was running his hands over her hair and face, down her neck and shoulders. When he encountered the mechanical contraption that confined her, Ryder swore again. Then he silently cursed himself when she drew a shuddering breath and began to tremble all over. He took her face in his hands and nuzzled her temple and ear, then her cheeks, seeking to comfort her, crooning endearments, wishing he could take her fear and pain into himself. "It's okay, baby. Don't worry, sweetheart. You're okay now, I promise, you're okay."

"Get me out of this, Ryder," Lauren said, shuddering as she strained against the steel bar entrapping her.

She felt his hands moving in the dark, testing the pressure of the bar. "Do you think you could wiggle out if I can force the bar just a little?"

She drew a shaky breath and tried to control the panic that clawed at her. It was so dark! And she was trapped so completely. What was a mere mortal's strength against the steel jaws of a monster?

It was just the way Clay had died.

She must have said the words out loud, because Ryder's hands went back to her head. "Hush, Lauren!" Cupping her face in his palms, he held her so that she knew he was looking directly into her eyes even in the dark. "You're not going to die. This is no time to panic. Don't think about Clay or anything except getting free of this damned robot." He waited a second or two and then, satisfied that she was listening again, he nodded. "I can get you out of here, sweetheart. It would be easier if I had some light, but—"

Lauren shook her head vehemently.

"But I don't want to leave you to try and find a flashlight."

"Hurry, Ryder...please."

"I will." He hesitated, one hand on her shoulder. "Uh, Lauren, you're wearing a bra, right?"

"Yes, why?" She was nearing the line between sanity and blind panic. Why was he talking about her bra?

"It's one of those with a steel wire." It wasn't a question. Obviously he knew. "I think you should take it off," Ryder told her. "The bar is snug against your midriff, but when you try to work your chest past the barrier, you need to have as much flexibility as possible." He cleared his throat, sounding suddenly uncomfortable. "Without the underwire supports, your breasts will have room to, uh—"

"Flatten out," Lauren finished quickly. "Fine. It fastens in the back. Can you reach it?" In the dark he could hear the rustle of silk, sense the movement of her hands as she swiftly unbuttoned her blouse.

"I'm sorry," he said, reaching around her, his breath caressing her ear. Sliding his hands over the skin of her neck and shoulders under the silk blouse, he fumbled a second or two with the clasp of her bra before it suddenly gave way. With another murmured apology, he slipped the straps off her shoulders. Her breasts, free of the satin and wire restraint, burst forth, lush and heavy. He swallowed thickly.

"It doesn't have to come completely off, does it?" she asked, for the first time thankful for the pitch-black darkness.

"No." He sounded curt, but his hands were gentle, as caring as a lover's as he readied her for the ordeal.

Ryder's hands went to the steel bar at her waist again and when he spoke, it was in the patient, almost tender tone he'd often used when dealing with Justin. "Now...when I force this, like I said before, you just wiggle a little and see if it's enough to— No, not in that direction, baby." He laughed huskily. To Lauren the sound was reassuring, but his hands weren't quite steady as he touched her midriff to show her the way he wanted her to move. "Think of your body as liquid, Lauren, and just let yourself go. I think it'll be enough. Okay?"

She nodded. "Okay," she whispered.

"Now, Lauren!" He grasped the bar and pulled again with all his strength.

Banishing everything from her mind except the concept of her body liquified, Lauren raised her arms and began. It was going to work! Inch by inch, she worked her way down. As her breasts encountered the cold steel vise, she winced.

"What?" Ryder demanded urgently, the strain telling in his voice.

"It's okay," she assured him, knowing there was no way to avoid bruising her breasts. There! Now, one shoulder...then the other. She turned her head slightly and...she was free!

Her knees gave way as though they were in fact liquid and she collapsed in a heap on the floor. With a muffled sound, Ryder went down on his haunches beside her. In the dark, she couldn't see anything, but she could feel his warmth, smell the musky male scent of him. She wanted... A sob rose in her throat.

"Are you in pain, Lauren?" He put a hand out and touched her hair. "Tell me where, baby." His voice was uneven, raw with concern. She could feel his breath caress her cheek.

She reached for him. "Please, Ryder," she whispered, "just hold me."

With a groan, he put his arms around her and gathered her closely. For a long moment, he let himself savor the soft, feminine warmth of her while rage and a terrible fear coursed through him. It had been a close call. Without realizing it his arms tightened convulsively.

"I was so s . . . scared," she told him brokenly, the words muffled against his neck.

"I know, baby, I know." One hand cupped her head gently while he sat on the floor beside her, stretching out his legs, and then leaned back against the wall and pulled her into his lap. "Are you in pain? Are you hurt anywhere? I know your ribs are bruised—" he ran a hand down her ribs and around to her breast "—and your breasts. Did it—"

Nestling under his chin, she shook her head, sniffing. "I'm fine. Just shaken up."

"Hell." Weakly Ryder rested his head against the wall, but his insides churned with a consuming wrath. She shouldn't have to go through any more pain . . . She shouldn't have to be afraid anymore . . . She shouldn't be so vulnerable . . . She shouldn't be so beautiful . . . She shouldn't be the one woman he wanted most in all the world.

Lauren felt him shift slightly and bury his mouth in her hair. She had been terrified just seconds before. But now, held close in Ryder's arms, she knew only how safe and utterly content she felt. And how right it seemed to be where she was.

"I need to get you out of here," he told her. He drew himself up and got to his feet, pulling her up with him.

"Wait," she said, freeing her hand with a tug. "M...my clothes . . ." she reminded him in a breathless voice.

Ryder stopped and waited while Lauren fumbled with the straps and hooks of her bra. She was still numb with shock, her fingers awkward as she rebuttoned her blouse. As soon as he sensed she was ready, Ryder wrenched open the door, halting her with a touch on the arm while he made a quick, thorough search of the brightly lit corridor. His eyes were a dark, turbulent blue, still roiling with the aftereffects of rage and fear.

The corridor was deserted. Almost eerily so. Another tremor passed through Lauren. Ryder felt it and wrapped his arm around her, pulling her against him.

"Who was that you called out to when Hercules went berserk?" she asked, shivering again with remembered fear.

"I don't know," he said, his tone hard.

She drew in a shaky breath. Someone had been there and had chosen to ignore her cry for help. She didn't want to accept what that meant. "Surely they could tell we were in trouble."

"Yes." Ryder spoke tersely but his arm tightened around her reassuringly. Lauren leaned into him gratefully.

"I don't know what the hell's going on here," Ryder said grimly, "but as soon as I take you home, I'm going to start asking questions. Somebody had better have some damn good answers."

RYDER DIDN'T LINGER once he'd dropped Lauren at her house. He took a minute to explain to Justin that he would have to put off helping him mount the birdhouse for a day and then got back into his Blazer and headed for the plant. He suddenly craved a cigarette even though he'd given up the habit over two years before. Heaven knew he needed something to calm the tempest raging inside him. His stomach churned with a dozen violent emotions. Ryder had been in many tricky situations—some downright dangerous—but he'd always managed to come through unscathed. He knew now that until today he'd never been gut-deep scared before.

Had it been an accident? The robot was still in an experimental stage. Bugs were common, as in all computer-operated equipment. If it wasn't an accident, was Lauren the target? Or had she walked innocently into a trap rigged for another victim? For him, maybe? And who was behind it? He thought again of the furtive movement he'd noticed in the first panicked moments just after the robot malfunctioned. His eyes narrowed, fixed on the darkened street ahead of him. He couldn't shake a sense of urgency. But more disturbing yet was this feeling of impending danger.

It was the way Clay had died. He remembered the anguished cry torn from Lauren as the robot's steel arm crushed her. Ryder's face contorted and his hands clenched on the wheel as he recalled his helpless panic and mind-blowing fear that he might not be able to save her. Thank God, this time he'd been able to do something. Next time...

Tonight's near disaster made a mockery of his vow to distance himself from Lauren. He wiped a hand over his face, not a bit surprised to find himself in a cold sweat. In that split-second moment when he'd been so close to losing her, he'd realized just how much she meant to him. That alone was almost as scary as the experience he'd just been through.

What the hell am I going to do now?

He draped a wrist over the steering wheel and stared into the night. He couldn't walk away and he couldn't take a chance on revealing his deception. He was in their lives for better or worse. He thought of Lauren's passion, the taste of her kiss, the smell of her hair, the feel of her soft body. Groaning, he felt himself grow tight and hard and hot while his level of frustration climbed. Because as long as he continued to deceive Lauren, he couldn't have her.

WHEN THE MAN WAS CERTAIN the widow and her protector were out of the plant, he scurried out of the empty office where he'd secreted himself. He made his way through the work stations, heading for the window that overlooked the parking area. He watched the taillights of the Blazer disappear into the lowering dusk and then, grunting with satisfaction, he turned away, intent upon one final task.

The accident with the robot had been an impulse. He was not used to acting on impulse, but the widow must be discouraged from dropping into his area whenever she pleased. He was certain now that she would hesitate before intruding again. He was already juggling a number of projects which were known only to his contact. Now that the robot's tendency for unexpected behavior was known, no one would venture too closely. Consequently the other secrets he protected would be safe.

Shrugging into his suit coat, he frowned. The new man would not be so easily deterred, he suspected. But he would handle him when it became necessary.

He pulled a set of prints out of a folder that was conveniently wedged in the tight space between his desk and a drafting table. Quickly he slipped it under his jacket. His contact's appetite for Holt secrets was insatiable. He thought briefly of the death of Clay Holt. It was sad. Still, he felt no shame. Only impatience. And anxiety. What was a man to do? There was his Anna to consider. His course was set. There was no turning back.

CHAPTER NINE

LAUREN AWOKE THE NEXT MORNING to the muffled sound of Justin's voice, eager and excited. She opened one eye to read the time and blinked sleep away. *Six-fifteen!* Was he outside already? Good grief, was there no limit to the energy of an eleven-year-old male? Frowning, Lauren reached out to throw the sheet aside and immediately groaned as her bruised ribs protested. Last night's long soak in a hot bath had eased the aches and pains inflicted by Hercules-gone-amok, but she wouldn't move without feeling stiff and sore for a while yet.

Halfway to the bathroom, she stopped. That wasn't only Justin's voice she heard. Mixed with his boyish enthusiasm was a deeper, more maturely masculine tone. Grasping the flower-sprigged sheet, she covered herself and went to the window.

Ryder!

Her lips parted soundlessly. While Justin buzzed around him like a little worker bee, Ryder was calmly shovelling something wet and gray and gloppy out of a wheelbarrow into a hole in the ground. He was shirtless in the morning sun. And sweating. She drew in a breath and felt a sudden rush of heat. She could see the sleek, lean muscles contract as he thrust methodically into the goo and then lifted and deposited it into the hole. His movements were smooth and even, a study in earthy male strength and grace. She had never seen a man look that good.

Suddenly Ryder looked up and saw her. Instead of dropping the curtain and stepping back, Lauren stood rooted to the spot, caught in the intensity of his gaze. Her shoulders were bare, her hair was a mess, she was sleepy-eyed and heavy-limbed. She was tousled, trembling, breathless... But with his eyes locked on her, she had never felt more like a woman.

"Mom, come on down!" Justin spotted her and grinned, screwing up his face in the sunshine.

"What's going on?"

"The birdhouse," Justin explained, sweeping an arm toward a white painted pole lying off to one side. The birdhouse, she noted, was already nailed securely to the top. "Me and Ryder are almost ready to hoist this baby up."

Baby, huh? Had her son already adopted Ryder's pet phrases? A smile touched her mouth at Justin's exuberance. Any reservations the boy had harbored about accepting Ryder's help had apparently been forgotten. As she watched, Ryder shifted his shovel and leaned against it, thrusting his hips forward. Nearby, Justin struck an identical pose, propping on a board he'd been using to mix cement. Involuntarily her smile widened. Standing side by side looking up at her, they looked remarkably alike.

"Can you be down in ten minutes?" Ryder asked, his mouth tilted in a half smile. "If so, we'll hold up hoisting this baby. But hurry, otherwise the cement'll set and we'll be in trouble."

"I'll be right down."

Ryder watched the curtain fall back into place, obscuring the tantalizing sight of Lauren, flushed and sleepy-eyed. Turning, his hands weren't quite steady as they closed on the handle of the shovel. He wasn't sure why he was here this morning, other than the fact that when he had awakened at daylight, nothing had seemed as important as seeing her. It had been hard to wait until she woke up.

He was filled with conflicting emotions. With a mighty heave, he tossed another scoop of cement into the hole, hardly aware of Justin poking the board into the mess, conscientiously making sure no air bubbles survived as Ryder had instructed. Justin and Lauren had awakened protective instincts Ryder never knew he possessed. The more he was around them, the more complicated everything became. And now that he suspected Lauren might be in some personal danger, he was honorbound to stay and see her through. He pushed the shovel into the cement, caught in a trap of his own design.

At the sound of the glass door sliding open, he turned. She looked cool and early-morning sexy in a big white shirt and faded jeans. Her hair had been hastily caught up and secured with a red barrette. Her amber eyes smiled into his as she headed across the patio, balancing two mugs of coffee.

"How are you this morning?" he asked, accepting one. He wiped the sweat from his face in the angle of his elbow and took a big swallow, concentrating on not eating her alive with his eyes.

"Stiff, sore, black and blue," she told him. "But other than that, undaunted."

His gaze fell to the deep V of her shirt where the creamy skin and the soft swell of her breasts tantalized. He looked away hastily. "You should take the day off," he said, dropping his voice so that Justin couldn't hear.

"Did you find anything last night?" she asked quietly.

He shook his head. "Nothing. The place was deserted—unusual for R and D, but not unheard of. I found Malcolm Stern's home phone number and called him to report the damage to his brainchild."

"I'm sure he was upset."

"He seemed to be."

"Oh, Ryder, surely you don't think Malcolm would deliberately sabotage his own work? He's devoted years to developing Hercules."

For a minute or two, Ryder studied the tiny dimple at the corner of her mouth and then stared at a point beyond her shoulder. All that loyalty and trust lavished on her employees. When it was all over, would she have anything left for him?

"You can't afford not to suspect any employee, Lauren. But don't worry, I'll take care of it."

Justin scrambled over the pole and began dragging it toward the hole. "Mom, we haven't got time to drink coffee. This cement's gettin' stiff. Put your mug down over there while we get this thing in the ground."

To Ryder, she lifted her eyebrows helplessly, and reached to take his mug. "Aye, aye, sir. What can I do to help?"

"Grab the other end," Justin ordered.

"Nothing," Ryder said in a tone that rang with authority. He looked at Justin. "We can manage without your mother, Justin. She can stand back and tell us whether we're straight or not. You guide the end into the cement and I'll lift the top."

Smiling, Lauren obediently headed for the picnic table carrying the coffee.

"Okay!" Justin shouted as he rolled the bottom end into the cement base. Bearing most of the weight, Ryder raised it. "How does it look, Mom?"

"It's off ten degrees," Lauren reported.

"Which way?" Both males stared at her. Again she was struck by the similarity of their expressions.

"Left."

"How's this?" Justin demanded.

"Perfect."

"All right!"

Hattie Bell slid the patio door open and stuck her head out. "Breakfast!"

Giving the birdhouse a final proud inspection, Justin wiped his hands on his backside and dashed toward the patio. "Boy, Hattie Bell, you timed that just right. I'm starved!"

"When is he not?" Lauren murmured, watching him fondly over the rim of her mug.

"He's either hungry or in a hurry," Ryder observed dryly, giving himself a quick once-over with a towel and then tossing it aside. Picking up his mug, he finished off the coffee.

"Or giving orders," she said, looking at him from under her lashes. "Like someone else I know."

"Habit," he said shortly, wishing he could openly claim the host of similarities between him and Justin. He was only now realizing how many small mannerisms he shared with his son.

"Thank you for helping him," Lauren said, scooting over to make room for him on the bench beside her.

He didn't sit down, but leaned a hip against the table, crossing his ankles. "He would have managed without me," Ryder told her. "He's stubborn and resourceful."

"Hmm," she agreed, sipping her coffee. "But I would have been drafted and subjected to a lot of male ordering around, and the thing would still have listed a lot more than ten degrees."

She glanced up and her smile faltered as she caught Ryder frowning at a mark on her throat. He put out a hand and brushed her collar aside, then gently examined the bruise. A slow flush spread over her skin. He raised his eyes to hers and she drew back at the blaze of emotion she saw there. "I thought you said you were unhurt. This looks like it extends beyond your collarbone. Are you this badly bruised all over?"

"It's not that bad, Ryder, Lauren said. "I'm ... My skin is pale. I bruise easily. I'm fine, really."

He pulled back and studied her. She didn't move or look away. She returned his skeptical look with grave amber eyes. With one hand, he took her coffee and set it on the table, and then gently pulled her to her feet.

When he spoke, his voice was low and hoarse. "Is Justin occupied for a while?"

Lauren nodded, still mute, and then her lashes came down weakly as he settled his hands on her waist and flexed his fingers into her soft flesh. She felt a tremor go through him as he drew her close.

"I couldn't sleep last night," he murmured against her temple. "I kept remembering you begging me to free you. I kept hearing the broken little sounds you made trying not to cry." He drew in a rasping breath. "I felt like I was tied in knots. I wanted to hit someone, Lauren."

She kissed the skin under his jaw tenderly. "It wasn't your fault."

"I wanted to get up and come over here."

She smiled against his neck. His skin was damp and tasted slightly salty. "You could have."

He lifted a hand to her hair, catching it so that he could tilt her head to look into her eyes. Long seconds passed as though he couldn't quite believe what he'd heard.

She smiled. "You could have," she repeated softly.

"Lauren." he bent and kissed the corner of her mouth. "You're so beautiful, did I tell you that?" He ran his lips over her cheek, across her nose, and then touched her mouth at the other corner. She sucked in a quick breath and held it, wanting, willing him to do more. She whimpered as his hand came up to stroke the line of her throat and his thumb found the soft spot under her chin, nudging it up until only a whisper separated her mouth from his.

"Lauren..."

She opened her eyes and wanted to melt into the midnight blue depths of his.

"Lauren, I know this is crazy, but—"

She made a sound of protest and without another second's thought, discarded the inhibitions of a lifetime. Rising on her toes, she kissed him. His mouth was warm, his lips soft and giving. Her arms went around his neck, urging him closer. She had the initiative only for a heartbeat. He tensed and inhaled sharply, and then he caught her face between his hands, deepening the kiss hungrily. Desire so intense she thought she would surely die from it exploded in Lauren, filling her mind and her senses. The sun was hot, the sounds of morning were all around them, but she might as well have been on a deserted island for all the notice she took.

Ryder's fingers brushed past the smooth skin at the base of her throat, seeking the softness that had tantalized him earlier. He slipped a hand in the deep V of her shirt, trembling with the effort to be gentle, and curled a hand around one soft, full breast. She made a small sound and he tore his mouth away, resting his forehead against hers. A sweet weight still nestled in his palm.

"Did I hurt you, sweetheart?" He was breathing like a man who'd run a marathon. His thumb moved slowly back and forth, savoring the feel of her satiny flesh. "I'm sorry, I'm sorry."

She put a hand on his wrist when he would have withdrawn. "No, don't stop. You didn't hurt me."

Lauren, Lauren. Her name was a wild song in his head, her appeal an irresistible lure. She was so sweet, so desirable, the most desirable woman he'd ever known. He had to close his eyes to cope with the emotion surging through him.

And he had to stop. It was broad daylight. Any moment Justin might appear. Placing one last soft kiss on the curve of her breast, reluctantly he withdrew his hand, but continued to hold her close.

"One of these days," Ryder said, a huskiness lingering in his voice, "It's just going to be the two of us . . . alone, nobody else around. I'm going to be able to kiss you the way I've always wanted to." His mouth was at her ear. She felt the warm vapor of his breath and shivered. "I'm going to take a long, long time and savor every beautiful inch of you . . ."

One hand crept slowly around the back of her neck, then inched down, down her spine and came to rest at the small of her back with just enough pressure to let her feel the strength of his need. "One of these days . . ."

Lauren took a small step back, her shaky fingers going to the open front of her shirt. "I guess we should go in," she said, flushed and breathless.

He stopped her with a touch on her arm. "Lauren, stay home today, okay? I had your car delivered this morning and left the keys on that little table in your foyer. But you don't need to go in. I'll take care of Armstead."

She sighed, tempted to let him do what he'd suggested. But that was the reason she was in the mess she was in. Playing a passive role while the men in her life—first Clay, then Jake, Michael, now Ryder—smoothed the way for her.

She gave him a helpless look, wondering how to put what she felt into words. "I can't Ryder. I have things to do and I really owe it to Michael to personally explain my decision to hire you."

He looked grim, suddenly. "Don't tell him the truth, Lauren."

"Michael isn't selling Clay's designs, Ryder."

"How do you know that?"

"I just do. He's been too supportive, too—"

Ryder straightened abruptly and reached for his shirt. "Maybe that's the operative word." He shrugged into a white pullover. "Personally I think he's a little too everything, too smooth, too pat, too accommodating."

"Ryder—" Lauren put a hand out, not wanting him to leave feeling angry after the beautiful moment they'd just shared. She touched him on the arm and felt the tension in him. "Look, already you suspect Michael and even poor old Malcolm Stern. I value your opinion, Ryder, believe me. But you'll just have to accept that I don't agree with you on everything. I do still run the plant."

"Fine. Great." Ryder swept up his car keys and donned a pair of sunglasses. Gone was the concerned, gentle protector she'd kissed only minutes before. In his place was a grim-faced stranger. "I'm telling you, Lauren, if you keep seeing all your people as saints, you're in for an ugly surprise."

He saw the cool mask descend, but he knew her better now. No matter how she tried, Lauren couldn't control that vulnerable mouth. He stopped suddenly, dragging a hand through his hair. "I'm sorry, sweetheart. I know how you feel about this damn company, about the people in it. But somebody's eating your lunch, Lauren. Somebody's systematically selling you out, and you make it simple for him by refusing to face facts."

She reached out but didn't touch him. She knew his point of view was well reasoned. "It's not Michael," she said stubbornly.

She could not see Ryder's eyes for the dark lenses, but she felt the power of his look and knew he was wrestling with an urge to give her a good shaking.

"Maybe not," he said, his voice soft. "But in my book, nobody's home free yet. And that includes your precious Michael." He was halfway across the lawn to the patio when he suddenly stopped. Turning, he pinned her with a look. "And get Justin back out to clean up and put away those tools. He gets away with murder around here!"

Ignoring her outraged gasp, he stomped across the patio and disappeared.

"DO YOU THINK Justin is spoiled, Clancy?"

"Hmmph," Clancy mumbled, tossing popcorn into her mouth. Her eyes were glued to the Little League field, where play action was interrupted by an altercation between the Bluejays's manager and the pitcher's father.

She stared at Clancy. "Is that yes or no?"

Clancy got to her feet. "Get on with it!" she yelled. "Let's play ball!"

"Clancy—"

"They ought to outlaw parents on the playing field," she told Lauren with disgust, sinking back down in her seat. "Oh, shoot, I spilled the popcorn." She brushed salt and kernels off her jeans. "What do you mean is Justin spoiled? Of course, he's spoiled. He's an only child, too bright for his own good and surrounded by adults who think he's adorable. The kid's only human, Lauren. He'll survive it."

A week had passed since Ryder's provoking remark, but Lauren had been unable to forget it. Justin's welfare was her Achilles heel. She was sensitive about anything that had to do with him. And—she admitted it—she was supersensitive to criticism of her performance as a parent.

Play resumed on the field and Lauren watched Justin neatly scoop up a foul ball and tag a runner who was attempting to steal home. Her heart swelled with pride and love. "Maybe I am too indulgent, Clancy," she murmured. "But—"

"What brought this on?" Clancy asked, looking at her curiously. Her eyes narrowed suddenly. "Has Jake Levinson been advising you on parenting in spite of his total ignorance of the subject?"

Lauren laughed shortly. "Not Jake... Ryder."

"Hmm... What'd he say?"

"That I let Justin get away with murder." She looked concerned. "Do I, Clancy?"

Clancy was thoughtful. "Well, I wouldn't say murder, but the kid is pretty fast on his feet, and who of us wouldn't weasel out of a few chores if we could think of a way to do it?" She reached over and patted Lauren's hand. "My advice is to forget it. Justin's a good kid."

They watched the ball game a few moments in silence.

"What's interesting," Clancy said then, in a speculative tone, "is what provoked him to say something like that in the first place."

Lauren sighed. "Justin failed to put away some tools and clean up after he and Ryder put up the birdhouse."

"A few tools and a little trash," Clancy murmured. "Doesn't sound much like murder to me. I don't suppose anything else was going down at the time?"

Lauren's eyes remained doggedly on the field. "Such as?"

"Such as a little contretemps between you two."

"We were having a slight disagreement," she reluctantly conceded.

"Yeah, I wondered how things were going at the plant."

"Fine," Lauren said. "He's very good at what he does. Some of his suggestions involve major changes, but he manages people so skillfully that I've had few complaints."

"Understandable," Clancy commented. "The job would hardly tax a man with the kind of experience Ryder has. How's Michael Armstead taking it?"

"Not very well. He was offended that I hired Ryder in the first place and spent the first couple of days trying to persuade me to put some restraints on him." Recalling the scene enacted in her office that morning, a frown appeared. Although she'd expected a negative reaction from Michael, she'd been startled at just how angry he had been.

Clancy nodded knowingly. "It must have been a new experience for Michael when you refused."

"What choice did I have?" Lauren demanded wearily. "With Jake's encouragement, I agreed to the plan. I couldn't very well fold at the first sign of resistance."

"No, of course not," Clancy murmured.

"But I refuse to see everyone at the plant as a suspect the way Ryder does."

"He does have a point, Lauren. Until you know who's stealing Clay's designs, everyone is a suspect."

"I know, but I feel so disloyal letting Ryder in the plant under false pretenses."

"Don't, it's necessary." Clancy dismissed Lauren's misgivings with her typical pragmatism. "You can beg their forgiveness later when Ryder has saved the plant and Clay's designs and made everyone's job secure for the next thirty or so years." She flashed a thumbs-up signal to Justin as he tagged another runner out. "So, what's this I hear about you almost being devoured by one of your beloved robots?"

Lauren stared at her. "How did you hear about it?"

Clancy shrugged. "Jake."

Lauren was momentarily distracted. "Are you seeing Jake again?"

Clancy's gaze followed a high fly ball. "He dropped by my place a couple of nights ago."

"Oh, Clancy."

"We talked, Lauren, nothing more. He's still mad as hell at me for taking that job in Washington."

"He was hurt."

"It was ten years ago, for Pete's sake! I was just a kid with big dreams. I wanted to be a journalist. I wanted to see the world. It would have been wrong for me to try to settle down in a sleepy town in Alabama with all those needs unfulfilled inside me."

"You were engaged, Clancy."

"I wanted him to go with me. He was a lawyer. He could have stepped into a fabulous job in Washington, but he wouldn't leave Mobile."

"Everybody's different, Clancy."

"Yeah."

"I think he's scared to believe you've changed."

"I'm ready now, Lauren. I've seen the world. I've proven myself as a journalist. I'm home to stay." She picked at a speck of popcorn on her jeans and looked up suddenly, her eyes fierce. "And I'm going to make him believe me if it kills me."

Lauren hid a smile. Although a decade had passed, the chemistry between Jake and Clancy was still there. Sparks flew whenever they were together. It was sad that their differences were still keeping them apart.

Clancy propped her chin dejectedly on her cane. "It beats me how Jake can admire Ryder the way he does and yet he puts me down for the very same reasons."

Lauren glanced at her friend in surprise. There were indeed similarities between Ryder and Clancy. Both were stubborn and single-minded; both had pursued exciting careers that had taken them to exotic places. Both were risk takers, and both probably disdained the caution inherent in Jake's soul—her own, too, Lauren admitted wryly. Jake envied Ryder, so why did he reject those selfsame qualities in Clancy? Cheers erupted around her, but Lauren was caught up in her thoughts and barely noticed. That was where she, Lauren, and Jake differed. She was done with playing it safe. She was ready to risk her cozy, comfortable existence for the unknown delights she knew instinctively she could have in a relationship with Ryder. If he wanted her.

A thought caused her brow to knit in a frown. Were Ryder and Clancy afraid of commitment? Maybe. Probably. Ryder enjoyed a life-style admired and envied by many men. Lauren couldn't see him giving it up. As for Clancy, she was ready at last to link her destiny with Jake's, and before long Jake would realize it.

Clancy touched her arm. "Look who's here."

"Ryder," Lauren murmured, feeling her heart soar like a high fly ball. Looking neither right nor left, he was heading directly for Justin, who had already spotted him. A chain link fence separated the players from the spectators, but Justin ran up to it, grinning, and curled his fingers around the steel mesh. As Ryder approached, Justin began to talk nonstop. Lauren watched them with mixed feelings. Justin was hungry for the attention of an adult male. He missed Clay and the masculine camaraderie they had shared. But not just any man would do. He had rejected the attention of several of Clay's old friends. It had been months before Justin had warmed up to Michael.

Now, in less than four weeks...

She watched Justin enthusiastically describe a play to Ryder, who, smiling faintly, gave every indication of listening intently. It wasn't difficult to understand why Justin had fallen so quickly under Ryder's spell. The ease with which he'd won over the men at the plant would work equally well with an eleven-year-old boy.

Pain sliced through her. *Don't let him be hurt,* Lauren prayed. Ryder might genuinely enjoy Justin's company, but it could only be temporary. A man like Ryder would soon be off again to some obscure corner of the world, resuming a life-style that had no place in it for a boy. It was one thing for her to risk her own heart, but she must somehow safeguard Justin's.

CHAPTER TEN

"RYDER? RYDER BRADEN! Jeez, man, is it really you?"

Still smiling over Justin's play-by-play recap of the game's first two innings, Ryder turned, mildly curious, and found himself face-to-face with Neil Putnam. His eyes widened with surprise as Neil grabbed his hand, pumping it and grinning. "How the hell are you, Ryder?"

"Fine," Ryder said, grinning, too. "Couldn't be better."

"What's up, man? How long have you been in town?"

"A while. I called your office and they said you were out of the country on some kind of cultural exchange program. Mexico, wasn't it?"

"Yeah, I took Patti and the twins. We just got back this week." Neil stood back, subjecting him to a long, friendly inspection. "You're lookin' good, Ryder. How long's it been? Five years?" He shook his head. "Time flies, doesn't it?"

"Hi, Dr. Putnam," Justin said.

Still focusing on Ryder, it was a second before Neil glanced down at Justin. When he did he smiled vaguely, and then the realization dawned. Neil shot Ryder a keen look before saying to the boy, "Justin, hey, what's happening?"

Justin shrugged. "Not much, I guess. Where's Cody and Jace?"

"In the stands. Since they haven't made it to practice, they're benched for the time being."

Justin kicked the fence. "Aw, no, we really need them. Curtis Wainwright is still out and coach is playing Shirley Beecham!" His tone was filled with disgust.

"Maybe they can suit up next week," Neil told the boy sympathetically.

"Justin! You're up!"

"Gotta go!" he shouted and dashed off in the direction of the dugout.

A moment of heavy silence stretched between them before Neil spoke. "What the hell are you doing, Ryder?" he demanded.

Ryder's eyes were on Justin at home plate. He watched the boy make a few practice swings, then step up for the first pitch. He connected for a base hit, tossing the bat willy-nilly before charging in a dead run down the line to first. Ryder's eyes were fierce with emotion when he turned back to Neil.

He laughed shortly. "I've been asking myself that same question for the past month."

Neil stared at him and then turned to the bleachers, searching for Lauren. "My God, I never thought— What did Lauren say when you told her?"

Head bent, Ryder curled his fingers into the steel mesh of the fence and kicked idly at the red ball field dust. "I haven't told her. Yet."

Neil swore softly. "I don't believe this."

Mutely Ryder shook his head.

"Well, it won't be long until she guesses."

Ryder glanced up sharply. "Why?"

"Jeez, Ryder, he's just like you."

Ryder's face contorted as a mixture of joy and pain wrenched his soul. He ached to claim Justin as his son. For the past eleven years, he had roamed the world with no ties, no family, no roots, and no particular desire for them. When had his thinking altered so drastically?

Neil's troubled gaze strayed back to Lauren. "Are you involved with her?"

"Yeah, I'm involved." Ryder studied the toe of his shoe, shaking his head wryly. Funny that Neil should put it that way. It was the one thing Ryder had vowed not to do. But involved he was and in every facet of her life, it seemed. In all the ways it was possible, he was involved.

"How, Ryder? Why?"

"I don't know." He shrugged helplessly. "I damn sure didn't plan it. At first it was business. Jake asked me to consult on the lawsuit. You must know about it." He looked at Neil, who nodded. "I met with Lauren a couple of times. Her husband was dead. She seemed vulnerable somehow. I thought she...needed me. I knew it was crazy, but I couldn't help myself. Then I saw Justin." He laughed a little, unsteadily. "I tried to back off then, but I couldn't, Neil."

Neil shook his head slowly. "You're playing a dangerous game, Ryder. I guess you know that."

Ryder rubbed the back of his neck. "I know I ought to tell her. Hell, I've got to tell her. But when it comes down to it, I'm scared. I don't want to lose them."

"So, what are you going to do?"

"I'm not sure," Ryder murmured.

Neil's eyes narrowed. "What does that mean?"

What did it mean? Ryder looked at Justin and felt a rush of hunger and regret for all the episodes in the boy's life he'd missed. His first smile, his first step. Who had taught him to ride a bike? Had he cried when he left his mother on the first day of school?

He watched as Justin paced just beyond home plate waiting for his turn at bat. He was relaxed and confident, carelessly tossing the bat from one hand to the other.

Someone yelled at him from the bench. He stepped up to home plate, laughing. No, he probably hadn't cried any more than he, Ryder, had cried on his first day of school.

Clay Holt and Lauren had done a good job raising Justin, but deep in his soul, Ryder felt proud of the obvious legacy he had bequeathed his son. Justin was healthy, intelligent, a born athlete. But more than that—he had grit and determination, an inborn fierce pride. What kind of man would he grow up to be? Ryder's eyes shifted from Justin to the bleachers where Lauren sat. How could he bear to walk away now?

"This is all my fault," Neil muttered, his blue eyes distressed. "I've kicked myself a thousand times for what I said that night, Ryder. It was an unforgivable breach of professional ethics. A damn stupid thing to do." He shook his head bleakly. "I'm more sorry than I can say, man."

Ryder's eye was on the playing field where Justin, now on third, was intent on stealing home. He danced tantalizingly out of range of the third baseman. Grinning, he ventured a little farther, ready to go for it. But the pitcher zipped one straight to third, forcing him to scramble madly back to the base, safe.

"Don't be sorry," Ryder told Neil softly, his eyes never leaving Justin.

Neil looked over at the bench where the twins, Cody and Jace, were on their feet yelling in unison for the Bluejays. After a minute, his expression thoughtful, he clapped Ryder on the shoulder. "Take it easy, buddy," he said, his tone gruff. "I'll see you around."

Ryder's brooding gaze followed Neil as the man made his way across the grass to the twins. Sandy-haired and blue-eyed, they were carbon copies of their father. He felt a twinge of envy watching the way they hurled themselves at Neil, laughing and jostling for position beside him like playful puppies. Ryder smiled slightly, remembering the night the twins were born. He'd been envious then, too, but only fleetingly. He had had places to go, things to do. That night—was it eleven years ago?—a family had been low on his list of priorities and a long way into the future.

When had that changed? When had he changed? A roar went up from the crowd. He turned, just in time to see Justin slide in to home plate and then scramble to his feet, flushed with success. He grinned at Ryder. It dawned on Ryder that he wanted the secrets and deception that clouded his relationship with Lauren cleared away. But how would she take it when he tried to explain? Would she even try to understand what he'd done and why? Or, once she knew the intimate connection they shared, would she order him out of her life?

She'd have to understand. He'd make her. Ryder clenched his fingers in the wire mesh of the fence, knowing if he really believed that he wouldn't be walking around with his stomach in a knot most of the time. Neil was right. He had to tell her. But first he would have to clear up the trouble at her plant. There was every possibility that Lauren might be in danger. That possibility took precedence over everything. Until he'd fixed the one, he couldn't do a damned thing about the other.

LAUREN SAT IN THE STANDS beside Clancy and felt her senses react as ever to the sight of Ryder, tall and broad-shouldered, making his way across the grass and then lithely taking the steps up the bleachers two at a time. Despite her best intentions she seemed helpless to control the butterflies that were suddenly doing aerobics inside her tummy.

"Wow."

Startled, she glanced at Clancy. "What?"

"Just 'wow,'" Clancy said, audaciously running her eyes over Ryder. "It's no wonder he has you ready to cast aside all your inhibitions."

Inhibitions. For a moment, Lauren thought how good it would feel to have Clancy's lack of them. Maybe then she wouldn't be walking around in a terminal state of nerves most of the time fantasizing about lovemaking techniques she knew little about and would probably be clumsy performing and not very skilled at, anyway. The brief taste of passion she'd had with Ryder only made her long for the whole feast.

"You're certainly not the only one smitten," Clancy said, patting Lauren's knee sympathetically. "From the way Justin was grinning all over himself talking with our hero, he's in love, too. What are they—bosom buddies?"

"Ryder spends a lot of time with Justin," Lauren said.

"Hmm," was Clancy's only response, but she had a thoughtful gleam in her eye that made Lauren distinctly uneasy.

"Clancy—"

"Sorry, excuse me . . . ah, pardon me." Ryder was making his way apologetically through the spectators in the stands, heading toward Lauren. People shifted obligingly to let him through.

"Hi," he said, stopping and looking directly into her eyes.

"Hi." She promptly lost the thread of her conversation with Clancy. Ryder, tanned and windblown, stole her breath away. Smiling slightly, outrageously male, he was indeed the kind of man to make any female heart flutter.

"Ryder," Clancy greeted him, inclining her head. Her eyes darted mischievously back and forth between the two of them.

"This is the cheering section for the Bluejays, I take it?" he asked, dropping down beside Lauren.

"It is," Clancy said, standing suddenly and balancing herself with her cane. "Here, take my seat. Our man behind the plate is having a super game. I think I'll just go down there and do like the rest of these pushy people—give the coach a few pointers."

Lauren looked alarmed. "Clancy—"

"Don't worry, I promise I won't embarrass Justin." She gave them a jaunty wave with her cane and started down the bleachers.

The bench was crowded, but Ryder shifted his shoulders, and Lauren found herself nestled snugly in the lee of his arm and chest. Instantly she was assailed by the scent of him— soap, she decided, and just plain warm maleness.

She hadn't spoken directly to Ryder since the morning he'd put up the birdhouse, but she had seen him every day at the plant. She was also kept well informed of his activities by everyone from the lowest ranking clerk to Michael Armstead. It seemed there was no way a man like Ryder could keep a low profile, especially in a plant the size of Holt with its family-oriented work force. That was the way they'd planned it, Jake and Ryder. But as the week wound down, remembering the kiss and her own part in it, she had found herself feeling the tiniest bit piqued by his failure to seek her out, even if it was only to inform her of any progress he was making. Her first effort to let a man know she found him attractive hadn't met with much success.

"I thought you might have found a minute to update me on what you've uncovered so far," she said coldly.

"When I know something for sure, you'll be the first to hear," he told her, his gaze on the field.

Why that statement should irritate her, she didn't know. "You mean the whole week's been wasted?"

"I didn't say that."

"Then you have found something…" She looked at him sharply. "Or someone. Who is it, Ryder?"

"I still only have my suspicions, Lauren." He gave her a deliberate look. "I've learned not to drop any names in front of you without hard-and-fast proof, so I'm still working on that. Besides, I'm not sure exactly what's going down at your plant."

Something in his voice and the grim line of his mouth made her forget everything else. "What is it, Ryder?"

"I don't know. The deeper I dig, the more tangled up I get."

She stared at him. "What on earth does that mean?" Her voice rose sharply, drawing curious stares from the couple sitting directly in front of them.

"This is no place to discuss it," he told her softly, squeezing her arm reassuringly. "Meet me at your office a little early tomorrow morning. We need to talk. You aren't the only one with questions."

The last thing Lauren wanted was to wait. If Ryder had something to tell her, she wanted to hear it. Now. Or rather, just as soon as the game was over. She would drop Clancy off and put Justin to bed and then Ryder could fill her in completely. She should have been getting daily briefings from him, she realized now, instead of tiptoeing around like a besotted teenager.

She was suddenly distracted by a flurry of noise and confusion at the Bluejays' bench. Beside her, Ryder caught her hand and hauled her to her feet.

"It's Clancy," he said, starting down the bleachers, sweeping Lauren along beside him. She craned her neck to see what had happened, and then drew in her breath sharply as she made out Clancy's petite frame lying face up in the red dirt of the dugout. Breaking away from Ryder, Lauren began running. Shooing Justin's team aside, she stared at Clancy.

"What happened?" she demanded, going down on one knee beside her.

"It's this damned—" Clancy's blue eyes swept over the whole Bluejays team that had gathered around and were now gazing wide-eyed at her. "Ah . . . this dadburn knee of mine," she amended sheepishly. "I was talking to the umpire, and suddenly I tripped and found myself flat on my back.

"You were yelling at the umpire, Clancy," Justin corrected, peering at her with the same wide-eyed interest as his teammates. "And then you started waving your cane right in his face. When he stepped back, you stumbled on those extra bats lying over there." Everyone, to a man, turned to look at the bats.

"Oh, Clancy, are you hurt?" Lauren ran a hand over the injured knee, jerking away as Clancy winced.

"I twisted it. It's nothing."

"It won't be 'nothing' in about fifteen minutes," Ryder said, bending down beside Lauren. "It'll swell to twice its size. Come on, I'll carry you to the car. Lauren can drive you home."

"What about Justin?" Clancy said, attempting to sit up. "The game's not over."

Lauren picked up Clancy's cane as Ryder bent and swung her easily up into his arms. Then he waited for Lauren to fall into step beside him. "Justin—" she began, glancing back.

"Don't worry," Ryder said. "You take care of Clancy, and I'll take care of Justin."

Wondering what he was up to, Lauren obeyed.

WHEN LAUREN ARRIVED at the plant the next morning, there were only two other vehicles in the parking lot. One she recognized as Ryder's Blazer, the other a black, low-slung powerful sports model she didn't recognize. She puzzled over it for a moment and made a mental note to find out who'd been conscientious enough to arrive so early.

Gathering up her briefcase, she climbed out of her car and promptly forgot about the driver of the black car. She hadn't had much sleep. For hours she had wrestled with unanswered questions and growing apprehension. Ryder had dropped Justin off, but had declined her invitation to come inside. In spite of her keen desire to question him, Lauren hadn't insisted. It was awkward trying to deal with the strong attraction she felt for Ryder while he was her employee. Not to mention the relationship that was developing between Justin and Ryder. She was frowning as she went up the steps to the entrance. Suddenly everything was so complicated.

To her surprise the main door was open. Shifting her briefcase, Lauren dropped her keys inside her purse. Ryder had probably left it unlocked for her. The sound of her heels echoed hollowly across the empty foyer. The area was usually filled with people and activity, but there was a strangeness about the area this morning that sent a little prickle along her spine. She turned the corridor to her office. Ridiculous.

Her door was slightly ajar, which meant that Ryder was already inside waiting for her. She felt a rush of anticipation and, taking a deep breath, she pushed the door wide.

What was that noise? A muffled thump—scuffling—and voices. Lauren's eyes quickly swept the interior of her office. It was too early to see without the lights. Why hadn't Ryder turned them on? Her hand went automatically to the switch, but never made it. There was another sound, and then a loud crash followed by a man's wrenching groan.

Her eyes flew to the storage room. It was brightly lit, the door wide open. Two men looked up, startled. Shocked, Lauren stared back. For a second or two, nobody moved. Both men had nylon stockings pulled over their faces. Someone lay on the floor at their feet. Her heart stopped. *Ryder!* He groaned and, raising one knee, tried to get up.

His movement seemed to galvanize the two. Without a sound, they headed directly toward Lauren. Her blood froze as she stared into features distorted by taut nylon. But the pair was bent on escape, not on attacking her. Brushing past her, they cleared the storeroom and then sprinted for the door of her office and were gone.

She started toward Ryder on legs that trembled and threatened to give way with every step. Sinking down beside him, she ran one shaky hand over his face. Blood came away on her fingers. "Ryder! Dear God, what did they do to you?"

Using his bent leg for leverage, he started to get up.

"No! Stay here, let me get some help."

He shook his head and got halfway up before groaning and clutching at his middle, his breath shallow. "I'm okay. They didn't have enough time to break anything." Ryder gave her a lopsided grin. "You arrived just in time to interrupt their fun."

Ignoring his attempt to put her off, Lauren slid an arm around his shoulders and helped him sit all the way up. His breathing was labored. Her amber eyes traveled over his face, darkening when she saw his mouth. "Oh, Ryder, you're still bleeding!"

He wiped it away with the heel of his hand. "I'm fine, Lauren. Really." He accepted the tissue she found in her purse and held it gingerly against his lip. "Did you get a look at them?"

She stared at him blankly. "What?"

"Did you see them?"

"Of course. They almost ran over me getting away."

"I mean, did you recognize them?" He began to get to his feet, wincing as he did so. Lauren scrambled to help him, putting an arm around his waist.

"No, those masks... Do you think anything's broken?" she asked anxiously, unconsciously stroking his chest through his shirt.

"Nah, just bruised. I've survived worse." He caught her hand in his and squeezed it. "I nearly died when you came through that door. I didn't know what they might—" He closed his eyes and leaned against an old filing cabinet.

Lauren's heart was in her throat as she reached up to touch his face. It was nicked and battered. His color was off. He turned his face into her hand. His mouth grazed her palm. Tenderness welled up in her along with another emotion far more intense and compelling.

"What's happening, Ryder? What was it all about?"

He pushed away from the file cabinet and, still holding her other hand, led her out of the storeroom into the outer office. Closing the door behind them, he headed for the leather couch and sat down. When he tried to pull her down beside him, Lauren refused. She was too shocked and upset to sit. Instead she went to her tiny bathroom and found a cloth which she wet with cool water. Coming back, she bent over him and touched his lacerated lip, murmuring when he jerked his head away.

"Sorry," she said, concentrating on the wound, not the intense midnight eyes that were fixed on her own mouth. "I don't think a bandage would help. Most of the damage is inside."

He raised his eyes then, and it was like looking into the turbulent, swirling waters of a stormy sea. She didn't get a chance to be this close to Ryder often, and she seized the moment to study him. His eyes, she thought, were oddly inconsistent with the harsh masculinity of his face. The deep blue was enhanced by a black ring and embellished with lashes that were lush and slightly curled on the tips. A tiny cut by the corner of one eyebrow would probably be another lasting imperfection. She found it strangely endearing.

"Somebody wants me to butt out of your business, Lauren."

She blinked. "What do you mean?"

"Those two thugs were waiting for me when I drove up this morning. They've probably been watching me the last couple of weeks. I get here early, before six, most days. They waited until I was inside and then jumped me in the storeroom."

A chill feathered over her skin. Watching her, Ryder felt it deep in his gut, along with an urge to gather her closely, to offer her his protection, to shield her from whatever the hell was going on here. But that was just the problem, he thought, frustration making him feel raw and powerless. He still didn't know what the hell was going on here.

"Maybe they were just after the missing plans," she said. He could feel her bewilderment, hear the fear in her voice. "I mean, you and I were thinking they might be in that storeroom. Maybe that's what they were after."

"No. They had a message to deliver and they delivered it. Get out of the plant and stay out."

"You mean they actually told you that?"

"They actually did," he said dryly. "And they were very insistent."

"I can't believe this," she whispered, sinking down beside him. "What can we do? Shall we call the police?"

"Yeah, I think we should report it, but we don't have much to go on. I didn't recognize their voices and we don't have anything but their general physical descriptions, thanks to those stockings."

"I saw their car, but I didn't notice the license plate."

"How about bumper stickers, special equipment... anything?"

Lauren shook her head. "It was black and powerful. Fairly new, that's all ... Seems like there was something on the back glass, but I can't ..." Sighing, she looked at him. "I'm so sorry you were hurt, Ryder. I never dreamed anything like this would happen. But I sincerely appreciate everything you've done. Even though we—"

"Whoa, lady." He reached out and caught her chin between his fingers. "You sound like you're kissing me off, talking in the past tense like that." He gave her a little shake. "I'm not going anywhere, especially now that they've decided to use muscle. I'm in for the duration, sugar."

"But—" Her eyes swept his battered face. "If I hadn't appeared just when I did, Ryder, who knows how far they might have gone? I don't want any more violence. We'll pursue this through the courts just as we were doing before you and Jake came up with this ... this scheme!"

Ryder got up from the couch, wincing only slightly. "It's not going to be resolved through the courts, Lauren."

"I know I stand to lose, Ryder. But it's a chance I'm willing to take. Besides, I won't lose the whole company, just the long-term royalties on Clay's designs. I can live with that. Justin and I—"

"Will you listen!"

Startled, she stared at him. He stood in front of her, his legs spread aggressively.

"It's not going to be resolved through the courts because I don't think we're dealing with a simple case of stolen designs. At least I don't think that's all that's going on here at your plant."

"What are you talking about, Ryder?"

He clamped a hand on the back of his neck and kneaded taut muscles. "I'm not sure." He moved over to the window behind her desk and stared outside. "I've been doing a lot of digging, Lauren. Things don't add up. Some of the projects going in Research and Development don't have a damn thing to do with industrial robotics." He turned back to her. "The Holt Company has never bid for any defense contracts, am I right?"

"No...ah, I mean yes, you're right." She shook her head, confused. "I assume you mean robotics to be used by the military on ships or airplanes, is that it?"

"Yeah, that's what I mean."

"No, never. Clay was a pacifist. He would never have consented to modifying his designs for anything other than peaceful, humanitarian purposes. He was an idealist in the truest sense."

"Somebody in the company doesn't share his philosophy, I'm afraid."

"Surely you..." Lauren shook her head. "No, it's impossible. Nothing like that could go on without my knowledge, Ryder."

"You said yourself you aren't technically qualified to run the company, Lauren. You can read a set of specs, but what if somebody is purposely keeping you in the dark?"

"But why?" she exclaimed, springing off the couch. "The company will never bid on a contract for anything other than peaceful purposes, I'd see to that. So what's the point?"

He faced her from behind her own desk. "I haven't figured that out yet. Frankly, I wasn't ready to tell you this much, since I still have more questions than answers. But because these people are beginning to play rough, it's time for you to know we're dealing with more than simple industrial espionage."

Lauren spread her hands helplessly. "To me, industrial espionage isn't simple," she said softly. "Anything beyond that almost boggles my mind."

He gazed at her a long moment. "I wonder if that's what they're counting on."

Her eyes clung to his. "Explain, Ryder. Please."

"You're harassed constantly by production breakdowns, late deliveries, a host of niggling problems," he reminded her. "Since I've been here, I've discovered other things. Last year, there was that fire in the old annex which caused a whopping increase in your fire insurance rates but conveniently didn't do any lasting damage to the main complex." He frowned. "Whoever's calling the shots has had it all his way—a woman alone struggling to cope with new, sometimes bewildering responsibilities and the added complications of a nasty court battle." He didn't say that he still had his suspicions about the accident with Hercules. In light of what had happened to Clay, he had gone over everything in grim detail, but had uncovered nothing.

Lauren was silent, considering Ryder's cool summation of the situation. "It does seem to make some sense when you put it all together that way," she murmured. She looked up suddenly. "Do you think NuTekNiks is in this all the way? I mean, not only Clay's designs, but the other military stuff as well?"

"It's hard to say, Lauren. There are plenty of unscrupulous types waiting to take advantage of a woman in your position."

The story of my life. If she had been more forceful, less passive, less willing to let other people lead her around, if she'd had a firmer handle on things, this probably wouldn't have happened, Lauren thought.

"You're right," she said. "If I hadn't been so naive, they never would have found the Holt Company so easy to sabotage."

He frowned. "That's not what I mean, Lauren."

"Let's face it, Ryder. If Clancy had been in charge of this company, she would have been on top of things from day one."

"What the hell are you talking about?"

"These people, whoever they are, have moved in because of me. You can believe that if I'd appeared more forceful or worldly wise, they would have had second thoughts."

Ryder leaned back, studying her thoughtfully. "No, I don't believe that. And I shudder to think of Clancy in charge. Only heaven knows if the company would have survived."

"Maybe so. But at least Clancy would have done something, not waited around for others to do it for her." Lauren drew in a deep breath. "Anyway, if you're right about these incidents over the past few months, whoever it is certainly won't welcome someone like you stepping in and having free run of the plant."

"Exactly. I'm surprised they waited this long to try and discourage me."

"And are you?" she asked, holding her breath.

His midnight eyes caught hers and held. "Am I what?"

"Discouraged."

Ryder's mouth was grim. "No, sugar. I told you, I'm in for the duration."

"I don't know what to say, Ryder. What if they try again? What if next time they do more than bruise a rib or two?"

"Don't worry, I don't plan to give them another opportunity. This morning, I was a sitting duck—the plant was deserted, I'd left the doors unlocked for you. I won't be that careless again."

Ryder moved from behind her desk and stood close beside her. Immediately Lauren felt reassured. Maybe it was his size and strength, or his innate masculine confidence—she wasn't certain. Whatever it was, she mustn't get too dependent on Ryder and his protection, she reminded herself bleakly.

He leaned over and picked up her telephone. "We both need a cup of coffee, but first the police." He punched out the number, slipping an arm around her waist while he waited.

Lauren leaned back and let him take charge, telling herself it was okay. This time.

THE POLICE CAME and Lauren gave her statement as calmly as she could manage, but she was still shaken. It was hard to believe the incredible things that were taking place in her world. Violence, industrial espionage, defense designs—what would it be next? She was relieved to see Ryder take charge as they prepared to dust for fingerprints and take photographs of the scene of the crime. The term made her shiver.

Handling her life on her own was her responsibility and no one else's, Lauren decided. The company was hers and Justin's. With that in mind, she picked up the phone and dialed the FBI. It was impossible to ignore Ryder's suspicions about clandestine defense work. She wasn't certain just how they would proceed to investigate such matters, but she was certain she should report it. She was also going to keep it to herself, she decided.

Michael Armstead was in Lauren's office minutes after the police departed. "Was that the cops?" He gave her a sharp look before striding over to where she stood watching Ryder and the two officers from her window.

Ryder had accompanied the men to their squad car. He wore his sunglasses, which concealed the scratches and cuts around his eye, but the damage to his lip—that full, sensual bottom lip—could be seen even from this distance.

Michael made a soft sound. "My God, he looks like he's been in a fight. What happened, Lauren?"

Lauren turned and studied Michael silently. His surprise appeared to be genuine. She didn't want to let Ryder's suspicions influence her. Was Michael a traitor and a thief? Could he be capable of the kind of betrayal—personal and professional—that appeared to be going on in her company?

"Lauren?" He was looking at her.

"Ryder was assaulted by two men early this morning, Michael." She waved a hand toward the storeroom. "In there. They had him down and were beating him and kicking him. If I hadn't happened along, there's no telling what might have happened."

Michael came closer, catching her shoulders. "Were you hurt? Did they touch you?"

She twisted slightly, so that his hands fell away, and retreated to her chair. "They didn't touch me. When I appeared, they ran away."

"Thank God." He was silent a moment. "What do you think it was all about?"

She looked directly into his eyes. "I don't know, Michael. What do you think?"

He turned away, thrusting his hands into his pockets. "I'm working on it."

She frowned. "What does that mean?"

"It means the whole company is down the tubes unless we find out what's going on and fast." He faced her suddenly.

"It's plain to me that Braden's snooping in areas that don't have a damn thing to do with production. I know, I know." He waved her silent when she looked as if she might speak. "You gave him a free hand. Hell, let him go. I want to know who the sleazes are in our own house as badly as he does."

He paused. "But I'm not going to just sit back and wait to see what Braden turns up, Lauren. I'm going to do a little investigating of my own. I'm telling you up front so you won't freak out if I turn something up that you don't like."

Lauren sighed, knowing what was coming. She had little doubt his suspicions centered on Ryder, but what would be the harm in giving Michael approval to snoop all he wanted? She knew he wouldn't turn up anything about Ryder, but he just might throw some unexpected light on the situation. Every little bit counted at this point.

"Go ahead, Michael. Give it your best shot."

He stared for a second, obviously surprised to get her blessing without an argument. He came up to her, fixing her with a telling look. "Braden has played his cards close to his chest, Lauren. I don't have to tell you we didn't have this garbage going on before he got here."

"No actual violence, no," Lauren replied.

Seizing his opportunity, Michael eased into the chair in front of her. "Maybe you should reconsider giving him total access, Lauren. At least until we know more about him. See what the police come up with on this."

"Jake knows him, Michael," she said patiently. "He trusts him."

Michael drew a long breath. "Jake isn't infallible. He hasn't been around Braden in years, Lauren. Things change. People change."

"But I trust him, Michael." And, for the moment, that wouldn't change.

THE MAN STOOD at the window. The day had seemed interminable. He had waited apprehensively while the police came and went. A tic appeared at his left eye. The whole episode had been stupid and ill timed. He had tried to tell his contact so, but she had not listened. Her greed was such that she was starting to make mistakes. Most important of all, she'd underestimated Braden. He was not a man to be put off by the threat of violence.

He turned away, thinking of his options now, before it was too late. And then weariness and despair settled on him like a dead weight. He had no options.

Anna. Oh, my Anna.

CHAPTER ELEVEN

"I'M DOING IT AGAIN, Clancy," Lauren said.

From a prone position deep in the luxurious depths of the sofa, Clancy watched Lauren refill the two wineglasses on the coffee table. Stretching out an arm, she accepted one of them. "Doing what, Lauren?"

"Waiting to be rescued."

Clancy took a taste of pale, crisp Chardonnay. "You want to enlarge a bit on that?"

"I've already told you what happened today. It was Ryder who was hurt, not me, but he insisted that I go home early, well before the office cleared, with instructions to bolt the doors when I got home and not to let Justin out unless I know exactly where he's going and who he's with. If I had allowed it, he would have cancelled Justin's camping trip."

"Speaking of that . . ." Clancy shifted slightly, favoring her knee. "I feel awful about dogging out on Justin, Lauren. But there's no way I could have hiked in the woods with this knee."

"Don't worry, Justin wasn't exactly thrilled to be going with two women."

Clancy grinned. "You're right there. Tell me, what lucky suckers got saddled with the job?"

"Curtis Wainwright's folks," Lauren said. "But even then, I had a time talking Ryder into letting him go. Just listen to this. Until further notice, I'm not to stay in my office for lunch if I'm alone or go into any restricted area of the plant unless I'm with Ryder. I'm practically a prisoner until this whole thing is cleared up. All for my own good, of course," she added bitterly.

Clancy straightened up and put her glass on the table. "I can see his point, Lauren. The situation does warrant caution."

"What if it's not cleared up for weeks? Months?"

"I think Ryder will probably have the situation in hand before long," Clancy said. "He's not the type to tolerate anybody terrorizing you or yours. He'll take care of the problem. Soon."

"That's just it, Clancy. I'm expected to sit here and let him take care of the problem." Lauren came to her feet and began pacing the floor. "As I said, I'm being rescued again. If it's not Jake or Michael, it's Ryder."

"You can hardly strap on a weapon and become Ms. Rambette," Clancy pointed out. "I don't see that you have much of a choice."

Lauren finished off her wine and set the glass down with a clink. "Look at me, Clancy. I'm healthy, sensible and reasonably bright. Why am I waiting for my destiny to be decided by other people?"

"Is this twenty questions?"

"You remember I told you I've always done the proper thing, always made the safe choices?"

"This *is* twenty questions."

"I've been thinking about something you suggested the other day." She went to the bottle and poured herself some more wine.

A bit wary, Clancy watched her friend begin pacing again. "What time is it?"

Clancy glanced at her watch. "Eight-thirteen."

"Justin's sleeping over at Scott's tonight, and we're going out.... We're going to the Blue Marlin, Clancy."

Clancy's eyebrows flew upward.

"You said yourself we could just drop in there casually and keep our ears and eyes open. Who knows what we might find out."

Clancy was shaking her head. "I didn't mean you, Lauren. You'd look as out of place at the Blue Marlin as...as..." Her eye fell on the pair of wineglasses—beautiful, fragile antiques—on the coffee table. "As those Waterford stems. Besides, somebody might recognize you."

"I plan to disguise myself."

Clancy was on her feet now. She propped both hands on her hips. "How?" she demanded.

"Makeup, hairstyle, a pair of glasses, clothes. You know yourself, Clancy, people only see what they expect to see. Nobody'll ever expect to see Lauren Holt at the Blue Marlin."

"I don't know, Lauren. I—"

"Please, Clancy. I'm going to do this and I'd feel a lot better if you came with me. After all, you said yourself you've done this before."

"That was in my past," Clancy argued. "The past I'm trying to put behind me. What if Jake finds out?"

"He won't. We're not telling anybody but Hattie Bell." She headed toward the kitchen. "With Justin camping out, I can't take a chance on being out of pocket in case there's an emergency."

"THEY DID WHAT?"

Holding Jake's gaze, Ryder's knuckles went white on the receiver as Hattie Bell repeated herself.

"Damn it to hell!" He slammed down the phone, pinning Jake with a black look. "Lauren and Clancy are at the Blue Marlin," he said. "Have you ever heard of anything as crazy as that?"

Jake resisted the impulse to relate a few equally reckless stunts Clancy had pulled that would make a Friday-night visit to the Blue Marlin seem like a Sunday School picnic.

"Come on," Ryder growled, grabbing up his keys. "We're going to get them."

They descended the steps of the old house two at a time. Ryder got in the Blazer and started it, waiting impatiently while Jake hurried around to the other side. Jake had arrived at his place a couple of hours before to discuss what to do next, now that the opposition had resorted to open violence. The last thing Ryder—or Jake—needed was for Lauren and Clancy to place themselves directly in the line of fire. Gunning the motor, Ryder tore out of the drive and down the lane to the main road driving like a man possessed.

"I didn't think Lauren would do anything like this," Jake murmured.

Ryder pointed an accusing finger at him and said in a tone that boded ill for somebody, "It was Clancy's idea, you mark my words."

"Probably." Jake clenched his jaw. He had just about had it with Clancy. It was just like her—tearing off without a thought for her own skin or Lauren's. If she was going to stay around Mobile as she claimed, she was going to get a glimpse of a side of him she hadn't seen yet.

Having his opinion confirmed seemed to pour more fuel on Ryder's wrath. He swore again and downshifted with a savage motion. "Why in hell can't you control your woman?" he demanded.

"She's not my woman," Jake said. "Yet."

"She sure wants to be!"

Jake grunted, his expression unreadable. "Nobody's ever been able to control Clancy. Me, least of all."

"Only because you refuse to see what's been planted in front of your face for weeks now," Ryder said, looking fed up. "When are you going to give the woman what she wants?" he demanded.

Jake leaned slowly back in his seat, his eyes on Ryder. "And what would that be?" he asked.

"She wants you, for God's sake! She's sashayed around you for weeks now getting about as much response as she could from a damned eunuch. If you'd act like the man I know you are, she'd melt like a snowball in hell. Instead, she's running around with time on her hands scheming up crackpot ideas, dangerous crackpot ideas. Damn it, Jake!"

Jake grunted again and thought of Clancy's fiery nature and how it would feel to have her beneath him, breathless and yielding, melting....

Ryder swerved around a pothole. "And now she's dragged Lauren into it with her! When I get my hands on—"

"Yeah," Jake said, his tone taking on a note of anticipation. "Me, too."

THE PARKING LOT around the Blue Marlin was crowded, forcing Clancy to circle twice before finding an empty spot. They were in her sleek little Mazda, since she had insisted on driving.

"We may have to make a quick getaway," she said in a tone that made doing so sound like a real possibility.

Lauren got out of the car, determined not to act as uncertain as she felt. Never in her life had she entered a bar without a male escort. And even with an escort, she'd never been inside a place like the Blue Marlin. Taking a deep breath, she headed for the entrance. But before they got there, she glanced back when a car, tires squealing, skidded to a stop a few spaces beyond them.

"Clancy!" Lauren's fingers closed on her friend's arm. "What is it?"

"That car, Clancy..." She pointed to the low-slung, black Trans-Am. Two men were inside, but as yet they made no move to get out. A light flared when the driver lit a cigarette. Suspended from the rear window was a yellow sign.

"Three Fifty-seven Magnum Aboard," Clancy read aloud. She looked at Lauren. "Friends of yours?"

"No! I'm not sure, but I think it's the car that was parked at the plant this morning. I knew there was some kind of sticker or something on the back window, but when Ryder asked I couldn't recall what it said."

Clancy caught her arm and began to haul her back the way they'd come. "C'mon, we're getting out of here. Those guys aren't the type to be gentle just because you're female. They'll recognize you and—"

Lauren pulled her arm free and stopped. "You're probably right if their treatment of Ryder is anything to judge by," she said, her face thoughtful. "On the other hand, this is the first opportunity I've had to connect anyone with the trouble I've had at the plant, Clancy." She gave the other woman a pleading look. "If I leave now or delay long enough to find a phone to call Ryder or Jake or Michael, the opportunity may be lost. The company is my responsibility, not theirs. I can't quit now. I have to do this, Clancy."

Clancy was silent another moment, and then said reluctantly, "Okay, but just do as I say, you hear me?" She turned and they started back toward the entrance.

Lauren squeezed her arm. "Thanks, Clancy. We're going in that bar and we're just going to melt right into the crowd. Nobody'll recognize either one of us. Bars are always dark."

"Oh, sure. And of course you speak from a wealth of experience." Clancy looked at her. "How are you going to see through those ridiculous glasses?"

"I'll manage." Lauren adjusted the oversized tinted glasses that covered a generous amount of her face then she firmly tugged at the tail of her shirt, unaware of the fetching sight she made with her derriere tantalizingly outlined in acid-washed denim. Her outfit was so unlike anything she would ever dream of wearing except in her own backyard that she was certain no one could possibly recognize her. Just in case, she had set her hair with hot rollers and arranged it in a wild tangle of curls that fell forward at her forehead and temples.

They slipped quickly inside the bar. Lauren had an impression of men, lots of men, loud music and laughter. She wrinkled her nose at the smell of smoke and stale beer. Clancy moved confidently beside Lauren and, taking a bead on a spot toward the back of the bar, headed for it. Lauren's courage faltered as she looked around. It seemed as though every male eye in the bar was on them.

"Look straight ahead," Clancy said in her ear. "And don't stop for anything or anybody until we get to that table way over there against the wall."

"Hey, you ladies need a drink?" A tall, bearded giant stepped in front of them, baring a lot of teeth. His chest was so broad that he seemed like a brick wall to Lauren, whose nose barely reached the third button on his shirt.

"No thanks," Clancy told him. "We're meeting somebody."

He put out a hand. "Well, I'm somebody, darlin'."

Clancy dodged the hand and didn't slow down. To Lauren's relief the giant seemed to accept the rebuff with good grace.

"Change your mind, you know where to find me," he called, still grinning.

Quickly they found the table and sat down. Lauren kept an eye on the front door while the barmaid appeared making one or two swipes over the tabletop with a large wet cloth. She transferred a lighted cigarette from one side of her mouth to the other with her teeth.

"What'll it be?" she asked, squinting at them through smoke.

"Perrier and lime," Lauren told her and then winced when Clancy kicked her on the ankle.

"Two beers," Clancy said.

"Light," Lauren said quickly. "Make mine a light beer." Even so, it would be a miracle if she could drink it.

"Two light beers," the woman repeated. "Coming up."

As the waitress left, Clancy studied the crowd while Lauren concentrated on the front door. "Those men should be coming in soon, wouldn't you think?" Lauren asked.

"Not for a while," Clancy replied, shifting so that the barmaid could set the two beers down. As soon as the woman left, she said, "They're getting high in the car."

Lauren stared at her. "How do you know?"

"Did you notice they were smoking?"

"Yes ... So?"

"That wasn't a regular cigarette, sweetie."

"Oh."

"You ladies want to dance?"

Startled, Lauren glanced up into the grinning features of a cowboy. At least, the man was outfitted like a cowboy, complete with Western shirt, jeans and worn boots. His silver and turquoise belt buckle was enormous.

Clancy laughed. "Both of us?"

Just then the jukebox blared out a new song, a blend of country and swing. "Sure, the Texas two-step," the cowboy said. "A pretty lady on each side of me is how I do my best work." he waggled his eyebrows suggestively. "Whadda ya say?"

"No, thanks," both "pretty ladies" said in unison.

"This might not have been such a good idea," Lauren muttered after they had finally convinced the cowboy to leave.

"No kidding," said Clancy, sipping her beer.

"Just sitting here, we're easy targets," Lauren said, frowning through the thick smoky haze. Behind them was a pool table. One lone man was just finishing a solitary game. After a final shot, he wiped the chalk from his hands and shelved the stick against the wall, where an array of pool cues were neatly racked.

As she watched, an idea came to Lauren. She turned back to Clancy. "Come on, let's go back to that pool table. If we're occupied, maybe they'll leave us alone."

After a moment of surprise, Clancy stood up. "Good idea. I forgot you used to play billiards with your daddy."

"And you probably learned to shoot pool in a place a lot like this one in some interesting corner of the world," Lauren returned with a smile.

"Germany."

"I knew it wouldn't be some everyday, ordinary place."

Clancy grinned. "It was the NCO club at an army base in West Germany."

Lauren saluted her with the chalk. "Rack 'em!"

In five minutes the crowd around the pool table was four deep and nobody was trying to come on to them—at least, not while the game was in progress. Clancy was obviously no shoddy player and Lauren found her own skill returning as they played. At first she was flustered by the audience, but after a few minutes she began to enjoy the men's enthusiasm.

"Bank the five and seven," advised one tough-looking dude.

"Nah, she ought to take that one straight," somebody named Joe countered.

"Whoo-eee! Did you see that shot?"

"Put some English on it, honey!" advised someone directly behind her whose gaze was fixed on her bottom.

"She's gonna run the table, hot *damn*!"

"Keep an eye on the door," Lauren murmured to Clancy as she neatly dropped the seven ball in a side pocket.

Pretending to chalk the end of her pool cue, Clancy leaned close to Lauren's ear. "They just came in."

Crack! The six ball went zinging across the table, striking a hair short of the corner pocket. A collective groan went up from Lauren's fans.

Getting into position for her shot, Clancy said for Lauren's ears alone, "Was that on purpose?"

Smiling enigmatically, Lauren allowed her gaze to drift beyond the crowd to the two men approaching the bar. There was nothing familiar about either one. Maybe if they wore stocking masks... She squinted through the haze, concentrating. But it was no use. Still she was certain the Trans-Am was the car she'd seen at the plant, and these men were probably the two who'd attacked Ryder. Fixing their features firmly in her mind, she turned back to the table.

"We can go now," she said softly.

Clancy nodded. "Nine ball in the side pocket," she murmured and then proceeded to do it.

"Game!" announced Joe. "Rack 'em up again. I'm gonna skunk this sweet thang." He winked at Clancy.

"No, you ain't!" The cowboy stepped up, pool cue in hand. "I already spoke to take on the winner."

"Oh, yeah?" Joe straightened up slowly. He looked the cowboy directly in the eye. "I don't think so."

The cowboy's fist shot out and connected with a thud, dead center in Joe's face. Joe grunted with the force of the blow. Shaking his head, he growled like an angry beast and charged at the cowboy, planting his fist squarely in the middle of the huge silver and turquoise belt buckle.

With the first blow, Lauren and Clancy began to back away hastily. But it wasn't fast enough. The cowboy crashed backward, sending them all to the floor in a tangle of arms and legs. Dazed, Lauren lay beneath somebody's thighs, vaguely aware of the pandemonium breaking out among the bar patrons who were still on their feet.

"What the hell?"

It was Ryder's voice. Lauren put a finger to the nose piece of her glasses, which were cocked at a crazy angle on her face, and straightened them. Looking up, she saw a ring of faces, all of them peering down at her. And Clancy. Blinking to clear the fuzziness from her brain, she focused on the man whose frown was the fiercest.

"Ryder," she said soundlessly.

Swearing, he reached out to pull her to her feet.

"Now just a damn minute," Joe began belligerently. "This little lady is with me. We—"

For the second time Joe was caught with an unexpected blow. Ryder's fist came out of nowhere and clipped him on the chin. He went down like a felled ox.

Without another word, Ryder took Lauren's hand and, turning on his heel, pulled her with him as he strode toward the door.

"What about Clancy?" she said, looking worriedly over her shoulder. She could see Clancy's red curls and—was that Jake?

"That's your lawyer's problem!" Ryder snapped.

JAKE SAVAGELY SHOVED the cowboy aside and pulled Clancy to her feet. "Of all the crazy, reckless, irresponsible—"

Her eyes wide and very blue, Clancy stared at him. "Jake—"

"Don't say a word, Clancy," he warned. Clamping both hands on her arms, he looked ready to explode.

"Hey!" The cowboy pushed Jake with a hand to the chest. "Don't be manhandling this little gal. Me and her gonna shoot a little pool. We don't need you, pal."

Jake was deadly quiet. Then he looked Clancy directly in the eye. "Is that right, Clancy? Do you have a date with this jackass?"

Eyes wide, Clancy shook her head.

"What?" said Jake softly.

"No. No, I don't have a date with this jackass."

Jake nodded and, moving her aside, turned his attention to the cowboy. "You heard the little gal."

Clancy put out a hand, suddenly worried. "Jake—"

Jake brushed her off with a twist of his arm. "You have a problem with that, cowboy?" His tone was still soft, but his gray eyes glinted with male challenge.

Cowboy put up both palms and backed off. "Hey, no problem, man. We were just gonna have a friendly game, but hell, we'll make it another time."

Jake's gaze never wavered. "Not with this woman, you won't."

He waited another deliberate second or two. Nobody made a sound. Jake's gaze passed over the men. Then, satisfied, he put his hand on Clancy's arm and guided her away from the pool table, across the tiny dance floor, through the chairs, past the bar and out the door.

"Where's your car?"

Clancy pointed toward the Mazda. For once in her life she was speechless. She stumbled slightly, having to stretch out her steps to match Jake's furious stride. At her car, she fished in her pocket for her keys. He took them and unlocked the car. She got in, but climbed across the steering console to the passenger's side. In Jake's mood, it was a given that he would drive.

Jake got in, closed the door and locked it, but he didn't start up the car. He still hadn't said a word. Turning in his seat, he looked through the back glass and located Ryder's Blazer. Lifting a hand, he signaled to Ryder, who waved in return. The Blazer started up, its lights flashing on. Ryder and Lauren were leaving. Jake grunted and, still without uttering a word, reached for Clancy.

Clancy let out a startled gasp as he hauled her over the console onto his lap and crushed her mouth with his. The kiss was hard and hot, wild and out of control. For time-less moments, Clancy was transfixed, stunned into unchar-acteristic submission. But not for long. She was where she'd longed to be. With a glad cry, her arms went around his neck.

RYDER LEFT THE NEON LIGHTS of the Blue Marlin behind in a cloud of dust. If that was possible on a paved street, Lau-ren thought, swallowing an urge to giggle. He hadn't said a word since the moment his fingers, feeling like steel clamps, had fastened on her wrist when he'd hauled her out of the bar. His jaw, she noted, stealing a quick glance, looked as if it was made of steel, too. His gaze had not wavered once from the centerline of the street.

A little shiver went through Lauren. She was in for a lec-ture, she guessed. But she didn't intend to cave in simply because Ryder, and Jake too apparently, believed her place was at home or behind the safety of her desk waiting pas-sively for them to solve her problems. He pulled up in front of her house with a squeal of tires.

Before he had a chance to start lecturing, Lauren had the door open and was halfway up the walk. In a few long strides, he was beside her. "Thanks for the ride," she told him, rummaging in her purse for her key, which she couldn't seem to locate.

"Would this help?" Ryder reached out and plucked the glasses from her face.

She grabbed them back and dropped them into her bag. Finally she found the key, and after fumbling with it, allowed Ryder to fit it in and open the door. When he pushed it open, she went inside, with him right on her heels.

"There's no way I'm leaving here tonight without getting a few things off my chest," he told her, taking her by one arm and shoving the door closed. "Where can we talk?"

"I don't need a lecture, Ryder. I went to the Blue Marlin tonight and—"

"How could you let her talk you into such a crazy thing?" he demanded.

"Who, Clancy?"

"Who else?" he asked impatiently.

Her laugh was short and harsh. "Of course, the whole idea had to be Clancy's," she said, speaking to the ceiling. "I'm a fully grown adult, but incapable of any decisive act, especially one that might hint of slight risk, even if the future of my company is threatened."

He stared at her. "I assumed it was Clancy's idea," he said, emphasizing each word, "because it *was* a risky thing to do. Not because I don't think you're capable of a decisive act. You've proved yourself over and over, Lauren. But you don't have to do everything yourself. Staking out the Blue Marlin was a crazy thing to do. We're dealing with dangerous people. What if you'd run into one of them?"

There was a certain amount of satisfaction in the look she gave him. "I did. Actually, I ran into two of them."

He was silent for a second or two, his eyes locked with hers while the air crackled with his frustration. Then, catching her by the arm, he led her from the foyer to the living room. The soft glow of a single lamp was the only light. Shaking him off, Lauren sat down on the sofa and then watched him take a seat on the edge beside her.

"You ran into two of them."

His tone was even, but she sensed leashed emotion in him. For some reason, it gave her a feeling of power to provoke him. "I recognized the black car that was at the plant this morning. The two men who were in it came into the bar a few minutes after Clancy and me. I made it my business to take a good look at them."

It was a moment before Ryder could speak. And then his lips barely moved. "That idiot cowboy one of them?"

She laughed. "No, he was just trying to come on to us."

"And the other one," Ryder said, barely managing to keep from exploding into a jealous rage. "The jerk who was stupid enough to think he had some claim on you—what about him?"

She laughed again. "Oh, I think Joe was more impressed with my talent at the pool table than anything else."

"Guess again," Ryder scoffed. "A man doesn't go to fist city over a woman just to shoot pool with her."

"Oh, come on, Ryder. I—"

"You could have been hurt! What if you'd taken one of those punches!" He reached out and flicked a finger at her curls. "What if one of those bozos had recognized you?"

Lauren pushed her glasses back onto her face and gave him a saucy grin. "I was traveling incognito."

Shaking his head, Ryder slumped back on the sofa. "Didn't you believe a word I said today, Lauren? You took a chance going to that bar, getting tangled up in—"

She giggled and tossed the glasses aside. "I was tangled up all right." Leaning back, she turned her head to look at Ryder. "And so was Clancy. I was floored to find myself flat out with some big ape on top of me."

"How can you joke about this? Don't you know you scared the hell out of me? Don't you know you could have gotten yourself in deep trouble?" His eyes on hers were tormented.

Lauren's playfulness vanished under the hot, dark look. The air between them was suddenly charged. He reached for her with a purely male, animalistic sound and hauled her into his arms.

"Don't you know you're driving me crazy?" Ryder groaned, burying his mouth in her hair. "If that big stupid jerk had touched you, I would have killed him."

In a heartbeat, he caught her to him and covered her mouth with his in a scorching kiss that burned all the way to her soul. It began as a bruising, punishing declaration of his dominance, but soon it gentled into something more compelling. Lauren responded eagerly, letting all she felt for him burst forth in physical expression. His mouth closed over hers, opening wide, while his tongue swept fiercely into her honeyed warmth, possessing and devouring, staking a claim.

He groaned, murmuring something she didn't catch, and pulled her into his lap, renewing the wild ravaging of her mouth with his. His hands swept over her shoulders to hold her fast, locking her against him, letting her feel the hard male thrust of his desire.

Lauren wrapped her arms around him. Here was the promise of pleasure and satisfaction she'd longed for, and she welcomed it with her whole heart. She loved this man. She tore her mouth from his to tell him so.

"Ryder—"

"Don't stop..." His tone was raw, ragged. "God, don't stop, Lauren. I need this, I need..." His words trailed off as he ran his mouth over her cheeks, her nose, her hair, her temples.

Sweeping his hands down, he sank his fingers into her soft buttocks, holding her fast so that she rocked against him in a heated, rhythmic cadence. Her head fell back while her body shuddered and strained against his pulsing manhood. Ryder groaned, pushed to the edge of his control. Suddenly, with one decisive motion, he tumbled her gently off his lap and onto the floor, coming down beside her. Quickly he stripped her jeans away.

"I want to see all of you sweetheart." He pulled feverishly at her shirt, and Lauren willingly lifted her arms. His voice was low and intense as his hands readied her. "This is crazy, I know it. But it's either this or go stark-raving mad. I may feel like a bastard later, but right now all I can think about is how much I want you." The words rushed over each other, tumbling from him like leaves in a whirlwind. His breathing was labored and uneven as he looked into her eyes. "We'll work it out somehow, sweetheart. I swear it." His hands went to the snap on his jeans.

"Hurry, Ryder." Lauren's eyes, dazed with passion, clung to his. "I want you, too. I love you."

The words hung suspended between them. At first Ryder didn't take them in. At first. Dropping his head until he almost touched Lauren's chest, he drew in an agonized breath and held it. Lauren felt the deep tremors that shuddered through his body as he struggled to control the raging passion that had driven him blindly to this point.

Ryder looked down the length of Lauren's body, open and defenseless to his, and the full extent of his deception hit him like a blast of cold air, twisting bitterly inside him.

"Ry-Ryder... What is it?" Lauren said, staring up at him in confusion.

Cursing himself, he rolled off her and then reached for her shirt. Taking it, she felt her face flame. Suddenly she was scrambling to her feet, shielding her nakedness with the shirt.

Ryder got to his feet and reached for her, intending to help her put her shirt back on. Her hand flashed out to ward him off. Turning from him, she quickly put on the shirt, unaware that he'd turned his back.

He sensed when she was ready and gathered the courage to look at her. She was staring at him, her eyes more golden than amber, he noticed, and glittering with tears and some other emotion. *Outrage,* he suspected. *Well, she should be outraged.*

"What was that all about, Ryder?" she demanded in a voice that was low and intense and slightly unsteady.

He raked a hand across his face. "I'm sorry. I—"

"Sorry!" Her tone rose emotionally.

Oh, God, what should I do? Ryder wondered, closing his eyes against the bewilderment and pain in hers. What could he say? Was now the right time to tell her everything? But suppose she decided to shut him out of her life? He groaned, caught in a trap of of his own making.

"I can't figure you out, Ryder." Lauren stared at him, her lips trembling. "You barge into my company like some bigger-than-life corporate raider, you insinuate yourself into every facet of my life, win my lawyer's confidence, charm Hattie, captivate my son . . ."

She turned, closing her eyes, and wearily kneaded her temples with her fingers. "You're everywhere when I need you and I seem to need you often, no matter how I tell myself that I won't." She laughed hollowly. "This will probably amuse you. You're the first man I've met since Clay died who has stirred any sexual feelings in me, and I let you know it. It wasn't hard, because, although you seem determined to deny it, there is something special between us."

His eyes, meeting hers, burned with emotion. But before he could reply, she stopped him with a shake of her head. "No, Ryder, just don't say anything. I think your behavior tonight says it all. When you've made up your mind what it is you want from me, then we can talk. Until then, I'd like for you to leave."

Seconds ticked by as Ryder stood unmoving. Eight, ten, twenty. And then, without a word, he brushed past her and went silently out the door. Lauren closed it behind him and rested her forehead against it for a moment. Then she turned away, squaring her shoulders, and climbed the stairs. She had never felt more lonely.

On the other side of the door, Ryder wrestled with an onslaught of emotion. Lauren's words echoed over and over in his mind. Little wonder that she was confused and feeling rejected. In his attempt to behave honorably with her, he had hurt her. Looking upward in the night sky, his heart twisted. He had been afraid to tell her everything, fearing that she would shut him out of her life. He would lose her, Justin, the hope of a life together with them.

Standing stock-still, he absorbed his own pain. The last thing he wanted was to hurt Lauren. He loved her, he realized suddenly. He wanted her with an intensity that surpassed anything he'd ever known—beyond sex, beyond reason, beyond the secret that linked them. Shaking his head, he stood silently thinking of her. He had fallen completely and totally in love for the first time in his life and he would never be satisfied until she belonged to him in all ways.

Ryder shoved his hands in his pockets and reminded himself of all the reasons he should wait to claim her. He had a feeling it wouldn't be long before he unraveled the conspiracy threatening her company. What was a few more days, weeks? He pulled a hand from his pocket. In his palm lay the key to Lauren's front door. Fate again? He turned and stared hard at the polished brass lock winking at him in the moonlight. Reason and logic and even honor paled when every instinct urged him to open that door and declare himself. He would tell her everything soon. When the time was right, he would know it. Deep inside him, desire and love were tearing him apart, compelling him . . .

Like a man in a trance, the decision was made. He reached out and put the key in the lock.

Inside, he hesitated at the bottom of the stairs, and then took them, two at a time. At the top, he looked down the hall. All the doors were open except one. She was in that room, he knew it. None of his considerable experience with women had prepared him for the way he felt as he approached Lauren's bedroom. Taking a deep breath, he lifted a hand and knocked.

"Lauren?" he thought he heard a soft, rustling inside, but she didn't answer.

"Lauren, it's me, Ryder. Can I come in?"

Still there was no sound. He reached for the door and found it unlocked. He debated two seconds and opened it.

Lauren scrambled off the bed and stared at him, her expression wary. He didn't go to her, but simply stood there, feeling his heart pound. Emotion churned in his throat. He wanted to charge across the room and sweep her up in his arms. He wanted to kiss away her hurt, love away her misgivings. He wanted to feel her body, soft and warm, against his. He wanted to be inside her, to feel her passion, hot and fervent, surround him.

"Why are you here?" she asked, wiping tears from one cheek with her hand. "What do you want?"

His eyes swept over her hungrily. "You," he said simply.

CHAPTER TWELVE

LAUREN BEGAN TO TREMBLE. Suddenly it was hard for her to breathe. She searched Ryder's face, not daring to believe him or the look in his eyes.

He didn't go to her, but began talking, the words pouring out. "You were right when you said we have something special going for us, Lauren, but at first I really fought it. I've never felt anything like this before."

He closed the door behind him and walked over to her until she was only inches away. "I tried to keep away from you, but everything conspired against me. I was just going to be your expert witness and when the case was done, move on. And then there was the trouble at the plant. I couldn't just walk away then." He caught her hand and brought it tightly to his mouth. "And Justin...I just kept getting in deeper." Sighing, he rubbed her knuckles against his cheek. It was rough with a day's growth, but to Lauren it felt delicious. "No matter how I tried, it was no good. The more I saw you, the more complicated my feelings became."

Listening, barely able to breathe, Lauren felt joy and hope spilling over inside her. His innate decency was revealed in every word as he tried to explain himself. She'd known all along Ryder was a man without roots, a man who couldn't stay long in one place. His relationships had been made up of brief encounters with no strings attached. She would surely have appeared unsuited for that kind of thing. Her heart filled as she realized he'd been thinking of her and of the eventual pain she would have when he moved on again when all she'd been thinking was how much she wanted him. He thought he knew her better than she knew herself.

He was wrong.

She drew in a shuddering breath and closed her eyes in relief and bittersweet joy. Maybe she couldn't have him forever, but the future and the illusion of security were not nearly as important as they once had been to her. She had chosen the ultimate in security when she'd married Clay and look what had happened. This time, she would risk whatever it took to know the joy of loving Ryder. If it couldn't be forever, then she could accept that.

He cupped her face tenderly in his hands. "I never meant to hurt you, sweetheart," he said, rubbing both thumbs over her lips. "Please believe that."

She made a soft sound and slipped her arms around his waist. He held her tightly, his mouth buried in her hair.

"I love you, Lauren."

Lauren felt as though her heart would burst. She'd waited so long just to know he wanted her the same way she wanted him. To hear him say he loved her...

"I love you, too," she said, holding him close, anchoring him to her to make the moment last and last.

"I want to show you how much," he murmured thickly, tunnelling his fingers through her hair. He brought her mouth to his for a kiss that was hot and hungry, rife with promise. It was potent and lavish and designed to make her crave more and more. Time was suspended as the kiss went on and on. When Lauren's body was melded to his all the way from her mouth to her toes, he finally broke off the kiss to urge her down onto her bed.

Ryder sat on the edge and reached for her hands. Bringing them to his mouth, he kissed them both. "I want to touch you all over, sweetheart. And taste . . . I want to taste you all over." His eyes flared when she shivered at the image his words conjured up. Lowering her hands, he took her mouth in a sweetly searing kiss. Her lips moved in instant, eager response.

"I'm going to love you in all the ways I've dreamed about," he promised huskily, putting aside his guilt and misgivings. "In all the ways it was meant to be with us."

They fell back together on the bed, and his kiss was suddenly no longer gentle. His mouth devoured her, sweeping over the curve of her brow, down her cheek to her parted lips. He kissed her with searing passion, his tongue plundering sweet, secret depths. His hand moved to her breast, holding it lovingly, and then she felt his breath, hot and heavy, through the thin knit of her shirt. She whimpered when he gently bit her nipple and then licked it soothingly. She caught his head and held him tightly against her, writhing and moaning, wordlessly urging him onward. She needed something . . . something . . .

Ryder groaned, almost out of control. He'd meant to be tender, to prolong the pleasure for her sake as well as his own, but she was making it impossible, twisting and turning, on fire as much as he. He rolled off her and reached for her shirt. As soon as Lauren realized his intent, she scrambled to help him, lifting her arms so that he stripped the shirt away and then ripped open the snap of her jeans and unzipped them. Ryder pulled them down and off and tossed them aside, leaving her clad only in her brief ivory bikinis.

The blood rushed to his head. He had never felt anything like the emotion that welled up inside him. He stood to remove his own clothes. Made clumsy by his need and by the sight of her naked, her skin like creamy magnolias, Ryder's hands trembled, fumbled at his belt buckle. Lauren was following his every move, unguarded hunger in her eyes.

Leaning back on her elbows, her hair was a riot of swirling, golden curls, spilling softly onto the pillow.

He groaned and came down to her, feeling a fierce triumph as she reached for him eagerly. "If you keep looking at me like that," he told her, resting his head between her breasts and breathing hard, "it'll all be over in about two minutes."

For the first time Lauren felt something deeply feminine flowering inside her, nurtured by the knowledge that she could arouse him this way. She kissed his hair and hugged him to her breast. He drew in his breath sharply and buried his mouth in the soft, giving flesh of her abdomen.

"I don't want you to wait," she said, feeling a quick rush when his tongue explored her navel and then began to venture lower. Her bikinis were just a tiny scrap of silk with a lace flower inset over the mound of her femininity. Holding her hips in his hands, Ryder tasted that flower and sent white-hot heat searing through her, pushing her to the edge.

"You're so beautiful," he muttered thickly, drunk with the scent and taste of her. "I want you so much. I love you so much."

She arched against him, his name a strangled cry. The sound seemed to galvanize him to new heights of passion. Quickly he stripped her bikinis off and took his place between her thighs. "I can't believe you're going to be mine at last," he said hoarsely. Almost hesitantly he bent and kissed her mouth.

"I am yours," she murmured against his lips. "Always for as long as you want me."

Forever, he thought. He wanted her forever. *If only that could be.* With his hand, Ryder stroked the curve of her buttocks and down the smooth line of her legs, then up the delicate skin inside her thighs. He found the soft, intimate folds of her femininity and sank his fingers into her warmth.

She was hot and ready for him. The knowledge filled him with fierce satisfaction. He anchored his hands at her hips, probing gently at her warm, creamy portal.

"Now, now," she urged, opening herself to him. "Take me now."

Ryder lifted his head and looked directly into her amber eyes. "What?" she murmured, sliding a hand along his hard jaw. She touched his mouth, her eyes sparkling with golden flame. "What is it?"

"I love you," he said, his voice unsteady, almost breaking. "Just promise me you'll remember that."

"I will."

"Promise?"

"I promise."

He nodded, everything he felt showing in his midnight eyes. And then, with a single hard thrust, he entered her.

He shuddered and went still, waiting for her body to accustom itself to his. She fit him perfectly. She was everything he'd ever dreamed she would be. He'd wanted her so long, waited so long. Could this really be happening? She stirred beneath him and his sex throbbed with its fertile burden. He squeezed his eyes shut and was flooded with feeling. He thought of that moment, twelve years before, when in a twist of fate their destinies became inextricably entwined. What would she say if she knew how fiercely he wished their child had been conceived this way, beautifully, naturally, lovingly?

"Come with me," he begged, breathless. Breathing deeply, he began to move in passion's instinctive, rhythmic dance. He gripped her hips, mounting a steady, loving assault that sent them racing toward completion. He felt the subtle ripples begin deep in her womb and it was like a gift from heaven. She sank her nails into the muscles of his back, making the small sexual sounds that had nearly driven

him wild before. Hearing her moan now, as they surged toward mutual satisfaction, he felt the immediate, urgent response of his body and was helpless in the wake of its
demand. Reaching as high as he could, he gave her everything.

WHEN LAUREN AWOKE, she was alone. It was not yet
morning, but the lightening shadows at her window told her
it soon would be. She stirred and passed a lazy hand over the
space next to her. It was still warm. She moved over and
buried her face in the pillow next to hers, inhaling deeply,
and smiled. It smelled musky and male, like the man she
loved.

She rolled over and sighed with pleasure. Never in her
dreams had she expected to know the kind of joy that filled
her heart. Ryder made her feel beautiful and cherished,
wholly feminine. Not a part of her was left untouched or
unkissed after their loving. Her body tingled and ached in
new places to prove it. And to her delight, she now had the
same intimate knowledge of his body.

After that first fierce coupling, when Ryder lay sprawled
and sleeping—or so she thought—Lauren had slipped out
of bed and into the bathroom. She was just sinking into the
tub when he had opened the door. The corners of his mouth
hiked in a sensual smile, Ryder had begun to move slowly
toward her. He had been big and rumpled, lazily relaxed in
the manner of a sated male. And naked, gloriously, beautifully naked. He hadn't even hesitated when he'd reached
the tub. He'd simply stepped in, hauled her up into his arms
and begun kissing and licking every drenched inch of her.
Recalling the moment, Lauren smiled and felt a delicious
expectancy, imagining pleasures yet to come.

Where was he, anyway? She glanced around the room.
The bathroom was open and obviously empty. She got up

and pulled on a deep blue silk wrap. In the hall, she saw the light in Justin's room. Curious, she walked that way.

OMIGOD, HERE IT IS. Ryder stared at the screen of Justin's computer. Everything fell neatly into place as he studied the complicated material displayed before him.

Who would ever have suspected? If he hadn't been curious to see the inside of Justin's room, if he hadn't been hungry to connect in a small way with Justin's everyday life, he might never have discovered this. But flipping through a box of diskettes, he'd found more than a boy's collection of video games. He'd stumbled on the missing schematics for Clay Holt's original designs!

Lauren was in the room before he became aware of her. She glanced curiously at the complicated material he had accessed, before turning her attention to him. He was wearing only his undershorts. Surrounded as he was by Justin's possessions and the youthful furnishings of the room, Ryder's body seemed even more rawly powerful than usual. Standing directly behind him, she slipped her arms around him and pressed a lingering kiss on the side of his neck.

"Oh, hi, sweetheart," he said huskily, but Lauren could tell that he was distracted.

"What are you doing in here?" she asked, wrinkling her nose at the monitor.

"Discovering lots of interesting things," he said, inclining his chin in the direction of the box of diskettes occupying the space beside the computer terminal. "See those?"

"Uh-huh." Justin's fascination with computers and all things electronic wasn't news to her. She certainly didn't find the subject interesting tonight.

"You'll never believe what I found tucked in among his video games," he said, tapping out a series of commands on the keyboard. To Lauren's amazement, up came something that looked like an electronic schematic. Even for Justin, it appeared complicated.

"What in the world?"

"Robotics," he said.

"Robotics?" She looked dumbfounded.

"Look here." Ryder shifted so that she could see the monitor over his shoulder. "You won't believe this."

Just then the air conditioner started up and Lauren shivered. Her silk robe was designed for beauty, not practicality. Idly Ryder slipped one arm around her, but his thoughts were obviously on the squiggles displayed on the monitor.

"I won't believe what?"

"All this time, we've been turning the plant upside down looking for the missing designs and they've been right here in Justin's room."

He reached over and flipped up the lid of the plastic case. "On these diskettes," he added, shaking his head. "The company's lifeblood carelessly tossed in among a bunch of video games, for Pete's sake."

Lauren stared. "Surely not."

"It's true. What the hell was Clay thinking about? These records are obviously vital, essential to the company's future."

She shook her head, mystified. Looking at the screen where the complicated schematic was still displayed, she tried to understand. "Clay was totally dedicated to his work," she murmured. "It doesn't make sense that he could be careless with so much at stake."

It made no sense to Ryder, either. Leaving the records of his multimillion-dollar business in the hands of an eleven-year-old, no matter how precocious, was just one more mystery in a whole string of them that didn't add up. His mouth was grim as he bent and switched off Justin's PC, determined to get to the bottom of things.

THE TELEPHONE WAS RINGING. Murmuring a complaint, Lauren awoke from a deep and dreamless sleep. They'd both gone back to bed. Reaching over Ryder's chest, she fumbled for the receiver, handling it gingerly, trying not to disturb him. But before she could carry it to her ear, Ryder's arms closed around her, pinning her close to his chest. She managed to get the receiver in place and was smiling into his eyes as she said, "Hello."

"Lauren Holt?"

Still smiling, she tilted the receiver up so that she could give Ryder a quick kiss. "Yes, this is she."

"The lady who owns the Holt Company?"

A tiny frown appeared, banishing her smile. "Yes, who is this?"

"I thought you might want to know that a bomb has been placed in the plant, Mrs. Holt."

She stared at Ryder, her face paling.

"Mrs. Holt?"

"What? What did you say?"

"You heard me, Mrs. Holt. There's a bomb in your plant and it'll go off in about—" he paused "—one hour and twenty-eight minutes."

Click.

"Dear God," she whispered, staring at the phone in her hand, unaware that she trembled with the fear and horror that suddenly coursed through her.

Ryder propped himself on one elbow, his eyes narrowed. "What is it, sweetheart? What's the matter?"

"There's a bomb at the plant."

"What!"

"It's going to go off in an hour and twenty-eight minutes."

Without another word Ryder grabbed the receiver from her and pressed the button to summon a dial tone. Swearing, he was on his feet and punching out the emergency number before she could scramble off the bed. In a few curt words, he explained the situation.

Behind him Lauren hurriedly riffled through a drawer and found both bra and panties, then quickly pulled on jeans and a shirt. When Ryder turned to her after hanging up, she was almost completely dressed.

"I'll just be a second," she told him, twisting her hair up and anchoring it with a sturdy clip.

"Would it do any good if I asked you to wait here?" he demanded, closing the zipper on his pants. His shirt was already on. He went down on one knee and found his loafers, then shoved his feet into them without bothering with his socks.

"Hardly." Lauren was already at the door. Impatiently, she looked back over her shoulder. He was at her dresser, sweeping up his keys and pocket change. "Hurry, Ryder!"

"I'm coming. But we need to tell Hattie to keep Justin close when he gets home from his sleepover. I don't like what's happening here, Lauren."

She nodded, still pale. Then, together, they went out.

A POLICE UNIT WAS WAITING when they got to the plant and so was Michael Armstead, along with his gofer, Jimmy Johns. He explained that he'd received an anonymous call about the bomb and, according to his responses to Lauren's questions, it appeared that the same individual had called both of them. Armstead appeared tense and grim faced. Watching him, Ryder had to give the guy credit. If he'd had anything to do with setting up the situation, he was covering it very well.

"I tried to call you at home," Michael said to Lauren, "but Hattie told me you had already left . . . with Braden."

Lauren barely heard him. Her eyes were on Ryder who was striding off to meet an arriving police van. *The bomb squad,* she thought, with a renewed sense of horror.

Armstead, too, was eyeing Ryder. "Braden seems pretty cool, considering the whole place might blow at any minute."

Startled, Lauren looked at him. "What are you suggesting, Michael?"

"I'm saying flat-out that he doesn't seem to be quaking in his boots." He shrugged, then added in a jeering tone, "Almost as though he knows something the rest of us don't. I'm still not convinced about Braden, Lauren. He acts like a con man, if you ask me."

Lauren struggled to hang on to her patience. "Your suspicions hardly constitute fact, Michael."

"Not yet, but—"

"You seem determined to concentrate on Ryder. Here's a suggestion, Michael. Check out the Blue Marlin where NuTekNiks's people hang out. Maybe you can turn up something more than innuendo."

"Uh, boss . . ." Jimmy Johns shuffled nervously at Michael's side. "Maybe we oughta go along with those bomb-squad guys while they check out the premises."

Lauren gave Michael a meaningful look. "Yes, maybe you should, Michael."

Armstead's jaw flexed in frustration as Lauren turned away abruptly and walked toward the growing number of people who were congregating at the entrance to the plant. In addition to Braden, the bomb squad and numerous uniformed cops, the press was also on the scene.

"Maybe you better back off bad mouthing Braden in front of the boss lady," Johns suggested.

"And maybe you better back off giving me advice!" Armstead snarled, more than ready to take his spite out on Johns.

"Okay, okay." Johns put up both hands. "It just looks to me like Braden's got the inside track right now, boss. She was ready to spit fire at you."

Armstead's eyes were on Braden and Lauren. "Yeah, it's going to take more than talk to shake her faith in that son of a bitch. He's managed to get her in the sack, Jimmy."

"A woman doesn't like to hear dirt about her lover," Johns observed sagely.

"Stupid, troublesome bitch," Armstead muttered, feeling another surge of frustration. "If we don't watch out, Braden's gonna move in and take everything. He's got to go, Jimmy. I didn't come this far to be robbed in the last inning." His expression was hard. "I just have to figure out how to make it happen."

THERE WAS NO BOMB. The search was abandoned that morning two hours past the eight o'clock deadline. The plant had been gone over with a fine-tooth comb and nothing suspicious had been uncovered.

The more Ryder thought about it, the more convinced he was that this event was just one more harassment calculated to annoy and distress Lauren, forcing her closer to a decision to dump the plant. But who was behind it and how far would they go? Would their next attempt be more personal? The questions came faster than answers in his head while his imagination supplied half a dozen ways a widow with a young son could be terrorized.

When Sunday night came, he was no closer to finding any solution. He paced the floor in Lauren's den, thinking about

Clay Holt. He couldn't prove Clay had been murdered, but deep in his gut, he was convinced that the man's demise was just too timely, too convenient. Whoever was behind this mess hadn't stopped at violence then, and Ryder wasn't willing to take the chance that Lauren or Justin, or both of them, might also be victimized.

The press was on the scent again and making the most of it. When they'd returned to Lauren's house the day of the bomb scare, a reporter had been parked out front, waiting. Ryder had sent him packing. Later he had refused three telephone requests for statements. There didn't seem to be any end in sight to the media harassment.

"I don't like any of this, Lauren."

Lauren leaned back in her chair and rubbed her forehead. "Neither do I."

Ryder stopped behind her and put his hands on her shoulders. Instantly she relaxed against him, sighing as his fingers found her tight muscles and began to work the tension away. His own body stirred and started to throb. Ryder smiled and let himself enjoy the task, thinking how he'd like to have the right to take care of her always. Every day. Until they were both old and gray. And beyond.

"You know what I hate most of all?" Lauren murmured, tilting her head sideways so he could reach one especially painful spot.

"No, what?"

"The publicity. I hate being in the news again. I hate them calling me on the phone and waiting for me at my front door. I just hate that, Ryder." She leaned her head back and looked up at him. Her face was upside down to him, blurred with fatigue, but beautiful, so beautiful. He bent and kissed her lingeringly on her mouth.

"I've got an idea," Ryder said, inching himself into the chair and moving Lauren so that she gave him room before he pulled her onto his lap, breathless and flushed. "This situation has too many questions and not enough answers. Somebody is obviously harassing you, and so far has limited himself to tactics that haven't harmed anybody. I'm worried that he might cross the line."

Ryder touched her hair, idly sifting through the silky pale strands and then, catching her face in his hands, he dipped his chin so that he could look directly into her eyes. "I want you and Justin to come and stay with me at my place until this is cleared up."

Joy flooded her at the thought of sharing the intimacy of his home even for a short time. Lauren hesitated, searching his face. He wasn't talking about commitment, she reminded herself. It would be temporary, just until the trouble at the plant was over.

"If you're worried about what people will say," he said, misinterpreting her expression, "don't be. I mean for Hattie Bell to come, too. We need her for Justin, and besides she's part of your family. There's plenty of room."

"Are you sure this is what you want, Ryder?"

He'd never been more certain of anything in his life. To have her and Justin under his roof, to have the right to offer them his protection, was a chance he'd never expected. Ryder drew her back against his heart, tucking her head under his chin and thought about fate. Something had brought him here at just this time and in just this place and had thrust him into her life. He was not a spiritual man, but there must be some reason, he told himself. He knew now that no matter how everything eventually turned out, he would never be able to live his life apart from Lauren and Justin. Last night he'd claimed the one woman meant solely for him, thereby taking a step from which there was no turning back. Her troubles were now his. Everything he had and was, was hers.

"What do you think Justin will say?" he asked.

She laughed softly. "He'll say, 'how soon can we leave?'"

For a second his throat was too thick to speak. "And Hattie Bell?"

"She already thinks you need a female to take proper care of that old house of yours." Lauren tweaked a sprig of dark, curly hair on his chest. "Provided she gets the job, of course."

He caught her hand and brought it to his mouth, and then kissed her palm with languid thoroughness, making full use of his tongue. "She's got the job."

"Mom! Mom!"

Alarm flared in Ryder's eyes. He lurched out of the chair, setting Lauren on her feet. Justin was just beginning to trust him and he wasn't taking a chance on ruining everything now.

Lauren didn't appear to be concerned. Laughing, she went to the door. "In here, Justin," she called.

Justin rushed in, real distress bringing a glaze of tears to his eyes. "Mom, I was just fooling with my computer stuff and somebody has been in my room! My dad's diskettes are missing, Mom!" He caught her hand. "Come on, I'll show you."

"No, Justin, they're safe," she said. "I took them." Stricken, Lauren looked at Ryder over the boy's head. "I meant to tell you today, but in the excitement over the bomb threat, I completely forgot. I'm sorry, Justin."

Justin looked confused. "You took them? But why?"

Ryder went to stand beside Lauren. "Your mother and lots of other people have been looking for those diskettes a long time, Justin," he said quietly. "Where did you get them?"

"My dad left them there," Justin replied.

As always, when reminded of the casual way Holt behaved, Ryder became irate. No doubt the man had been brilliant, but he seemed to have been sorely lacking common sense. His carelessness in leaving those diskettes lying around might well have endangered both Justin and Lauren. "Did he tell you anything about them, Justin?"

Justin shook his head slowly. "Just that all diskettes should be kept closed up and all, so that they wouldn't get damaged." He looked at his mother. "I'm real careful about that, huh, Mom?"

She ruffled his hair. "That's true, Justin."

"Once in a while I'd take a look at them," he continued ingenuously, "but I couldn't understand much when I displayed them, so I just put them in the back of the case."

Lauren stared at him. "You didn't once think that I might be interested in looking at them, Justin?"

"Not really, Mom."

She opened her mouth, but Ryder spoke before she could say more. "Does anybody else know about the diskettes, Justin?"

Justin shook his head solemnly, then looked anxiously from his mother to Ryder. "Did I do something wrong?"

Ryder put his hand on the boy's shoulder, smiling faintly. "No, you didn't. Don't worry about it, Justin. Sounds like you and your dad really enjoyed playing around with your computer."

"My dad was always fooling around with my computer," Justin told him proudly. "And when he took me to the plant, he showed me a lot of things his big one could do."

Ryder nodded absently, his mind still on the valuable design diskettes. "I'll bet your dad used your computer sometimes when he was at home, probably to review whatever he was working on. Maybe he forgot to collect them the last time he did that.''

Justin shook his head. "No, he didn't forget them. The night he was using my PC, he had to go back to the plant for something and he told me if I turned it back on, to be careful and not damage his diskettes." He looked at his mother and then away quickly. "That was the night he had the accident . . . the night he . . . he . . ."

Ryder looked grim.

Lauren put her arms around Justin and hugged him tightly. "It's okay, love. We just wondered how they came to be in your room. And now we know. You've taken very good care of them."

Blinking back tears, she looked at Ryder, whose expression was troubled. She was glad to see that he was not insensitive to Justin's pain. She put out a hand to him and he took it, then pulled them both close.

CHAPTER THIRTEEN

THE NEXT TWO WEEKS passed in a blur of happiness for Lauren. It was the height of foolishness, she told herself, but loving Ryder and being with him all the time made it impossible to feel threatened and stressed out as she had so often in the past year. Besides, in that magical two weeks, nothing awful happened at the plant or in the lawsuit. It appeared that she was at long last enjoying a rare spell of peace and quiet, even prosperity.

She loved Ryder's house. Even though the place still needed a lot of work, it had so much potential that it was all she could do to maintain any kind of decorating restraint. It was exactly the kind of house she had always wanted. From her first glimpse of it that morning with Jake, she had appreciated its charm and grace. But now, more than that, it was special because it was the only home Ryder had ever known.

Getting to know Ryder was almost as satisfying as loving him. One afternoon, they took Justin and a picnic lunch and fishing gear and whiled away one whole afternoon beside the bayou that wound through the rear of Ryder's property. But Justin was the only one with enough energy to fish. Ryder sprawled out in the grass after propping his own fishing rod on the ancient boat landing and enjoyed Hattie's lemonade with real honest-to-goodness lemons in it. Hattie pampered Ryder outrageously and he loved it. Sitting beside him, sharing the peace and summer sounds of the lazy afternoon, Lauren couldn't resist a chance to learn more about him.

"You must have been very happy as a boy growing up here—woods, a bayou with fish in it, birds and animals everywhere," she said, looking around. "Did you know how lucky you were?"

He looked at her. "Lucky?" He leaned away and tossed out the ice from his drink. "I didn't have a lot of time to enjoy it. I had a job from the time I was nine years old."

She frowned, secretly shocked. "I thought you played baseball."

"I did. I worked the games and practices around my jobs, whatever they happened to be at the time. Mama Jane planned for me to get an athletic scholarship, but I broke my wrist in an accident on a job in a grocery store and that shot my chances in the big leagues."

Lauren felt a pang for the advantages he must have missed. "What about your parents?"

"What about them?"

She watched him squint out over the bayou. The set of his shoulders and the hard, grim line of his mouth told her his childhood memories weren't happy ones. She suspected his thoughts were as dark and held as many secrets as the murky bayou bottom.

"I was raised by my grandmother," he told her, his voice low and deep. "She worked two jobs until I got old enough to help out. As for my parents, I wouldn't know. I can't remember either one of them."

With a quick, unexpected movement, he tossed a pebble far out over the water. The peace of the afternoon had vanished.

"How old were you when they died?"

Ryder turned and looked at her deliberately. "If a kid doesn't have any parents at home, they must be dead—is that how neat and tidy your world has always been, sweetheart?'' He shook his head, his mouth twisted in a humorless smile. ''My parents aren't dead, Lauren, at least not that I know of.''

Her voice was barely a whisper. ''I'm sorry, Ryder.''

''Apparently it was the age-old situation,'' he said dryly. ''Pregnant teenage girl and immature youth forced into marriage. My mother had visions of becoming a country singer, so she split first. Took off to Nashville, I think. I was about eighteen months old, according to Mama Jane. But my old man . . .''

Ryder gazed at the wooden landing where Justin sat fishing. Lauren sensed he wasn't really seeing Justin, but was trying to conjure up a memory. Ryder blinked. ''Yeah, my old man stayed a little longer. It was either Australia or Alaska he decided to try. He was a sailor with the sea in his blood.'' Ryder held Lauren's eyes. ''That was a direct quote, in case you're wondering—Mama Jane's stock answer when I wanted to know where the hell my father was. I'm not sure how old I was when he left, about four, I guess. Some people claim they can remember things back when they were four years old, but I can't. Not even bits and pieces.''

''Maybe it was too painful,'' Lauren said softly, feeling the sting of tears behind her eyes for an abandoned little boy. ''Maybe you just blocked everything out.''

Ryder rubbed his thumb against his chin. Lauren could hear the soft rasp of day-old beard. ''You may be right,'' he said. ''As a boy it was my father's desertion that bothered me the most. I had Mama Jane as a surrogate mother. She gave me all the nurturing any kid could ever need. But I wanted a father.''

Lauren reached out and touched him. ''You would be a good father.''

He smiled softly and pulled her close so that he could nuzzle her hair. "What makes you say that?"

"The way you are with Justin," she told him. "And the way you are with his friends when they're over and at the ball field. You're a good role model. You teach by example when you can and you're tactful, caring of their feelings."

Watching Justin first, Ryder slipped a hand under her shirt and rubbed her stomach. "Their egos, you mean."

She smiled back, glad to see some of the shadows leave his eyes. "I'm happy to hear a man admit that the male even has an ego." She waited a moment. "Did you never want children of your own?"

His hand on her stomach went still. "My marriage was too rocky to risk bringing a child into it."

His marriage. Lauren felt a quick, sharp jolt and realized it was jealousy. And longing. Ryder had loved enough to marry once. She wished...

"How long... I mean..." The words trailed off, incomplete. There was so much she longed to know. She stared up at his profile, wordlessly urging him to tell her more.

"I got married about five years ago." He inclined his head so that he could see her face. "Do you remember the night we met? We danced..."

"I remember," she murmured.

"It was right after that. One of those whirlwind things. I was on a job in California. I met Stephanie. We got married."

Ryder closed his arms around Lauren and thought about Stephanie. She had been a lot like Lauren—pale ash-blond hair, warm hazel eyes, a cultured background. She'd even had a soft Southern drawl—from Texas, not Alabama. After the sexual heat between them had cooled, their differences started to cause problems. It had taken them only a few months to realize what a gigantic mistake they'd made.

Stephanie had married Ryder to share his free-wheeling life-style, not because she loved him. As for Ryder, what he'd done was just now becoming clear to him. And why.

"What was she like?" Lauren asked softly.

"She was from Texas."

"No, I mean . . . what was she like?"

His tone was suddenly teasing. "Blond, hazel-eyed, five-four, a size eight."

She pinched him lightly on the arm. He kissed her on the neck. "She was a very nice lady, but it was just never meant to be."

"What happened?" Lauren whispered, closing her eyes as she felt his breath, hot and erotic, against her skin.

He lifted one shoulder. "Same thing that happens to one out of two marriages today. We got a divorce."

"But why?" she asked, distressed for him, for herself for reasons she didn't want to know right now.

She wasn't you. He had fallen for Lauren that night five years before, and he had married a woman who looked like her and talked like her—God forgive him—a woman who had soon sensed she did not have his heart. A woman who could never *be* Lauren.

"Ryder! Mom! I caught one. Look!"

Grinning, Justin stood on the landing holding up his line with a catfish dangling from it.

"Be careful," Lauren called. "A catfish has fins that—"

Ryder silenced her with a finger over her mouth. "He knows that, sweetheart. I showed him weeks ago how to get it off his hook without getting a fin stuck in his thumb."

Sure enough, Justin had already netted the fish. As Lauren watched, he flopped it on the pier and put one foot—safe in his Reeboks—on it. With a deft twist using a screwdriver or something—she couldn't tell what—the fish was free.

"He's too little!" Justin informed them and tossed it back into the bayou.

"Good job, Justin." Ryder settled back on one elbow, smiling at Lauren's chastened expression. "Cut him some slack, Mommy."

Staring at him, she allowed herself to dream for a moment. He was wonderful father material, whether he knew it or not. Her eyes roamed his rugged features, stopping at the tiny cut still visible beside his eyebrow. Now that she'd seen the two thugs in the Blue Marlin, she realized Ryder might easily have been killed that morning in the storeroom.

Impulsively she reached out and touched him, using one finger to trace the faint red line. "It's going to leave a scar," she murmured.

"Mmm, it sure won't be the first." He rubbed his cheek against her hand.

His shirt hung open, revealing a dark mat of chest hair. She slipped her fingers through it slowly. Ryder was like a big, lazy cat sometimes. He loved having her touch him and stroke him.

"You know what I thought that first day in Jake's office?" she asked softly, finding another jagged scar below his collar bone.

"Hmm..."

"You looked world-weary and battle-scarred," she said, her palm flat on his chest. "I thought you were the most beautiful man I'd ever seen." Her fingers moved lower. She felt his stomach muscles clench.

"Lauren—" Ryder glanced toward Justin, who was busy baiting his hook.

"And dangerous." Lauren's laugh was soft, self-mocking. "Of course, I denied it like mad." Careful to keep

her back to Justin, she caressed Ryder through the heavy
jeans.

A frustrated groan was torn from his chest. Ryder closed
his eyes and fought to keep from surging against her hand
like a wild man.

"How do you like the new, uninhibited me?" Lauren
asked huskily.

His features were heavy and flushed and his breathing was
uneven. "As soon as I get you alone," he told her in a rusty,
rough tone, "I'll show you."

"WHAT'S THE MATTER, Justin?" Lauren pushed open the
bedroom door and stepped inside. It was Saturday afternoon, and Justin and Ryder had spent most of the day
working on the old house. Usually nothing short of a hur-
ricane could dim Justin's enthusiasm for the renovation.
Why was he up here lying on his bed?

"Nothing."

She hesitated, studying him a moment longer. Like hers
Justin's relationship with Ryder had flourished. They spent
hours together—working or playing; it didn't seem to matter. Ryder's world travels were a source of wonder to Justin, and he was full of questions, which Ryder patiently
answered. But what they both seemed to like best was
working on the house. Ryder spent hours patiently demon-
strating how to use a hammer, tear up and replace floor-
boards and how to replace wobbly railings. Sometimes the
lesson would be how to caulk and paint properly. Or re-
shingle. There didn't seem to be anything Ryder considered
beyond Justin's abilities. He even gave him a plumbing lesson when the ancient pipes in the bathroom began leaking
from the strain of unaccustomed use.

"Weren't you going with Ryder to the building supply
place this afternoon?"

Avoiding her eyes, Justin got off the bed. "I changed my mind," he said.

She didn't believe that for a minute. Maybe Ryder had decided he'd get more done without an eleven-year-old underfoot. "Well, maybe you'd like to give me a hand with the old pedestal table in the kitchen. I'm taking the finish off and it's turning into a messy job."

He shifted his weight onto one hip and looked dejected. "I don't think so, Mom."

She studied him shrewdly. Maybe he was simply bored with grown-ups. "You want to give Scotty a ring and see if he'd like to come over?"

He didn't answer, but sat back down on his bed. "Mom, what do you think Dad would say if he knew that you and me and Ryder were friends?"

A sharp pang went through her. Lauren had tried to shield from Justin the sexual nature of her relationship with Ryder. They were very discreet, but Justin was bright and perceptive. Did he suspect? Or was he simply worried about his own growing affection for Ryder?

She sat down closely beside him. "I don't think your dad would object to our friendship with Ryder," she said softly. "Ryder is a good person, Justin. He's been helpful to me at the plant and he's opened his home to both of us when we needed a friend. Why do you think Clay would object to that?"

Justin plucked at a loose thread on one knee. "That's not what I mean, Mom. I know Dad would think that's okay." He looked at her. "I like Ryder a lot, Mom."

"So do I, Justin."

"He teaches me a lot of things."

"I know."

"He's almost as good at teaching me things as Dad was."

Her heart aching with tenderness, Lauren put her arm around his shoulders. Justin wasn't thinking she was disloyal. He was feeling disloyal himself. Staring at his firm little chin, she searched for the right words to reassure him.

"Your dad was blessed with lots of talent, Justin. He was an engineer and a scientist and an inventor. And although you were very young, he taught you many things, giving you as much information as you could understand." She caught his chin and turned his face so that she could look at him. She laughed softly. "But remember how he hardly knew a hammer from a screw driver?"

Justin's blond head bobbed up and down.

"Everyone has different talents, Justin, you must have noticed that." He nodded. "Then you must have noticed that Ryder handles a hammer and a screwdriver like a pro right?" He nodded again. "He's an engineer, too, but his talents are different from Clay's. Still, Clay would want you to learn everything Ryder is willing to teach you, Justin."

"You think so?"

"I know so, Justin. I believe your father would think you've been lucky to find a friend like Ryder."

THE NEXT DAY was Sunday. Ryder invited Jake and Clancy over to cook steaks out on the grill. After they'd eaten Lauren and Clancy took tall glasses of ice tea outside and sat down in the old swing in the backyard, grateful for the deep shade of a giant live oak tree.

"So, what's the latest at the plant?" Clancy asked. Using her foot, she gave a gentle push that sent the swing into motion.

Lauren shrugged. "Nothing. No incidents, nothing. Maybe whoever it is has decided there's too much risk involved."

"Now that you're under Ryder's obvious protection, you mean."

Lauren closed her eyes and felt color rise in her cheeks. "Oh, dear," she said faintly. "This is not what I meant when I said I was going to become less inhibited, Clancy."

"Don't look so shattered. Anybody who matters knows the circumstances, Lauren. Your safety—and Justin's—has been threatened. Besides, with Hattie Bell chaperoning, your behavior is perfectly respectable. Forget it, for Pete's sake. Let's enjoy the lull in hostilities, even if it's only temporary."

There was a lull, and for that Lauren was thankful. Another week had passed with no harassing incidents at the plant.

"What about those two goons in the Trans-Am?" Clancy gave her a wry look. "Or is the subject of that night at the Blue Marlin as touchy between you and Ryder as it is between Jake and me? I've had strict orders not to try my hand at covert operations again."

"I've been meaning to ask you about that," Lauren said, resting her glass on one knee. "When I saw Jake drag you into the car that night, he looked like a man getting ready to do something drastic. What happened?"

Clancy grinned. "Something drastic."

Lauren studied her friend in silence. She knew how much Clancy loved Jake. Had she finally overcome his doubts about her? Had Clancy convinced him that she was home to stay?

"You and Ryder missed it when he faced off the whole crowd at the pool table," Clancy told her, smiling at the memory. "I was busy planning how I could get us out of there in one piece, but he didn't need me, Lauren. He was terrific!"

"I've always known Jake was terrific, Clancy."

"Yeah, well—I don't mean that Southern gentleman stuff that you seem to bring out in a man. I'm talking physical stuff. To my amazement, not a one of those guys seemed willing to take him on." She shivered and looked like the cat who licked the cream. "Then he marched me off to the car and took out his frustrations on me."

"I can see how outraged you are," Lauren said dryly.

Wearing a dreamy expression, Clancy looked over in the direction of the men under discussion. "This may sound schmaltzy coming from a totally liberated woman, but Jake makes me feel one hundred percent female. It's like I've been looking for something for a long time and now at last I've found it." She looked at Lauren with a crooked smile. "I tease him about being stuffy and overly conservative, but actually Jake appeals to me like no other man ever has. I think he's sexy as hell."

"From what you say, he wasn't stuffy and conservative at the Blue Marlin," Lauren observed.

"Hardly. Here's the amazing part—I thought he was holding back because he was convinced that when the spirit moves me, I'd simply take off. That was only part of it. What he really feared was that he wasn't exciting enough for me, that I'd soon be bored with him." Clancy shook her head. "I think he made that grandstand show at the Blue Marlin out of some crazy mixed-up notion that he had to prove to me that underneath he was as macho as . . . as Ryder, if you can believe that."

Lauren *could* believe that. Hadn't she been thinking the same thing about herself and Ryder? How long would it be before Ryder moved on?

"I'm glad it worked out for both of you," she told Clancy, giving her a quick hug. "You and Jake must be meant for each other, even if it took ten years to happen."

Clancy bent over to place her empty glass on the ground. "Speaking of 'meant for each other,' you and Ryder certainly are."

"I don't know about that," Lauren murmured, her eyes on her lover. "The time may be right for you to settle down, Clancy, but Ryder is still a vagabond at heart. Oh, I think he'll stay here until my troubles at the plant are resolved and the lawsuit is finished, but I'm not counting on a future with Ryder."

Clancy looked distressed. "I think you're wrong, Lauren. He loves you."

But not enough to make a permanent commitment, Lauren thought. And because he wouldn't, she tried not to let herself dream the impossible. She tried to manage as much of the business independently of him—and Michael—as she could. She already accepted that the two men would never be able to work together. But getting along without Ryder at the plant was one thing. Getting along without him in her personal life was another.

"Well, we'll just have to see." Sounding brisk, she finished off her drink and set the glass down beside the swing. Deep down, she was anything but casual about her relationship with Ryder and its tenuous nature, but the day was too beautiful and the company too enjoyable to dwell on it.

Clancy's eyes were on Ryder and Jake, who were sharing an intense conversation on the back porch. "I wonder what those two are talking about?" she murmured.

Lauren looked at the two men. "I was just wondering the same thing." Whatever it was, Ryder would tell her in his own good time, especially if it was something that might distress her. He was constantly trying to shield her. It was a daily struggle, trying to get him to treat her as the owner and CEO of the Holt Company first and his lover second—

which didn't help in her campaign to control her own destiny.

"As for those two goons at the Blue Marlin," she said, "we know they work at NuTekNiks in the shipping department. Only we can't prove they were the two who attacked Ryder in the storeroom that morning." As she watched, Ryder reached into a cooler and got out a beer. He tossed it to Jake and then took one for himself. Still deep in conversation, the men came down the steps and started across the lawn.

"The only thing we have connecting them to the attack is my uncertain identification of the car. It's not enough."

"It was a good start," Ryder said, sitting down on the grass opposite the swing and stretching out his long legs. "Jake and I were just discussing the situation. We've got feelers out here and there. Some of them are beginning to pay off."

"Really?" Clancy perked up, her blue eyes going from one man to the other. "Like what? How? Is somebody staking out the Blue Marlin?"

Jake leaned back against the trunk of the big oak and crossed his legs. "Relax, relax, the deed is done."

"Well, tell us, for heaven's sake!" Lauren demanded.

Ryder grinned and saluted Jake with his beer. "My old buddy here has been enjoying happy hour at the Blue Marlin lately."

Clancy stared speechlessly at Jake and then at Ryder and then back to Jake.

"Can you believe this, Ryder?" Jake's mouth curled in a slow smile. "Clancy's struck dumb."

Everyone laughed as Clancy gazed at Jake with unabashed wonder.

A dull flush started at Jake's neck and spread upward. "What's the matter?" he demanded gruffly, "You think you're the only reckless fool around here?"

"Frankly, yes," Clancy said, still amazed. Suddenly she frowned. "Seriously, Jake, that's a rough place. We already know these people aren't playing games. I don't think you should—"

"Listen to this," Jake addressed the sky. "The original thrill seeker is giving me a lecture on prudence."

"I'm not kidding, Jake. Don't go back there. Please."

For a long moment, they seemed to forget Lauren and Ryder and simply stared at each other. Lauren could see that Clancy was truly shaken. Now that she had Jake's love and the promise of a future together with him, there was a new vulnerability about her. She wasn't as impulsive and free-spirited as she had been. The hint of a threat to Jake shook her. Lauren wondered what it would take to work some basic changes in Ryder. If he loved her...

Jake moved away from the tree and came toward Clancy. Taking her hand, he pulled her up from the swing and looped his arms around her. "Hey, what's this?" he teased. "I never thought I'd hear you urging caution. I thought you'd be impressed."

Clancy moved back so that she could see his face. "You mean after we knew first hand what a dive the place is and the kind of people that hang out there, you went anyway just to prove some macho principle?"

"No, I went for the reason we discussed when the idea originally came up."

"You said then that it was risky and you were right."

"Lauren is my client and I felt obligated."

Clancy's mouth trembled. "You could have been hurt!"

"But I wasn't." Jake reached out and gently touched her cheek. "What d'you say we go home and discuss this?" he suggested in a husky voice.

"Wow." Lauren's expression was a mixture of wonder and bemusement. She watched Clancy and Jake, oblivious to everything except each other, drift off toward their car after hurried goodbyes.

"Uh-huh." His eyes dancing, Ryder rose to his feet and brushed the grass off his cutoffs before sitting down beside her on the swing. Putting one arm around her, he brushed a kiss on her temple and then gave a shove that sent the swing gently in motion.

"I guess it's obvious what they plan for the rest of the day," she said, snuggling up against him.

"Hmm." Lazily he began unbuttoning her shirt. "Afternoon delight I believe it's called." One deft twist and he'd unsnapped her bra. Her breath caught as he touched her nipples and she shivered, closing her eyes.

"Come here." Ryder shifted in the swing and pulled her over onto his lap. As soon as he felt the softness nestled warmly against him, he groaned and moved urgently, searching for her mouth. Their lips parted and fused hungrily, tongues greedy and bold. For Lauren, the world and everything in it ceased to exist.

She clung to him, her body melting into his. When his mouth left hers, she whimpered at the loss until she felt him string a line of soft, open-mouthed kisses down, down, past her chin, her throat, then to her breasts.

He murmured something, rubbing his whole face against her, his beard sensually abrading her skin. Lauren, almost purring with pleasure, arched her body up, up...

"Nobody in the world could feel as good as you," Ryder whispered.

"Nobody but you," she said, straining against him, cuddling her softness against the hard ridge between his legs.

"I have a taste for afternoon delight myself," Ryder said, in a raw, rough voice. With a little growl, he pushed her shirt low on her shoulders and bared both pink-tipped breasts. Framing them between his hands, he renewed the slow, tantalizing seduction with his mouth. She felt dizzy and disoriented and it had nothing to do with the fact that she was being ravished in a swing. Her breath caught as his hand burrowed under the elastic waistband on her shorts and spread over the satin flesh of her stomach and then ventured lower to rake the soft, curly triangle. She arched, moaning, when he stroked the tiny core of her desire. Mindless, and thrumming with a thousand sensations, Lauren ached for more.

"Ryder, Ryder, let's go inside."

He made no move to stand. "Is Hattie Bell gone?"

"She's at the movies."

Losing all pretence of control, Ryder stripped off her shorts and panties, tossing them aside. Fumbling, breathing hard, he freed himself and positioned her so that she was astride him. Controlling her with his hands at her waist, he looked into her eyes and slowly lowered her, groaning as he sheathed himself in the warmest, farthest reaches of her femininity.

Lauren moved cautiously at first, unsure but eager for yet one more sensual lesson. But her wariness vanished with the quickening of Ryder's body and dissolved into shivering, mindless pleasure. She threw back her head and surrendered herself completely to the feeling. When Ryder found his own satisfaction, calling out her name hoarsely, she knew the deepest joy.

"I can't believe I did that," she murmured as soon as she could catch her breath. "In broad daylight, too, right out in the backyard, even if it is in the country." She was cuddled on Ryder's lap with her arms draped around his neck, still in the swing.

"It was awful, was it?"

She buried her face in his neck. "It was wonderful and you know it."

He chuckled softly, molding the curve of her hip with a languorous hand. "And you were the one who wanted to go inside."

"What do I know?"

"You know enough to make me the happiest man alive," he said huskily, closing his eyes and pulling her close against him.

The swing squeaked softly, the sound gentle in the lazy afternoon. The mockingbird that resided in the side yard was perched on a limb high above them, its song a clear, melodious tribute to the peace and beauty of the day.

"When's Justin due back?" Ryder asked after a while.

"Not until seven."

He frowned. "The movie can't be that long. He's with Scotty and Curtis, isn't he? What's the plan for afterward?"

"They're going from the movie to the plant to see a demonstration of the robot that flips hamburgers. Michael volunteered to—"

"Damn!" In one swift motion, Ryder was on his feet. "What in hell—do you mean to say he's with Armstead?"

"Yes." Lauren glanced at her watch. "He is by now." She sighed, knowing what was coming. "Ryder—"

"I thought I told you Justin's freedom was to be curtailed until we got to the bottom of whoever and whatever's trying to destroy you, Lauren! Didn't you hear me?"

"I don't take orders from you, Ryder."

He dismissed that with a wave of his hand. "Who's taking them?"

"Scotty's dad," she said coolly. "Michael was to meet them there at six." It was now past that time.

"*Damn it!* I don't believe this."

Without replying, Lauren turned on her heel and started toward the house. Ryder caught her before she'd gone three steps and whirled her around. "Do you know who Jake saw when he was hanging out at the Blue Marlin?"

"Take your hands off me," Lauren ordered.

He complied with an impatient look. "He saw your precious Michael Armstead, that's who!" Ryder said, his expression fierce. "Armstead was with a woman—the secretary to NuTekNiks's chief engineer, Laurén. Michael Armstead is the traitor in the Holt Company, the man who's masterminded all the grief you've suffered this past year, and now you hand him Justin."

"That's ridiculous, Ryder. How many times do I have to tell you that Michael is not the one?"

He stared at her incredulously. "What do I have to say to prove it to you? The man's a thief, a criminal, for heaven's sake, maybe worse!"

"He is not, I tell you!"

Unable to find words, Ryder swore savagely and started toward the porch steps, his pace literally eating up the distance. "I'm not wasting any more time trying to reason with you. I'm going to get—"

"You are going nowhere," she said, the words dangerously soft. "You have no right to dictate to me about Justin."

Ryder took the porch steps in a single bound. "We'll see about that."

Lauren had to run to catch up with him. She reached him at the door. "We won't see anything, Ryder. You're mistaken if you think you can dictate to me. I know I'm living in your house and I may have gone along with your suggestions at the plant, but none of that gives you the right to make decisions for me, especially concerning Justin."

Ryder didn't answer. He couldn't. Fear and frustration churned inside him. Armstead could be a killer. Clay Holt had almost certainly been murdered and everything, *everything* pointed to Armstead.

"Did you hear me, Ryder? You do not have any rights where my son is concerned."

Inside Ryder, something tight and hard suddenly gave way. He didn't stop to consider the consequences of his next impulsive words.

Angrily, he turned and looked straight into Lauren's eyes. "Oh, yes, I do have a right," he said softly. "He's my son, too."

CHAPTER FOURTEEN

LAUREN LOOKED AT HIM, her expression blank. "What?"

Ryder took a deep breath, gazing beyond her shoulder. His voice, when he at last spoke, was quiet. "I said, he's my son, too."

She shook her head, bewildered. There was something about the way Ryder looked that sent a chill down her spine. "Wh-what are you trying to say?"

She watched him rake his fingers through his hair, absently noticing that his hand was shaking. Apprehension grew, settling in her middle like a cold stone. He turned and his eyes, dark and compelling, met hers.

"Lauren, I know how Justin was conceived."

Her heart started to pound. "What . . . ? How . . . ?"

"God, there's no easy way to tell you."

Ashen, Lauren put a hand to her throat. "Tell me what?"

"Let's sit down over here first," he said gently. Unresisting, Lauren let him lead her to the ancient rocking chair. Her eyes followed him as he began pacing. "I was a student at Alabama twelve years ago," he began. "My roommate was in pre-med. He got involved in a research program that had to do with infertility."

He glanced at her quickly. Pale before, now she was as colorless and lifeless as a marble statue. Only her eyes seemed alive, and they were a bright, cold flame.

"What does this have to do with me?" Lauren whispered, her lips barely moving.

He looked away. "I donated sperm in that program."

She swallowed, trying to capture the whirlwind of her thoughts. What was he saying? *Dear God, what was he saying?* No one knew. *No one.* The doctor was dead. The records were supposed to be sealed forever.

"My roommate told me I was a good match for the...the father. I would never know his name or anything about him, I was assured of that. I was reluctant at first, but they finally persuaded me. I told myself a couple who wanted a child so desperately would be good parents. There would be an abundance of love for this baby, more so than some babies conceived naturally."

She stared at him in disbelief. What he was saying was so incredible, so overwhelming, that her brain sought frantically to deny it. She shook her head furiously.

"They never reveal who receives whose sperm."

He didn't quite meet her eyes. "Not intentionally, no."

"Then...?"

"I..." He swallowed hard. "Someone told me."

Lauren's eyes closed weakly. "That's despicable," she whispered, hardly aware that she spoke out loud. "As if the pain of being childless isn't enough. To think we were the object of snickering, behind-the-scenes gossip." Head bent, she rubbed her forehead with unsteady fingers. "I...it's..."

"No, you're wrong," Ryder said urgently. "It wasn't like that. It just happened. It wasn't a malicious breach of ethics. We were out celebrating the—"

"Celebrating." She sprang up from the rocker, her brain spinning with the sheer enormity of it. *Twelve years ago, it was Ryder's sperm that was used to impregnate her!*

"Lauren, if you'll just hear me out..."

"How much did you get paid?" she demanded coldly.

"I swear to God, Lauren, it was a purely humanitarian thing. It was just a fluke that I ever found out."

She lifted her chin, pinning him with a look. All of her strict, rigid upbringing was in that regard. "A thousand dollars, ten thousand? Twenty? Fifty?" Her voice dripped sarcasm and repugnance. "How much was your precious seed worth, Ryder? How much for you to sire Justin?"

He bowed his head.

She struck him on his shoulder to force his eyes to hers. "Because that is who we're talking about here, isn't it, Ryder? Not some nameless, faceless child spawned out of your *humanitarian* impulse to benefit a poor, sterile couple," she mocked him. "Hardly. We are talking about Justin Claymoore Holt, my son, aren't we, Ryder?"

"Yes."

"You bastard!" she whispered fiercely. "You lying, deceiving *snake*!"

Ryder felt real fear trace an icy finger down his spine.

"I can't believe this!" Her eyes, suspiciously bright, swept the ceiling.

"Lauren, listen—"

"Listen?" She laughed harshly. "To what? More lies, more deceit? I may seem like a simpleton to you, Ryder, but once I'm burned, I don't stick my hand back in the fire."

When he would have spoken again, she interrupted. "God, what a fool I've been," she said, regarding him with tortured eyes. "You must have been laughing your head off at me, the poor deprived, sex-hungry widow—so ready, so eager to fall into bed with you."

"Lauren..."

"I never had a clue," she said as if he weren't there. "I never dreamed it was all part of a...a mean, cruel plan."

Ryder came close and put his hands on her shoulders. "There was no plan, Lauren. I came home because of my grandmother's death. Jake called me about the expert witness thing, and then the situation at the plant heated up. It was almost as though fate brought me here and then one by one, things happened to involve me deeper and deeper in your life. In Justin's life.''

"Fate.'' She shrugged off his hands, her tone derisive. "You're asking me to believe fate, not you, made you do it.''

"No, I'm just saying it wasn't something I planned and plotted for. But once I got involved—''

"Does Jake know?''

Ryder shook his head. "No, he would never have contacted me in the first place if he had known.''

Lauren considered that, realizing what he'd said was probably true. Jake would have no part in such a vicious deception. And how clever Ryder had been, manipulating her with his sexual technique, holding her at arm's length, letting her desire for him grow. By the time he'd judged her ripe to fall into his bed, she'd been literally panting for him. Fury and outrage and wounded pride mixed in her like a poison. The truth rose bitterly in her throat. He had not kept his distance for fear of commitment, or because he was too decent and too honorable to drag her into an affair that would go nowhere. Instead, every move he'd made had been part of a carefully orchestrated scheme. *Get close to Lauren and thereby closer yet to Justin.* It wasn't her he'd wanted, but Justin.

Fear now combined with other emotions, as the significance of his parentage dawned on her. His real motive was to insinuate himself in her life and then seize his chance to take custody of Justin when the time was right. Reaching deep into some secret well of strength, she drew a long breath. It was Justin, not her pride, who was at stake here. Fortified by an intense, almost primitive instinct to protect her son, she forced herself to look at Ryder.

"It amazes me that I was too stupid to see the truth," she said. "The physical similarities are remarkable. You stand alike; you walk alike..." She thought of Justin's athletic ability and poor Clay's ineptitude at all sports. "You even smile alike," she said bitterly.

He reached for her, but she moved away. "Don't touch me, Ryder."

"Lauren, I know I have a lot of explaining to do," he said urgently, "but right now I need to go to the plant and get Justin. It's unsafe for him to be with Armstead. Surely you see that now."

"I see no such thing."

"Be reasonable, Lauren! I just told you that we've linked him to the NuTekNiks people at that bar. You may be willing to trust him with Justin, but I'm not."

"Michael was in the bar because I sent him there," she said coldly, enjoying the incredulous look he gave her.

"When he insisted on doing his own investigation—with you as his chief suspect, I might add. In fact, I suggested he check out the Blue Marlin for starters. Apparently he decided to do just that."

Ryder stared at her, his jaw clenched. "I don't believe this!" he shouted. "If he is the informer, you've alerted him! Are you crazy?"

"I must be, to ever have trusted you!" In her fury she, too, was almost screaming.

"You don't know what you've done, Lauren."

"I know I'm still the owner of the Holt Company," she said, "and as such I have the right and the authority to exercise my best judgment in all matters." She lifted her chin imperiously. "All matters, Mr. Braden."

Exasperated, he propped a hand on the porch railing and prayed for patience. "Then what would you say to the fact that someone in your plant is not only furnishing the sleazes at NuTekNiks with Holt designs, but that same individual is also passing more important, sensitive robotic secrets to a country in Eastern Europe."

Nothing surprised her anymore, but still the news hurt. Lauren put a hand to her throat.

"Yes, *Mrs.* Holt. One of your precious employees is a spy. A real spy." His eyes were cold. "The kind they charge with treason."

"It's not Michael," she said, her voice stony and unyielding.

"I don't want to waste any more time talking about this, Lauren. I'm going to get my son."

She caught his arm, her eyes flashing. "That's all this is about, isn't it, Ryder? Your son. You've planned and schemed and manipulated and . . . and cheated just to get your hands on Justin. There is no spy. Isn't that the truth, Ryder, or do you even recognize the truth when you hear it?"

"What about this truth! Have you forgotten that Justin told us Clay familiarized him with the computer at the plant? We've searched high and low for the key to Clay's records. What if Justin holds the key and doesn't even know it? What if he possesses information that could endanger his life if the wrong person finds out about it?"

"That's for me to worry about, not you!"

"Are you so blind you're willing to place Justin's life on the line, Lauren?"

She stared at him mutely, suddenly not certain of anyone's innocence, but unwilling to admit it to Ryder.

He took her hand from his arm. "We'll discuss this when I get back. Now go inside and wait for me."

"I'll do no such thing!" Lauren started down the steps, but just then the telephone rang.

He stopped. "Are you going to get that?" he asked evenly.

"No."

"It might be Justin," he snapped.

Without another word, Lauren turned on her heel and climbed the stairs, furious. The telephone was on the wall just inside the kitchen. She snatched it up. "Hello."

"Mom, could you come and get me and Scotty and Curtis?" Justin asked.

Through the screen door, she could see Ryder watching her, his mouth a straight, grim line. "Where are you, Justin?"

Ryder's eyes narrowed, and he started slowly toward the door. "At a pay phone. Get this, Mom, we caught a ride here with Scotty's dad after the movie just like Uncle Michael said, but he never showed up. Now we're stuck, Mom. You'll have to come here and get us, I guess." He paused, then added with undisguised hope, "Or maybe Ryder could pick us up." Fresh enthusiasm was infused in his voice. "Hey, he knows some stuff. He could show us the burger-flipper, couldn't he, Mom?"

"I don't know about that, Justin." She frowned. "Where exactly are you?"

"At the Timesaver on the corner by the plant."

"Stay there, Justin. Don't speak to any strangers and don't leave, don't take—"

"I know, I know, Mom. I'm not a baby."

"I'll see you in fifteen minutes, Justin."

" 'Bye."

She replaced the receiver slowly, her eyes on Ryder, who was watching her from the open doorway.

"We'll go get him together," he said quietly. "And when we get home, we'll talk."

LAUREN SAT in stony silence as Ryder drove to the plant. It was just as well, he decided. There wouldn't be enough time for him to try and explain everything to her before they picked up Justin and his friends. And there would be no opportunity to talk once the boys were in the car, until after they'd been dropped off at their respective homes. Justin was already overly sensitive to his mother's moods, and Ryder had no intention of jeopardizing the growing affection or the trust the boy had for him. If Justin had a hint that his mother was angry with Ryder, he knew where the boy's loyalties would lie. Ryder didn't plan to let that happen. There was too much at stake.

He made an excuse when Justin asked him to demonstrate the burger-flipper and, though disappointed, Justin accepted the decision with good grace. He'd had a full day anyway, his mother pointed out. Ryder felt suddenly desolate. He wouldn't be spending any more time with Justin, if Lauren had anything to do with it.

He knew she was going to insist on moving back into her own house, and he was just as determined not to let her go.

Once Scotty and Curtis were dropped off, Ryder cautioned Justin not to mention that he had some knowledge of the computer at the plant. He had no desire to alarm the boy, but he had to make certain that Justin understood the seriousness of the situation.

"Your dad's ideas were very unusual, Justin. Some of them could be dangerous in the wrong hands."

Justin was occupying his favorite spot in the Blazer—in the middle directly behind the front seats. In the rearview mirror, Ryder could see him weighing the implications of what he'd just heard. Lauren stared straight ahead.

"You mean good ideas can be used for bad things," Justin said, looking at Ryder for confirmation.

"Exactly," Ryder replied.

"So we have to be sure nobody bad gets my dad's ideas."

"That's right."

Justin thought a moment. "So far nobody knows I can pull that stuff up on the big computer," he said.

Ryder swallowed hard, hearing the boy confirm his worst fears. Such knowledge was deadly. "Are you sure?"

"Nobody but you," Justin said brightly. "And Mom, I guess."

"Well, let's be sure and keep it that way," Ryder told him, resolving to take Justin to the plant himself and let the boy show him just how much he did know about the computer. Hopefully it wouldn't be much. It made his blood run cold to think that Justin might be the key to unlocking Clay's secrets.

"Okay," Justin said agreeably. "I won't tell anybody anything. Except you."

Trust was implicit in the boy's tone and the expression on his face. Ryder pulled up in front of his house and stopped. He had Justin's trust. Now he had to regain Lauren's.

"I'M GOING HOME." Lauren stood poised at the door, one hand on the knob. They were alone in the room that Ryder had converted to a den. Justin was upstairs playing video games; Hattie Bell was in the back of the house watching a Sunday-night special miniseries.

"You can't go home, Lauren." Ryder faced her, careful to keep some distance between them. From the look of her, it wouldn't take much to send her flying from the room and out of his life. "None of the reasons why you came here in the first place have changed."

"Don't bother trying to fast-talk me out of this, Ryder. I'm not staying under this roof with you another hour. Another minute."

"Lauren, stop thinking like a betrayed woman, for heaven's sake, and remember what's at stake here. It's just not safe for you and Justin to be alone in that house until this whole thing is cleared up and whoever's responsible is out of business."

"I'm not going to be at the house. I'm taking Justin and we're leaving town." She turned, fumbling at the doorknob.

"Leaving town?" Ryder felt a cold chill feather down his spine. "No, you can't take him—"

She rounded on him furiously. "I can take him anywhere I please, and don't you forget it!"

He put out his hands to try and calm her. "Okay, okay..." He cleared his throat. "Am I allowed to know where you're going?"

Lauren relaxed a little, her shoulders sagging. "Clancy's got a beach house on Dauphin Island," she said wearily. "I'm going to ask her if I can spend a few days there."

"Just the two of you, alone?"

"Yes."

"I know you need to think this over," he said hesitantly, "but won't Justin be bored and restless with no friends? Won't he be more of a distraction than you need right now?"

She looked at him. "What do you suggest, Ryder? That I let you baby-sit, and when I get back to town, maybe, just maybe my son will be here? Maybe you won't have decided to stake your claim and whisked him off to... to Saudi Arabia or some other godforsaken hole in the world?"

"You know I would never do that," he said quietly. "I would take care of him for you right here in my house."

"I wouldn't let you take care of my goldfish!"

He stared at her, anguished. "Lauren, I love you."

Instantly her eyes flooded with tears. "Don't—" she whispered, putting up a hand as though to hold him off. "Don't you dare say those words to me."

"I want to marry you, Lauren."

"Well..." She dashed a hand across her eyes and sniffed. "That would be the simplest way, wouldn't it?"

He reached for her again and she jerked away.

"What was it, Ryder? Were you like Clancy? Did you get lonely traipsing around the world alone, never having any roots anywhere, never anybody waiting for you at night, no one to care whether you lived or died? Did you wake up one day and discover it was time to have children while you were still young enough to see them grow up? What did you say— hey, I've got this readymade kid out there?" Her eyes shot daggers. "Almost as simple as ordering a baby right out of the Sears catalog, huh, Ryder? Was that the way it was?"

He stared at her, a million words, excuses, reasons trembling in him, but he knew nothing he said right now would make a difference.

"When were you planning to tell me?" she asked in a conversational tone.

"I don't know," he admitted with stark honesty. He thrust both hands through his hair. "A lot of what you said is true. I have felt for a while that my life was empty. I was lonely and bored. And when Mama Jane died and I came to Mobile, I just stayed. I don't know why. I didn't know Clay had died. I didn't know your company was in trouble. Once I did know, I'd intended to keep my distance. I knew the complications that would arise if I told you who I really was. I never intended to fall in love with you, Lauren, but I did."

"I don't believe you."

He expelled a tired sigh and just looked at her. "I didn't tell you at first, because I was going to help you out, as Jake suggested, and then get right out of your life."

"The old rolling stone maneuver," she said, nodding with heavy sarcasm. "It's probably gotten you out of a few tight scrapes before."

"And then I met Justin." He clamped a hand against the back of his neck. "I told myself I'd just spend a little time with him, get to know him, and then I'd move on. What could it hurt?"

"Oh, sure. What's another loss in his life? His father—" she emphasized the word "—a year ago, and you this year?" Her eyes accused him. "But who's counting? He's a tough little kid."

Ryder closed his eyes, stung by the lash of her words, feeling her pain because it was his own. "It just snowballed from there. I didn't tell you then because I was afraid of what you'd do. I was afraid you would never trust me again, that you'd send me away. Everything I ever wanted was in the palm of my hand—the woman I loved, my son, a real honest-to-goodness home." He stared earnestly into her eyes. "Can you understand that? To tell you the truth meant I might lose everything. Is that really so wrong?"

"You were right about one thing," she told him coldly. "I can't trust you, and I'm not staying in a house with a man I don't trust."

"Lauren, don't do this . . . please."

Ignoring him, she walked to the telephone and, turning her back, deliberately punched out a number. Clancy answered and she went right to the point, foregoing the usual small talk.

"Clancy, is that offer to let me use your beach house still good?"

"Sure, just say when, and it's yours," Clancy replied.

"How about now, tonight?"

Clancy laughed. "You and Ryder ready for some much-deserved privacy, hmm? No problem. The key's with an agency there on the island. I'll give them a call right now and all you have to—''

"Ryder won't be going, Clancy."

Clancy was silent a beat or two. "Umm, you're going to the beach alone?"

Sighing, Lauren squeezed the receiver a little tighter. "I'll be taking Justin."

Another short silence. "What does Ryder say about this, Lauren?"

"Why should he say anything?"

"He's just letting you go?"

"I don't need his permission."

"Wait a minute," Clancy said. "Am I talking to the same woman who entertained me this afternoon at Ryder's house..." There was a significant pause. "The same woman who's under Ryder's protection, who's madly in love with Ryder—and as long as we're being frank—sleeping with Ryder. A woman who hasn't had a thought or said a word in the last three weeks that isn't somehow connected to Ryder? Is this that same woman?"

Oh, Lord, she's right. Am I that hopelessly infatuated? Lauren clenched her teeth. "May I use your beach house, or not, Clancy?

"Had a little spat, hmm?"

"And would you please give Jake a message for me?" Lauren continued. "Tell him that I'll be back on Friday, in plenty of time for the deposition he has scheduled with the expert witness."

"Tell him yourself. He's right here."

Lauren wilted suddenly as it dawned on her what she'd probably interrupted. "Oh, Clancy, I'm sorry, I didn't think—"

"Don't apologize, you ding-a-ling. Jake's not going anywhere." In the background Lauren could hear the low rumble of Jake's voice. And soft laughter. His and hers. Had it been only half an hour since she and Ryder had been exchanging the same loving sounds? Lauren felt a clutch of pain.

There was some shuffling on the other end and then the sound of Jake's familiar voice. "Lauren what's this about you leaving town? You can't leave town, babe. I thought Ryder would have laid down the law since he tends to take his protective instincts to the max when it comes to his ladylove."

Ladylove. Lauren's mouth trembled suddenly. Turning from Ryder's sharp gaze, she closed her eyes.

"If he hasn't said anything, the phone's not the place to discuss it," Jake continued.

"If you mean Michael and the spy and the lies and the security breaches and who knows what else, he's already told me." Her voice was trembling.

Jake was silenced momentarily. "Well then, you understand. You can't leave town, babe."

"But Jake, I have to," she whispered urgently.

"Not this time, love," he said firmly. "It's not safe and it's not smart. Just stay put. You're in good hands right where you are."

When Jake hung up, Lauren stayed at the desk with her hand on the telephone until the line began to beep its electronic reminder. She replaced the receiver slowly and turned to face Ryder.

"Jake seems to think I should stay in town," she said quietly. "But I won't stay here."

"You and Justin can't stay alone in your house, Lauren," he argued desperately. "Just think. He knows too much. Somebody else might suddenly put everything together and come to the same conclusion we reached. He's full of energy and a child's innocence. If you'll just stay here with me, I'll hire a couple of men—''

"Bodyguards?"

He nodded. "Yes, bodyguards. Don't worry, we won't alarm Justin. We'll tell him they're professional associates of mine or something."

Looking at him, Lauren was reminded of her first impression that day in Jake's office. She had thought then that there was probably nothing much life could dish out that would intimidate Ryder. And soon she'd turned herself and Justin over into his keeping without a doubt that he would keep them safe.

But that was before!

He moved close to her. "Please stay, Lauren. I won't touch you, I swear. I'll stay out of your way. You won't have to see me except at the plant."

She covered her face with her hands. "Oh, God," she whispered, "I don't know what to do."

He put a hand on her shoulder, aching to take her fully in his arms, knowing that it might be a long time before she would welcome him again. If ever. "You can't go, sweetheart. You have to stay."

Without a word she turned from him and walked to the door, her chin up, her eyes dry. It opened soundlessly. Only last week, the door and several boards in the stairs had been so squeaky that she'd teased Ryder and Justin about the resident ghost. Ryder had oiled the hinges and braced the stairs that very day. She climbed them now slowly, trailing a hand along the beautiful old banister, polished to a gleam by her own hands. And then she was in her room, the one she'd taken so much pleasure in fixing up at Ryder's insistence. Her eyes swept over the Queen Anne desk she'd refinished, the rocker that had been Mama Jane's own and the big brass bed with the elaborate curlicues where she and Ryder had loved . . .

Only then did she let the tears come.

On Monday Lauren got up, determined to get a handle on whatever it was that was going on. The sooner she did, the sooner she would be free of Ryder. The problem was—who could she trust? Her self-confidence had been badly damaged. She'd been taken in completely by Ryder. As for Michael, she'd tried to call him Sunday with no luck after the broken appointment with Justin, but it worried her that he was out of pocket. The FBI agent she'd contacted after the attack on Ryder had turned up nothing on Michael or the men who worked closest with him. Michael himself was hellbent on finding something incriminating in Ryder's past. If that's what he was doing, he had his work cut out for him. Ryder's career had taken him around the world.

At the plant Cheryl met her with word from Michael. He was on to something, the message said, but it would take a few days to get all the details. He didn't say where he was, but he remembered to apologize for failing to honor his appointment with Justin and the boys at the plant. He would explain everything when he got back.

Ryder was skeptical, as usual.

"I don't want to argue with you about Michael anymore," Lauren said wearily. "He isn't the informer."

She seemed so positive. It was almost enough to make Ryder doubt his own instincts. "What makes you so sure?"

Some of the starch seemed to go out of her, as though the battle was just not worth the struggle. "I think it's Malcolm Stern."

His eyes narrowed. "Malcolm Stern? The old guy?" he laughed incredulously. "The father of Hercules?"

"When you mentioned your suspicions about the clandestine Research and Development work, I requested a background check on the employees I felt had enough technical qualifications to be suspect. The information on Malcolm is extremely incriminating."

"Such as?"

"His wife and son are being politically detained in East Germany. He's been trying to get them out for years."

Ryder was stunned. "Who did it for you? Who else knew about it?"

"The FBI. Who else do you call if you suspect espionage? And nobody knew except me." She looked at him, her chin slightly lifted. "If someone in my employ is engaged in research for hostile purposes, it is my responsibility and mine alone to find him."

"But Malcolm Stern..." Ryder was still trying to take it in. "Can you prove anything?"

"Not yet, they told me they would handle it."

THE CLOCK on Malcolm Stern's desk told him the hour was late. But still he sat staring at the small framed photograph. Anna, himself and their small son, all smiling. The intricate scrollwork decorating the frame was worn smooth in places from the many hours he'd handled it, touching, stroking, caressing. Poor substitute for the warm, vital flesh of his beloved Anna.

God willing, the waiting was almost over. Although—he frowned. What they planned next was foolhardy, a venture destined to fail. The widow's protector, Braden, was a threat to the entire operation and must be eliminated, so said his contact. Whether to drive him away or to kill him outright was a decision not yet made. *Fools,* he thought contemptuously. Had they not yet discovered the kind of man Braden was? He would not be intimidated once he was set on a course. Braden loved the widow. There was only one way he would leave her unprotected. He would die first. Stern shrugged. It was not his concern.

Carefully he replaced the photograph in the small, velvet-lined box that was its special place. He had carved the box himself of the dark, strong wood from the famed Black Forest of his homeland. As he did, more and more frequently now, he let his mind drift back to happier days. Anna, his beautiful Anna, beckoned. And the boy... smiling. He moved toward them, his arms wide.

The clock, a marvel of German craftsmanship, ticked on.

CHAPTER FIFTEEN

SIGHING, LAUREN SHUFFLED another file over to the "hold" stack on her desk. Another decision she'd make...tomorrow. Tossing her pen aside, she made a face. Her desktop overflowed with an accumulation of paperwork. She was finding it more and more difficult to concentrate, when her thoughts kept straying from her work to the situation with Ryder. Without opening another file, Lauren turned her chair slightly and stared out the window.

The past four days had been miserable. True to his word, Ryder kept out of her way at his house, though he always found time for Justin, she noted bitterly. They hammered and nailed and sawed and painted just as though nothing was wrong. Ryder was always excruciatingly careful never to take Justin out of her sight. Why did that fact, instead of making her feel perfectly justified and reasonable, make her feel mean and ungenerous?

Lauren wasn't sure when he ate or slept. At mealtimes he was never around. In the evenings he was in his study and he stayed there after everyone else was in bed. If they bumped into each other in the hall, he treated her with the same courtesy he showed Hattie Bell. Or Clancy. Or Murphy or Jannsen, the bodyguards he'd hired, who had taken up permanent residence in two spare bedrooms in the rambling old house.

The idea of bodyguards for Justin had appalled Lauren, but Ryder had them in residence bright and early Monday morning. He told Justin they were carpenters hired to speed up the job of restoring the old place.

She rubbed her forehead wearily. Surely everything would be resolved soon. She might have been able to bear up a little better if she weren't living and working with Ryder every day.

How could you miss someone when you were living right in the house with him? And how could two people seem like strangers when they spent the whole day working together? And most disturbing of all—why did Lauren feel as though she had somehow been unreasonable and unfair?

She missed him. With a deep, dark longing that reached to the bottom of her soul, she missed him. Even knowing that he had lied and deceived her, that he'd only been with her so that he could get to know Justin, even then, she missed him.

THE WEEK FINALLY wound down. Almost. The expert witness's deposition was scheduled for mid-afternoon Friday. Lauren and Jake were already in her office waiting for him, a man named Collier Steele, recommended by Ryder. Jake had also asked Ryder to sit in.

Jake leaned back in the deep leather couch, placed at an angle to her desk, and studied her for a few seconds in silence. "I'm trying to decide whether to mind my own business or stick my nose in something that could very well cost me a client and blow a perfect friendship at the same time."

Lauren was immediately wary. Jake knew her well, but even a stranger could tell that something was wrong with her lately. There were circles under her eyes, and she appeared as thin and fragile as hand-blown glass.

"Hmm, sounds serious," she said, trying for a light note.

"You and Ryder haven't patched it up yet, hmm?"

"It can't be patched up, Jake," she said. "Just be satisfied that yours and Clancy's story has a happy ending."

"You want to tell me about it?"

She stared down at her hands. "It's . . . personal, Jake."

"Is it so dreadful—whatever he's done—that you can't forgive him?"

For one wild crazy moment she imagined telling him everything. *You see, Jake, Clay could not have children and so Justin was conceived by artificial insemination. Ryder just informed me a few days ago that it was his sperm that was used to impregnate me. Ryder is Justin's natural father. Isn't that amazing, Jake?*

"It's too bad." Jake shifted on the couch, resting one ankle on his knee. Lauren blinked, then scrambled mentally to pick up the thread of the conversation. Watching her intently, Jake said, "Justin will miss him."

Pain ripped through her so sharply that she actually made a small sound.

"Amazing how they took to each other, Justin and Ryder, wasn't it?" he said.

Her nod was barely perceptible.

Jake studied his shoe. "A lot alike, those two."

Lauren's head came up and she stared at her lawyer. "What are you getting at, Jake?"

He met her gaze directly. "Does your disagreement with Ryder have anything to do with Justin?"

She looked at him speechless. *Did Jake know, too?*

"I have some legal files which Clay left with me for safekeeping," Jake said, "in the event a problem should ever develop regarding Justin's trust fund. It was established at his birth. The details of his conception and birth are there, Lauren."

Lauren put a hand to her throat.

"Stop me if I'm butting in or offending you, and I will drop the subject," he told her softly. "I give you my word, we'll never speak of this again, Lauren."

Her eyes were wide, smoky with emotion. "No, it's...it's all right."

"Does Ryder know any of this?"

She cleared her throat. "Yes," she whispered.

"Ryder is the donor, isn't he?"

He watched her turn to gaze distractedly out of the window. She nodded her head mutely.

"And is that a problem?" He went on when she didn't answer. "Ryder loves you both—it's obvious to anyone who sees you together. I know lawyers are the original cynics, but when I put it all together..." He stopped, shaking his head. "By God, what were the chances?"

"Ryder knew," she said bitterly. "He's known all along, Jake, from the moment of Justin's birth."

His eyes narrowed. "Are you sure?"

"I'm sure. He came here knowing, and when he thought he had Justin and me dependent on him, then he told me who he really was."

Jake frowned. "Is that what this is all about?"

"Isn't it enough?"

"He didn't ever have to tell you, Lauren."

She got out of her chair abruptly. "And it would have been a thousand times better if he hadn't."

He thought that over. "Why? Because then you'd never have to wonder if he really loved you, or if he just deceived you so that he could be with Justin forever."

She regarded him with eyes filled with pain. "Can you blame me?"

At the sound of voices in the outer office, Jake started to get to his feet. "This is not just your own hurt and wounded pride at stake here, Lauren," he said. "You'll be throwing away Justin's chance to know his natural father. Just remember that.''

ALL THROUGH the deposition Jake's words kept going round and round in her head. Was it just her own pain, her own wounded pride that made it impossible for her to believe Ryder? Suppose he hadn't come to Mobile for the express purpose of insinuating himself in her life. Suppose he really *hadn't* meant to get involved. It was easy to believe that once he'd seen Justin and gotten to know him, he couldn't have helped but love him. Had he kept his secret for fear of losing what he'd just found? She tried to imagine his dilemma. Would he want to marry her if she weren't Justin's mother? God help her, she wanted to believe that more than anything. Over and above the technical dialogue of the deposition, she was intensely aware of Ryder's brooding gaze on her, his dark eyes saying to her...what?

She had found no answers by the time they started back to Ryder's place. The beltway was crowded with Friday traffic. Lauren watched Ryder's hands on the wheel of the Blazer. He drove with the same competency that he brought to most things. But just then he made a turn with a little less finesse than usual, and she glanced quickly at his face.

"I'm going to have these brakes checked this weekend," he said quietly. "They seem a little low."

They exited the beltline then and headed south. Soon they were off the main highway and on the winding country lane that led to Ryder's property. Out of the traffic the Blazer picked up speed. They'd be home in a few minutes.

Home. Lauren turned her head on the seat and idly watched the passing scenery. How quickly she'd learned to think of Ryder's place as home. And so had Justin. And Hattie Bell. They'd moved in without a backward look at the house in town. It was as though they'd all finally come home.

She felt urgent and unsettled suddenly. She and Ryder needed to talk, she decided. She wanted to hear everything and this time she would— She heard the startled sound Ryder made and then became aware that he was having trouble steering the Blazer. She saw with alarm that they were nearing a dangerous hairpin curve and that he was not slowing down.

"The brakes are gone!" he told her, glancing quickly to see that her seat belt was fastened. His was not, she noted, and felt horror clutch at her throat.

It couldn't have taken more than fifteen seconds, but the whole world and everything in it seemed to de-escalate to slow motion. They approached the curve, tires screaming on the worn asphalt. The first quarter of the turn they made, just barely. But then they hit a pothole. At that speed the wheel was wrenched out of Ryder's hand. The Blazer began to slide. Moving sideways, it hit the edge of the pavement and soft shoulder, out of control.

Lauren was frozen with terror, but her brain registered the deafening sounds, topsy-turvy scenery, the gut-wrenching jerk of her seat belt, glass shattering. And Ryder coming toward her, his arms reaching out for her, his body covering hers, shielding her. And then—truly in slow motion, it seemed to Lauren—the Blazer rolled, end over end, and came down with a bone-jarring crunch.

The cessation of all noise was shocking to her rattled senses. Stunned, she was incapable of any thought for a few seconds. She was not unconscious. She stirred and became aware that she was trapped somehow.

Ryder. Ryder was on top of her.

Moving cautiously he lifted his head until he could look into her eyes. Never, Lauren thought, if she lived a hundred years, would she forget the expression on his face at this moment. Urgent, terrible, fearsome. Wild, turbulent emotion churned in the blue of his eyes, turning them almost black.

"Are you all right?" he asked hoarsely, lifting his weight only slightly from her.

She wiggled a bit experimentally. "Yes, I think so."

His eyes were anxious, searching her face. "Are you sure?"

Her hands were trapped against his chest. She pulled them free and threw them around him, hugging him close to her heart. "I'm not hurt."

"Thank God, thank God." His eyes closed and he leaned his forehead against hers, while a deep, convulsive shudder shook his whole body.

She ran her hands over the heavy masculine shape of his shoulders and back. He didn't move except for the clenching of his hands anchored around her. She swallowed thickly. Maybe he was hurt. Maybe he couldn't move. "Ryder..."

"I'm okay," he said, his voice muffled against her temple.

She breathed a silent prayer of thanksgiving and relief and humility. They could so easily have been killed, Ryder especially, since his seat belt had not been secured. It had been crazy of him to throw himself over her like that, shielding her with his body. He should have— Light dawned, and her thoughts went flying. Using his body to protect her had been the instinctive act of a man whose first thought had been for her, not himself. Amid the dusty, steaming wreckage, she drew a deep, unsteady breath, not daring to believe what that meant.

"I have never been so scared in my whole life," Ryder said in a shaken tone. He lifted one hand and began stroking her hair. Lauren could feel the fine tremors still racking him.

"All I could think about was how would I get you to a hospital? This road is so isolated. If I had to leave you to run to the house, how long would it take? But then I knew I couldn't leave you—" He made an anguished sound and buried his face in her neck.

"You thought all that, while we were tumbling all over the road?" Smiling softly, she threaded her fingers through his hair and kissed his ear. "You are a remarkable man."

He lifted his head, then, and stared at her. His gaze seemed to go right through her to the very gates of her soul. "No," he said slowly. "Not remarkable. An ordinary man who just came too close to losing the person who matters most to him in the world."

"Ryder..."

"I love you, Lauren." The words were low and urgent. "I know you don't believe me, but just now I have to say the words or else go crazy. I love you so much."

Without giving her a chance to say anything, he suddenly straightened up. "No, just be still until I get you out of this, sweetheart." His voice was still not back to normal. He fumbled with the lock on her seat belt, finally releasing it. Then with a word of caution to her, he pushed open his door and came around to her side. After letting her out, he moved back, watching her as she straightened her clothes and smoothed a shaky hand over her hair. "You're sure you're not hurt?" he demanded anxiously.

Her knees were a little rubbery, but she gave him a reassuring smile. "I'm fine. No lumps or broken bones, maybe a couple of bruises, that's all." Her smile faded. "Thank you.'"

"For what, for God's sake? I almost killed you."

"For using your own body to protect me. If the window had shattered, you could have been cut seriously. Or worse." She shivered, turning away as though to block out the thought.

When he didn't say anything, she raised her eyes and looked him over more closely. Particles of glass clung to his clothes and his hair, but she didn't see any blood.

"Let's go," he said, turning away to check the deserted road for any sign of life. Her gaze fell to the back of his jeans, midway down his left thigh. Her eyes widened.

"You are hurt! There's blood all over, Ryder."

Raising his arm, he stretched backward, trying to see it. "I don't think it's bad. When we get home, I'll see to it."

Lauren didn't even bother to reply to that. She reached into the Blazer and rummaged under the front seat for the box of tissues she knew was there. Grabbing a handful, she told Ryder to turn around. The tear in his jeans was long and jagged. She shivered at the thought of the damage it could have done to his neck or a vulnerable artery. Thank God for tough denim.

There was a lot of blood, anyway. She located the cut and pressed the tissue to it. "I'm scared to press very hard," she told him, her whole attention centered on the wound. "If there's glass still inside, I could do more damage than good."

"Don't worry," he said, touching her hair. "Fortunately we're only two or three minutes from the house. No one's likely to come along to give us a lift, so we'd better start hiking."

Chewing her lip, she had to face the fact that they had no choice but to start out on foot. Using the belt from her skirt, she secured a thick fold of tissue over the wound, and then fell in step beside him as he turned toward home.

"It was rigged; I guess you know that."

"I was just thinking the same thing," Lauren said, wrapping her arms around herself to control a shudder.

"You know what it means."

She clamped her jaw hard. "These people mean business, Ryder."

"Yeah." His mouth was a grim line.

Ryder felt the intensity of her gaze. She'd been sending those little looks his way every thirty seconds since they started walking. He kept his eyes straight ahead. Otherwise, no power on earth could have stopped him from turning to her and closing his arms around her and promising her the moon and the stars, anything that would take that bruised, vulnerable look from her face. But she would know his promises weren't worth spit, because he couldn't fight shadows and suspicion. And that was all any of them—the FBI, Jake, the police—had to go on.

They were entering the tree-lined lane that led to the house. With every step he took, Ryder's rage had risen a notch. He didn't care a damn for the scratch he'd taken. What incensed him and scared him to his toenails was how quickly and finally Lauren could have been taken from him. For days he had guarded against doing anything that would have made her shy away. He knew she was having a tough time dealing with his deception. But he hoped she would come around. He had been telling himself that, every hour on the hour, for days now. Everything that made his future worth living she held in the palm of her hand.

He touched her elbow as they started up the front porch stairs. The problem was he didn't know if he could keep his emotions in check after what he'd just been through. He just wanted to put his arms around her and never let her go. Instead he opened the door and, without touching her, waited for her to step inside.

"First we need to call the sheriff's office," he said, steering his thoughts in another direction. Sounds came from the backyard, Justin's yell and the deeper tones of Murphy and Jannsen in a game of touch football. Just as well, he thought. He didn't want Justin alarmed. He headed for the telephone.

"Ryder, your leg—"

"In a minute, sweetheart."

It wasn't a minute. It was more like three hours later, when Ryder allowed Lauren to hustle him into the bathroom to tend to the cut on his leg. First the wrecked Blazer had been towed, then the Sheriff notified, the FBI advised, Justin's questions answered and Hattie Bell calmed down. The house was finally quiet.

"What if it has glass in it?" She watched him shrug out of his tattered shirt, shuddering at the sound of tiny particles of the Blazer's windshield tinkling to the floor. "And your hair! I can see the glass in your hair, Ryder."

"I'm going to take a shower," he told her, popping the snap on his jeans. "That'll take care of it. It's also the most efficient way to clean the cut. Just give me a few minutes, sweetheart."

"Well—"

Sensing a subtle change in him, she raised her eyes to his. "Unless you want to get in that shower with me, lady, you'd better run."

She didn't. At least not right that minute. Instead she subjected him to a long, long look. Heat shafted through Ryder like lightning splitting a pine. He could see her fear, her doubts, her desire, her love. He could no more have prevented himself from reaching for her than he could have stopped a lightning bolt.

But she slipped past him in a twinkling and he was left staring at the wrong side of the door.

In the bathroom adjoining her bedroom, Lauren had her own bath while Ryder showered. She didn't take the time to luxuriate in the steamy tub, because when Ryder finished, she wanted to see for herself that his wound was truly nothing to be concerned about. Hurriedly she put on an ivory silk caftan and, still pulling the sash around her, made her way down the hall to the master bedroom.

He was just coming out of the bathroom. He was damp and steamy. His hair was dark and still wet and clung to his head. He was naked except for a towel that rode low on his hips. Her breath caught at the sight of him, because he would always take her breath away. He had already bandaged the cut. White gauze laced with surgical tape circled his left thigh.

He stopped short and stared at her. She glanced at his thigh. "Was it bad?"

"No."

"All the glass is washed away?"

"Yes." His gaze caught her and held her with its intensity. "Lauren—"

"While you were with the sheriff, I called Agent Sommerfield at the FBI," she said, her tone husky.

It took a moment, but his brain finally clicked into gear. "I wonder if the Feds' right hand knows what the left hand is doing," he muttered, thinking that that pale silky thing made her look virginal and innocent and vulnerable. He had a hunger for all three. "I've been dealing with an agent named Whitman."

"I guess I should have told you when I called the FBI." Her hands fluttered as though she was having trouble finding a place for them.

"You didn't quite trust me," he replied, and then held his breath for her answer.

"It wasn't that. I just felt I needed to take full responsibility. After all, I knew you'd be leaving."

For the first time in his life, Ryder let his heart show in his eyes. "I won't be leaving unless you tell me to go, Lauren." He looked away, ran agitated fingers through his hair and looked back at her. "I know I promised not to touch you, but..."

Without even thinking about it, she was in his arms.

He caught her up close, crushed her to him as though he could absorb her very essence through his body. For long, timeless moments it was enough just to have her in his arms again. He knew exactly what he needed: the feel of her softness giving way against him, the brush of her hair on his face, the scent of her.... Ah, the scent of her.

Somehow he had her pressed against the wall, and his hands were in her hair. His mouth covered hers; hers yielded, opened, blossomed inside his. Every cell in him was alive to the smell and taste and feel of her. Hoarse sounds came from deep in his throat. She must think she'd unleashed a wild man, he thought.

But if so, she seemed undaunted. Her hands were eagerly fumbling with the fold of the towel. It gave, and her hands went around him, pulling him into the inviting softness below her waist. He groaned, and his mouth left hers to skim down her throat to the soft hollow there. He kissed it, openmouthed, his tongue hot and hungry. Lauren clung desperately, melting with feminine need. He felt powerful, with her in his arms, invincible, ready to leap tall buildings. Without her, he had discovered how bitter *lonely* could feel, how bottomless *empty* could be.

He was aching, swollen, throbbing with his need for her. His hands swooped down the delicate curve of her spine and fanned out over her soft buttocks. She was sleek, silky smooth warmth. She whimpered, wordlessly encouraging.

The sound tore through him. He wanted—needed!—to touch the hot, sweet treasure that was so close, needed to bury himself in that most vulnerable, secret part of her.

"Lauren, Lauren..." Her name was an agonized cry as he tore his mouth from hers. Breathing like a man who'd run a marathon, he leaned against the wall. "We can't do this here, Lauren."

Her nose was buried in the curls on his chest. She laughed shakily, warming him all the way through. "I know. The bed's only a few steps that way, darling."

For a second he couldn't speak. Then he swept her up in his arms, his own laugh a little unsteady. "I may make it."

"LAUREN?"

"Hmm?"

"Does this mean you've forgiven me?" Ryder raised his head high enough to look down at her.

Her gaze was soft as she regarded him. "Yes."

A groove formed between his dark eyebrows. "You're sure?"

She smiled at him. "Yes." He lay back and she resumed her place, snuggled close against him, her arm draped across his chest, their legs entwined.

His arm went around her waist. "I do love you."

"I love you, too."

"I meant it when I asked you to marry me," he told her, and she heard the faint tension that laced his voice. His muscles felt taut beneath her cheek. "Say you will, Lauren."

She smiled against soft, curly hair. "I will."

He relaxed a fraction. "Can I tell you something?"

"Yes," she said dreamily. For a moment nothing disturbed the deep, quiet stillness of the night. It was late, and they were drowsy, love-laden, sated in the afterglow of passion.

"Five years ago, when I met you at that party, I felt like I'd been hit by a truck. There was something about you—I still don't understand it." He dipped his chin so that he could see her, could judge her reaction.

She was quiet. She hadn't forgotten his strange behavior that night.

"I knew the name of the couple who'd had my child, but until that party, I'd never seen you." He stared earnestly into her eyes. "And I never intended to, I swear that, Lauren."

"You were so cold and abrupt that night," she murmured, her eyes smoky as she recalled the way he'd held her when they danced.

"One look," he said, settling back. "Just one look and I ran like hell. I left the party and Mobile that same day as if I was being chased by a demon. You were happily married to a good, decent man. Justin had exactly the life I'd imagined he would have. After that, I didn't come back to Mobile until Mama Jane died."

He took a deep breath. Intense emotion made his voice rough. "They say everything has a purpose, Lauren. We were meant to be together with Justin. I was here; you needed me. It wasn't my plan, Lauren, but it was someone's plan. It was meant to be. I believe that."

Listening to him, she felt her throat grow tight and achy with emotion. At last he was telling her what her heart longed to hear.

"And something else, Lauren. I want to know about Justin, about his babyhood, everything. I want to see pictures of him when he was christened and when he went to kindergarten and in his pee-wee uniform and when he lost his front teeth. I want to know all those things I missed even though I know I don't have any right to ask." He turned his mouth to her temple. "I have so many years to catch up on. Tell me you understand, Lauren."

She brushed a kiss under his jaw. "I do."

He pulled her up until their lips touched, parted, touched again. Whispering incoherent things, his mouth skittered over her face. Her hair fell forward, forming a golden curtain enclosing them. Lauren made a soft sound, seeking the full satisfaction of his kiss. His tongue spiraled deep into the warmth of her mouth, questing and seeking, tender and wild. Instinctively her hips began the rhythm. Ryder stretched out his legs. Lauren arched and bent her knees. They came together, his hardness to her softness.

She gasped his name.

He sighed hers.

LAUREN WAS IN Mama Jane's garden when Michael Armstead drove up the next morning.

"I thought I'd find you here," he said, looking oddly excited.

Slowly she began to pull off her gloves. "It's no secret where Justin and I are staying, Michael. And Hattie Bell, too," she tacked on pointedly. She could also have mentioned Murphy and Jannsen, she thought sardonically, but it wasn't important. She didn't need to justify anything to Michael. However, he did owe her some answers.

"Where on earth have you been, Michael?"

"Florida, for starters," he told her. "And then New Orleans. I ended up in Denver."

Her mouth fell open. "Denver?"

"We've been operating in a hotbed of intrigue, Lauren."

She was in no mood for drama. "Please, Michael. Between the FBI and bodyguards and robots running amok,

I've just about had it. Now, please tell me what you came to say."

"Malcolm Stern is in love with a woman who works for NuTekNiks."

"What?" Lauren squeaked, holding back laughter with an effort.

"He's the one who's been selling Holt designs to that lousy outfit."

That could well be true, she thought, but Malcolm... in love? No, it was too much. "Malcolm Stern, my... our Malcolm?"

"The inventor of Hercules, yes."

"How did you find that out, Michael?" she asked faintly.

"After that incident with you and Hercules, I was suspicious of him." He paused, meeting her eyes. "It was too similar to what happened to Clay. I decided to follow him one night."

"To the Blue Marlin?"

"No, he didn't go there; the woman did."

Lauren looked confused.

"She and Stern met at a restaurant, but left in separate cars. It was odd, but I didn't realize the significance of it...then. The next night, I did as I told you I would. I went to the Blue Marlin and she was there. Imagine my surprise when I discovered she was the secretary to Jonathan Green."

"NuTekNiks's president?"

"The same. I had to drink a lot of beer and listen to a lot of macho bar talk, but I found out she's his secretary."

She sighed. He was truly enjoying playing private detective. "And what does that prove, Michael?"

"We know they're getting our technology some way. It has to be Malcolm. He's doing it for love of a woman," Michael said, his contemptuous tone revealing his own opinion of that. "Selling us down the river for sex."

She drew in a deep breath. "I appreciate you making such an all-out effort on this, Michael, but what you've told me doesn't really prove anything." She rubbed her forehead. "It's pretty incredible to think of our Malcolm nursing a grand passion." What about his wife and child in East Germany? she wondered. Was the FBI on the wrong track?

"That's not all I discovered, Lauren."

"What else?"

"Braden is not the sterling character you believe him to be," he said.

"Oh?" The tone of her voice cooled noticeably.

"I know you trust Jake Levinson's judgment. He found Braden and persuaded you that he was trustworthy." He was suddenly defensive. "I definitely think some of the blame for this belongs at his door."

"Get to the point, Michael."

"Do you remember the contract that so conveniently fell into our laps the same week Braden showed up?

"Hy-Tech in Pensacola?"

"Yes. Braden's been on their payroll for years. I checked. Throwing that contract to our company was a shrewd move on his part. It was a way to line his own pockets at Hy-Tech and get a firsthand look at sophisticated Holt designs and techniques."

"Next, he talked you into setting him up as production manager where he'd have access to anything else he might decide he wanted. He's an expert in the field and uniquely qualified to siphon off anything he had a buyer for."

Lauren stared back at him wordlessly.

"Where is he, anyway?" Michael inquired, seeming to recall suddenly that he was on Braden's property.

"He's . . . he went to the sheriff's office."

He frowned. "Sheriff's office?"

"To file a report." She waved a hand vaguely, speaking through lips that barely moved. "We had an accident in the Blazer last night. Someone cut the brake line. He discovered it this morning."

"My God, were you hurt?"

"No."

"Well . . ." He seemed distracted for a moment. "What do you plan to do about all this, Lauren?"

She pinched the bridge of her nose, feeling as old as . . . as Malcolm Stern. "I don't know, Michael."

He cleared his throat and moved slightly closer. "Lauren, we never get any time together anymore, but I've been doing a lot of thinking about your situation."

Oh, no, she just wanted him to go. Her head was throbbing, trying to absorb everything he'd turned up about Ryder.

He caught her hand. "Lauren, you need someone to turn to who you can trust now. We're good together, and you know how I feel about you. Ever since Clay died, it's been you and me together, when you get right down to it."

She pulled at her hand, and reluctantly he let it go.

"Braden just happened along at a time when you needed someone with his experience," he told her with a smile that did nothing to reassure her. "It was a mistake to let him take over like he did, but fortunately we found him out in time."

"I didn't let him take over, Michael," she said coolly.

He hardly heard her. "Forget him, Lauren. You and I can make a go of this plant, and we can do it as man and wife."

She stared at him, totally repelled. Why today of all days had Michael decided to propose? "It's not a good time, Michael. I'm upset and worried. Ryder—"

"Didn't you hear me, Lauren? Braden's got irons in the fire from here to infinity! Pensacola and New Orleans are just the beginning. He's hooked up with some outfit in

Denver and if I'd had more time, I could have chased down leads in L.A. and Honolulu."

"He's a consultant, Michael."

"Consultant!" He swore. "He wants your company. Are you too hung up on him to see it?"

He sliced the air with one hand. "Forget Braden! Don't be a bigger fool than you've already been. Is he so fantastic in bed that you're going to hand him the plant?"

She froze him with a single look. "I think you'd better leave, Michael."

Instantly he realized his mistake. "Lauren, I'm sorry. I shouldn't have said that."

"But you did, and now I know your true opinion of me personally and my judgment and my ability to run my company." She mustered her tattered dignity and looked him directly in the eye. "I'll just say this. I don't need you or Ryder Braden or any man to help me hold my life together. And if you plan to keep your job, I suggest that you remember it."

She forgot Michael and his clumsy attempt to manipulate her almost before his car disappeared. The real challenge was not to panic over what she'd learned about Ryder. Deception and a betrayal of trust had nearly destroyed her relationship with him once before. She paced restlessly, longing for him to return. Everything Michael said was so *plausible*.

Her head spinning, she thought back to the day when the Hy-Tech contract had come to them. As Michael pointed out, it was right after Ryder had come on the scene. Was he getting money under the table from Hy-Tech? Was he managing production in her plant so that he could get his hands on all the designs, instead of just the few that Nu-TekNiks had stolen? She thought about the first night they'd made love, how she had awakened and found him gone from her bed. She'd found him in Justin's room, jubilant over finding the lost designs.

She cringed with a growing sense of foreboding. What if she'd been worried about the wrong thing all along? What if he didn't really care anything about Justin? A searing, twisting pain caught at her heart. After all, he had known about him for eleven years and had done nothing. Her thoughts raced ahead, darting first one way, then another. Did he care about his son? Or her? She sat down, feeling sick. Dear God, was it her business he'd wanted all along? Did he want the Holt Company? She had to have some answers.

WHEN RYDER CAME from the sheriff's office, she was waiting for him. He was dusty and tired looking and utterly appealing. She hardened her heart, watching him cram his sunglasses into his shirt pocket and head toward her. He was going to kiss her; it was in his eyes.

"Why didn't you tell me about your connection with Hy-Tech?"

He stopped, the kiss forgotten. Something—a frown, a flare of surprise, she couldn't be sure—came and was then gone from Ryder's face. "Hy-Tech?" he shrugged. "I guess because it never came up in conversation. I've consulted for them for years. Why, Lauren?" His tone was quiet, not a bit like a man with something to hide. "Why do you ask now?"

She was put off momentarily. "Did you get—" she waved a hand, trying to come up with a term that wasn't too offensive "—ah, anything from Hy-Tech for arranging that contract with my company?"

He eyed her narrowly. "You mean personally?"

She met his look squarely. "Yes."

"No."

For the life of her, she couldn't think what to say to that. She could believe him, or not. But he was a man who had secrets; she already knew that. She needed to know more.

"I knew they had the work going," he told her. "And it was no secret your plant needed work. I put the two of you together."

"You could have accepted a gratuity from them," she said. "A finder's fee . . . or something."

"A kickback," he said bluntly.

Oh, she was no good at this. Since Michael had left, all she'd done was chase chaotic thoughts round and round in her head. Her first impulse had been to pack and leave, but there was too much at stake. Maybe he could explain everything. If he couldn't, and he really wanted the company, instinct told her that barring him from the plant would cause him more dismay. Now she just didn't know. It wasn't that he couldn't explain; it was that her trust in him was too shaky, untried. He'd deceived her before. Was he deceiving her again?

"Ryder, why did you take the job as my production manager?"

Ryder turned from her and went to the window. She would hardly believe the truth, he thought, feeling the pain of disappointment and deep hurt. Everything he had done since coming into her life he'd been compelled to do, compelled by something beyond logic, beyond rational thinking. His heart had sought to seal the connection between them. Would she believe that?

Still not looking at her, he said, "Why do you think I did?"

"I don't know!" she cried. "You're overqualified, you don't need the work . . . you tell me. Clay's designs are valuable. Only a few people could understand them even if they saw them. You could. And you have the connections to market them.''

A tiny muscle moved in his jaw. Still he didn't turn.

She swallowed around the tightness in her throat. ''Or you could marry the widow and have it all,'' she said.

He closed his eyes. ''I see you've done some thinking since I left.''

''Please answer me, Ryder.''

He turned and looked at her. ''Don't forget Justin. I could have you and the company and Justin.''

She had been pale before. Now she looked like a ghost.

''What happened, Lauren? Last night I thought we reached an understanding. I told you that I love you. I want to build a life with you and Justin. When I left this morning, you were a happy, satisfied woman. Now you're full of suspicion and accusations.''

''Michael came while you were gone.''

''Michael.''

''He'd been doing some…investigating. He told me about Hy-Tech.''

''Did he also mention the FBI is looking for him?''

She frowned. ''No.''

''They're on their way to pick up Malcolm Stern right now. The evidence against Armstead is inconclusive, but not for long. Where did he go?''

''I don't know. To his apartment, I guess.''

He regarded her steadily for a long moment, before moving abruptly from the window and striding across the floor. At the door, he turned. ''I've just about had enough of your precious Michael.'' He reached into his pocket and pulled out some keys. ''I'll have to use your car since the Blazer is wrecked. Stay put,'' he ordered, heading for the porch steps with Lauren at his heels. ''And keep an eye on Justin. Murphy and Jannsen are off for the weekend.''

She caught his arm. "Ryder, I . . . I may not be here when you get back," she told him.

He pinned her with a look. "Then you'd better find a good place to hide," he told her grimly. "Because you and I have unfinished business, lady."

"MOM . . ."

"I told you, Justin, go to your room and pack your things."

"But why? Won't Ryder wonder why we up and left like this?"

Lauren set her jaw.

"Mom, I heard you and Ryder fighting."

"It's rude to eavesdrop. I've told you that." She unsnapped the clasp on a piece of luggage and flipped the lid open.

"Don't you love him anymore?"

Her hands hesitated, but only for a second. How did he *know* these things? "You're too young to understand, Justin."

"I like living here with Ryder, Mom."

She closed her eyes. "Go pack, Justin. I'm not telling you again."

Only after Lauren was ready to go, did she realize she didn't have a car. Hattie Bell didn't bother to conceal her relief.

"You're making a big mistake running away like this, honey. You haven't done anything this silly since you were a teenager."

"I know you think Ryder has no faults, Hattie, but there are things you don't understand." She ran a distracted hand through her hair. Was she making a mistake?

"I understand he won't be happy when he comes back here and finds you and that boy gone," Hattie muttered darkly.

Clancy. She could call Clancy and ask her to pick them up. Of course, she would be subjected to a third degree. She hesitated, her hand hovering over the phone. Maybe it would be a good thing. Having to justify her decision to Clancy would force her to think it over. Her whole life was at stake here, her future with Ryder, Justin's relationship with the one single man in the world who was the perfect father for him. She picked up the phone.

Busy! Damn it, was everything going to go wrong today? She slammed the receiver down and looked around for Justin. When she couldn't locate him in the house or up in his room, she went outside. After calling him several times and searching the immediate area, she felt a tiny tremor along her spine. Panic wouldn't help, she reminded herself and hurried inside to find Hattie Bell. Together they began calling and searching in earnest.

She tried to tell herself he would be just around the next bush or the next tree. Although it wasn't like him to flagrantly disobey her, it was possible she'd pushed him too far. He wasn't leaving Ryder's place willingly. She put an icy-cold hand to her throat.

She called his name again. But all she heard were crickets and early night sounds. It was getting dark. Her mouth dry, she forced herself to think where he could be. The place was so isolated, he couldn't have walked to the nearest neighbor. Besides why would he? She refused to think the word that hovered on the edge of her mind.

"Lordy, do you think he's been kidnapped?" Hattie Bell moaned, putting both hands on her cheeks.

"Oh, Hattie..." Lauren took a deep breath. His bike. Was his bicycle gone? Hurrying around the corner of the house, she saw that it was missing from the bike stand Ryder had made for it. Her heart pounding, she sank down on the porch steps. It was dark, and the only road out was long and lonely. Where was he? Was he alone? Was he hurt?

"We gotta tell Mr. Ryder!" Hattie Bell said, heading for the phone.

Oh, Ryder, I need you now.

AT THE PLANT Malcolm Stern shuffled down the hall heading for the data-control center. This was his last mission. If he failed he would never see Anna and his son. His contact had been most emphatic about that. Authorities were closing in, she informed him. So be it. He would make this last effort and then... He patted his pocket where the gun weighed heavily. He was very tired.

If he had any regrets, they were that he hadn't acquired all the access codes from Clay Holt before arranging the accident. Muttering to himself, he made a mental review of the particular design that his contact demanded from him not later than tonight. How much simpler all his tasks would have been this past year with the access codes. Maybe then, Anna's release could have been arranged.

Hearing a noise, he stopped abruptly. There should be no one remaining in the plant, especially in the computer room. He had waited until everyone authorized to work on Saturday had departed. Even the janitors were in another area. Frowning, he peered through the small window in the door. He blinked in amazement. It was Clay Holt's young son seated before the monitor. Stern's gaze narrowed suddenly at the screen. The boy was not playing one of the silly video games. The schematic displayed on the monitor was familiar. Stern himself had been privy to Holt's early work on the design. Soon after, Holt had become more secretive with his

work, an attitude that had made Stern's mission very difficult.

He stepped back from the door, his face thoughtful. He
remembered the frequency with which Holt had brought his
son into the plant. Always the boy had gravitated to the
computers. He was intelligent. On the occasions Stern had
spoken to him—always in the company of his father—he
had been impressed. Did the boy posses the precious access
codes?

There was only one way to find out. His expression intent, Stern pushed open the door.

CHAPTER SIXTEEN

ARMSTEAD HAD NOT BEEN at his apartment. Fed up with Lauren's right-hand man and the horse he rode in on, Ryder's temper was simmering just shy of hot, as he pulled up at the plant in a squeal of tires and spraying gravel. Right behind Armstead's fancy Jag. He didn't know what the creep was doing here on a Saturday night, but he intended to make it his business to find out.

He was out and halfway up the steps when a car pulled in off the street and stopped. Frowning, he watched as the passenger door was flung open and Lauren scrambled out, before the driver, whom he could see now was Clancy, had a chance to open her door.

Lauren felt a moment's uncertainty as Ryder stared at her from his position on the steps. Would she always feel this overwhelming instinct to fly into the safety of his arms when she was frightened? A feeling of relief and rightness suddenly bloomed deep inside her, and she knew she would. Always. Who else could understand the depth of her fear for Justin except Ryder?

"Ryder, Justin's missing!"

He started toward her, concern etching a sharp line between his eyebrows. Automatically he opened his arms as she reached him and caught her up hard against him.

"Wait, calm down, sweetheart." His tone was soothing, the words spoken against her temple. She knew he could feel her trembling, but some needy part of her that had been as cold as death sought the warmth and reassurance only Ryder could give her. He caught her face in his hands and made her look at him. "Now, tell me."

"Oh, Ryder, I got ready to leave, and he didn't want to. I told him we had to, that there were things he didn't understand, and you know how he hates to be told that. It was only a few minutes later that I came to my senses, but by then he was nowhere around." Her eyes clung to his, frantic. "Nowhere, Ryder. Oh, God, please don't let this happen."

He pushed her head against his chest and held her there for a second or two. "Don't cry, darling. And don't panic. We'll find him." He started up the steps with his arm around her and remembered Clancy.

"Go get Jake," he told her. "Tell him to get Whitman at the FBI." Clancy nodded and without a word turned and ran back to her car.

"Now, when did you last see him?"

"It was when I told him to go and pack." Desperately she tried to think back. "It was a good hour and a half ago, Ryder. Oh, what do you think could have happened to him?"

"Did he say anything that might give us a clue?"

"No," her voice rose. "Nothing, nothing."

He hugged her again, his hand warm and reassuring at her waist. With an effort, she tried to keep her teeth from chattering. "He couldn't have gone far," he said, thinking out loud. "The place is deserted and—"

"His bike was gone."

"Good." When she started and glanced up at him, he explained, "That means he meant to leave. If he'd been taken against his will, they'd have hardly bothered with his bike.''

A rush of complicated emotion was released with his statement: relief that he hadn't been kidnapped; fear that he'd started out on that deserted road alone; guilt that she'd caused her son to run away from home.

Standing on the steps in front of the plant, Ryder thought of the possible places Justin would go. Scotty's or Curtis's, maybe. His gaze drifted over the small landscaped area where the flagpole and the iron bench were. His eyes stopped and flicked back again. Justin's bike was leaning against the flagpole.

"Lauren..." He touched the soft underside of her chin and turned her head gently in the direction of the bike. "He's here."

For a second she simply stared. And then she slumped against him with a cry.

"He's inside with Armstead," Ryder said in a tone laced with menace. "Stay here."

"No."

"I mean it, Lauren. Let me handle this."

She put both hands on his arms. "I'm not arguing about your rights where Justin is concerned anymore, Ryder. But I have some rights, too. I'm not waiting out here."

They entered the plant quietly and did not turn on any lights, at Ryder's insistence. Outwardly Lauren still staunchly defended Michael, but Justin's disappearance and the accident in the Blazer and Michael's new hostility had shaken her. There were depths to Michael she had just glimpsed.

They headed directly for the data center. While they were still in the hall they heard voices. The place was brightly lit. The door was wide open. Ryder put out a hand to caution

Lauren. She looked up at him and nodded. Urging her to stay slightly behind him, they peered in between the door and the doorjamb.

Justin was sitting at the keyboard. Michael Armstead was standing a few feet from him. At his shoulder was Malcolm Stern. Stern had a gun and it was pointed at Armstead.

Ryder heard Lauren's involuntary gasp and quickly covered her mouth, frowning at the evidence before his eyes. He was startled to discover that Armstead wasn't in league with Stern, but that wouldn't help Justin, whose cheek, he noted with a grim hardening of his jaw, was bruised. All of his years of survival rushed to the forefront of his mind, readying him for the supreme challenge—to protect and defend his son. Standing flush against the wall, he restrained Lauren with one arm. He could feel her whole body quaking. Quickly he reviewed his options.

Armstead was speaking. "You're making a big mistake, Malcolm. Let the kid go. He's accessed the stuff you wanted, and you've got a printout. They're on to you, believe me. I'm not making this up."

Stern looked defeated suddenly. "It does not matter. I am committed for this last mission."

"Haven't you done enough? Clay was supposed to be your friend, man. You've sold his designs to NuTekNiks; you've sat back and watched them practically push the plant down the tubes. His widow's been hounded and harassed. Give it up, for God's sake."

Neither man appeared aware of Justin seated between them, listening.

"One moment, if you please." Stern gave a short bark of a laugh. "You speak as though you yourself have the interests of the widow at heart, Armstead. Do not bother to lie. My contacts are aware of your petty attempts to, as you say, hound and harass—a bit of arson, shipping mix-ups, malfunctioning equipment.''

"You're crazy, Stern!'' Michael gave Justin a quick look.

Malcolm Stern nodded slowly. ''Well, we shall see. Nevertheless, we must proceed here.'' He made a gesture with the gun. ''I know what I have to do, and nothing you say can persuade me otherwise.''

"And what is that, Malcolm? What do you have to do?''

A spasm of emotion twisted Stern's mouth. ''She promised, this one last time. She promised.''

Michael shook his head. ''Who, Malcolm? Who promised what?''

"Evelyn . . .''

"Jonathan Green's secretary? Your lover?''

Stern's laugh was pitiful, but his eyes were wild and unfocused. ''Lover? I have no lover. There's just my wife.'' His face crumpled suddenly. ''My wife, my Anna.''

Michael's eyes narrowed suddenly. ''You killed Holt, didn't you?''

Stern seemed to focus his mind on the question. He straightened a bit, still pathetic in his dingy lab coat. ''I arranged an accident. He was an impediment that had to be eliminated.''

"Impediment? He was a genius!''

"He would not be reasonable.'' He gave Michael a simple look. ''My contacts demanded his designs in exchange for Anna's release.''

Michael stared. ''You did it for some dumb broad? You are crazy!''

"Stay there!'' Stern brandished the gun menacingly and forced Michael back against a row of file cabinets. He turned to Justin. ''Now, boy.'' He nudged Justin's shoulder with his free hand. "You must print out that document you located in the index."

Justin turned his face up to Stern. "I don't know whether I can call it up or not, Mr. Stern."

Stern put out a finger and touched the bruise on Justin's cheek. "I do not want to cause you pain, boy," he murmured, looking regretful. "But if I'm ever to see Anna and my own son again, you must obey me."

Lauren had never felt such terror. Malcolm Stern was obviously a deranged man, a traitor and a murderer. The things he said were muddled and incoherent, but he was desperate. It wouldn't take much provocation to push him over the line. And Justin could be the victim. She looked up at Ryder, her eyes full of anguish and a mother's fear.

He bent to her. "Don't make a sound," he whispered. "I think I can slip inside behind those files and then work my way over to them." She started to object, but he caught her arm and squeezed it with sudden authority. "Do as I say, Lauren. Justin's life is at stake here. Now, go into that little office—" he hiked his chin to indicate the door across the hall "—and don't come out until I say you can. Okay?"

She gazed at him a moment, torn, instinctively feeling a mother's reluctance to walk away from her child. And then she looked at the deadly little scenario across the room, where Justin was at the mercy of a crazed man.

The decision was taken from her when, incredibly, something prompted Justin to turn slightly and see them. He stared directly for a second or two, and then without a flicker of an eyelash he turned back to the computer console.

"Mr. Stern, I have to go to the bathroom," he said a moment later. *Cool, Justin,* Ryder thought, swamped with pride and admiration at the boy's courage. He would have to come through the doors where Ryder and Lauren waited, to get to the bathroom.

"Not now, boy." Stern adjusted his bifocals to focus on the monitor.

"I'm sorry, Mr. Stern, but I really have to go."

Michael cleared his throat. "I think you'd better let him," he suggested.

"I'm not playing games, young man!" Stern admonished, holding the gun up as a reminder.

Justin looked properly chastened, but undaunted. "If I don't go, I don't see how I can keep my mind on this stuff."

Stern sucked in an exasperated breath. "Then we will all have to go." Justin stood up quickly. Stern jerked his head toward Armstead. "You go after the boy and remember, I will use this if I have to."

Michael warily stepped behind Justin, but when he would have put a reassuring hand on the boy's shoulder, Malcolm Stern uttered a sharp objection. Michael obeyed, but he was clearly prepared to use Justin's tactic, somehow. If Armstead caused a hair of Justin's head to be hurt, Ryder vowed the man would wish Stern had used the gun on him.

Ryder touched Lauren's shoulder and urged her toward the small room. With a last, agonized, backward look, she went. He flattened himself against the wall and waited, while Justin calmly led the group of three to him.

Justin's karate yell startled everyone, Ryder included. But mostly it was Malcolm Stern who was rattled. The old man's nerves simply couldn't stand up to a martial arts cry. Justin quickly dropped to the floor, rolling into a ball that Michael Armstead couldn't avoid. They both went down in a tangle of arms and legs. Stern bellowed once in rage, pointing the gun at the downed pair. Ryder stepped out and delivered one sharp chop to the back of Stern's neck. He dropped like a puppet whose strings were suddenly cut.

There was an instant of quiet as they all stared at Malcolm Stern. Sprawled on the floor, he looked old and pitiful. The gun had flown out of his hand and lay against the baseboard where it had landed.

Justin blinked once or twice, his valor all used up. And then he scrambled to his feet and launched himself at Ryder, whose arms opened to receive him. Eyes closed, throat tight, Ryder could do nothing for the sheer power of his love for Justin. Wordlessly he treated himself to another second or two of the joy and relief of having his son, unharmed, in his arms, and then he let him go.

"Where's Mom?" Justin asked with eyes suspiciously bright.

"Right here." Lauren fumbled with the door of the tiny dark office and rushed out. Justin ran to her, and she swept him up, her eyes closed in heartfelt thanks. *She could so easily have lost him!*

"Are you hurt?" she said, her voice tight with emotion. Leaning back she inspected his face, wincing when she saw the bruise.

"I'm okay, Mom."

Michael was on his feet again, favoring his elbow which was skinned and bleeding from the tumble in the hall. He was watching them warily. "Umm, how long have you been here?"

Ryder gave him a hard look. "Long enough."

"Well..." He gestured to Stern. "He came in and found Justin at the console. He knew Clay and Justin had spent a lot of time here together. He decided to use Justin to get all the files, once he discovered he had such complete knowledge of the system."

Not a muscle moved in Ryder's face. "Clear your desk, Armstead. You're fired."

Armstead sent a challenging look to Lauren. "Are you going to let him do that, Lauren?"

"We heard everything, Michael. Do as he says."

Everyone turned at the flurry of sound down the hall. "That'll be the FBI," Ryder said. "A little late."

Michael frowned. "Why are they here?"

"For starters," Ryder said with obvious satisfaction, "to pick you up, Armstead."

"What!" he blustered. "Now look here, Braden. The Feds don't have a thing on me and neither do you. I—"

"Tell it to them," Ryder said, taking Lauren's arm and putting a hand on Justin's shoulder.

"Are you mad at me for leaving the house without telling you?" Justin asked, looking warily at his mother and Ryder.

Lauren put a hand on his shoulder. "Not mad, Justin. But you certainly gave us a good scare. Striking out in the dark on your own was very dangerous. Why did you do it?"

Justin dropped his eyes. "I knew what was causing the trouble between you and Ryder. It was all that missing stuff—my Dad's designs and the secrets in the big computer at the plant...." He looked at Ryder. "And maybe a little bit Michael Armstead. I couldn't do anything about Ryder disliking Michael Armstead 'cause I didn't like him much myself."

Ryder felt a little spurt of satisfaction. It might be unfair, but still it was gratifying to know that Justin shared his disdain for Armstead. He glanced at Lauren, who refused to look his way.

"I knew you would probably be mad, Mom," Justin said. "But I figured if I was able to do any good with the big computer, maybe you wouldn't stay mad at me very long."

One look at his anxious, bruised face and Lauren forgot the stern lecture he deserved. Since Ryder was so eager to exercise his parental authority, she'd let him take it from here.

Ryder shot her a wry look, unwilling to scold his son when the sight of Stern's gun pointed at him was still fresh in his mind. Besides, he was too busy feeling pleased over how far Justin had been prepared to go to fix things between his mother and Ryder. He cleared his throat. "You meant well, Justin, but next time remember the house rules—you don't go anywhere without asking permission."

"Yes sir."

Some disciplinarian, Lauren thought, secretly amused.

"Can we go home now?" Justin asked, stretching his legs to match Ryder's strides.

"Yes." Ryder squeezed his son's shoulder and pulled Lauren into the place that seemed designed for her under his arm.

"Your place?" Justin inquired, dividing a look between his mother and Ryder.

Over his head, their eyes met. "Yes," they said together.

Outside, they lagged behind when Justin dashed toward the car.

"Poor Malcolm," Lauren murmured, thinking of the old man with his broken dreams. "Michael was right in a way. He did do it all for love. For his wife, Anna."

"And his son," Ryder put in. "Evelyn, the woman, was his contact to a communist agent. She promised him papers for Anna and his son in exchange for Holt secrets."

"Incredible."

"But she was greedy," Ryder said. "As secretary to NuTekNiks's president, she recognized the overall value of Clay's designs. She had Malcolm hooked, anyway. She simply coerced more and more from him."

She had probably ordered Clay's death, Ryder thought, but he kept that idea to himself. Later he would talk to the authorities. Right now, he was worried about Justin and Lauren. He wanted to take them home, where they could talk about Clay and the way he had died.

"Jonathan Green was in it with her," Lauren said, marveling at the audacity of people.

"Yes." Ryder hugged her to him suddenly. "Your lawsuit will be dropped, all the harassment that NuTekNiks instigated here in your plant will end, and you'll have to look around for somebody to replace me as your production manager."

She paled. She had known all along that he was not the settling down kind, but . . .

"What's the matter?" he asked, tipping her face up.

She licked her lips and watched as something flared in his eyes in response. "You're resigning as my production manager?"

He angled his head back, and she got a look at the devil dancing in his eyes. "Well, I kind of thought I might be in line for a promotion. Now that I finally managed to get Armstead booted out, how about making me general manager?"

Her lashes fell. "I'm not sure I can afford you."

"We can probably strike a bargain." He squinted, looking at her with his head to one side. "The price might have to be negotiated, but I'm a reasonable man."

She smiled. "Okay, what's your price?"

He didn't hesitate. "Marriage, sugar. You promised and I'm holding you to it. I want you and Justin and Hattie Bell set up permanently in that big old house. Work as long as you want to at that plant, but I'm betting you're going to be a very busy lady at home."

Pale pink color stole into her cheeks as joy stole into her heart. "Doing what?"

"Making babies."

She made a soft, faint sound.

He added emphatically, "The old-fashioned way."

Harlequin Superromance.

COMING NEXT MONTH

#374 SILKEN THREADS • Connie Rinehold
At age thirty-two, fashion designer Sabrina Haddon
finally met the daughter she'd given up sixteen years
earlier—and the girl's irate adoptive father. The sparks
between Sabrina and Ramsey Jordan were instant, but a
relationship was impossible. Sabrina could only hope
that in time the delicate threads of their individual lives
could be woven together.... .

#375 HANDLE WITH CARE • Jane Silverwood.
Dr. Jim Gordon barely made it back alive to Maryland
after being held hostage overseas. Wounded in spirit,
he felt rejuvenated when he met Dory Barker and
her teenage daughter. But he failed to realize that
the pretty pottery instructor was also one of the
walking wounded....

#376 REMEMBER ME • Bobby Hutchinson
While researching a children's book, Annie Pendleton
met ambitious pediatrician David Roswell, and before
she knew it Annie was as hard-pressed to balance the
duties of single parenthood as her lover was to balance
his work load. Perhaps this stress explained Annie's
chronic physical pain, but maybe it was David's
opposition to decisions she'd made—decisions that
dramatically affected them both.

#377 WORDS OF WISDOM • Megan Alexander
He'd broken their engagement, and he hadn't said why.
All Jenny Valentine knew for sure was that men like
Luke Beaumont ought to come with warnings tattooed
on their foreheads. Luke thought he'd done the noble
thing by breaking their engagement. Well, he'd had
enough of being noble. Only now it seemed that Jenny
had had enough of *him*....

JAYNE ANN KRENTZ
WINS HARLEQUIN'S
AWARD OF EXCELLENCE

With her October Temptation, *Lady's Choice*, Jayne
Ann Krentz marks more than a decade in romance
publishing. We thought it was about time she got our
official seal of approval—the Harlequin Award of
Excellence.

Since she began writing for Temptation in 1984, Ms
Krentz's novels have been a hallmark of this lively, sexy
series—and a benchmark for all writers in the genre.
Lady's Choice, her eighteenth Temptation, is as stirring
as her first, thanks to a tough and sexy hero, and a
heroine who is tough when she has to be, tender when
she chooses. . . .

The winner of numerous booksellers' awards, Ms Krentz
has also consistently ranked as a bestseller with readers,
on both romance and mass market lists. *Lady's Choice*
will do it for her again!

This lady is *Harlequin's* choice in October.

Available where Harlequin books are sold.   AE-LC-1

Harlequin Intrigue®

High adventure and romance—
with three sisters on a search . . .

Linsey Deane uses clues left by their father to search the Colorado Rockies for a legendary wagonload of Confederate gold, in #120 *Treasure Hunt* by Leona Karr (August 1989).

Kate Deane picks up the trail in a mad chase to the Deep South and glitzy Las Vegas, with menace and romance at her heels, in #122 *Hide and Seek* by Cassie Miles (September 1989).

Abigail Deane matches wits with a murderer and hunts for the people behind the threat to the Deane family fortune, in #124 *Charades* by Jasmine Crasswell (October 1989).

Don't miss Harlequin Intrigue's three-book series The Deane Trilogy. Available where Harlequin books are sold.

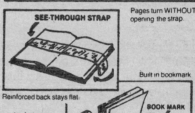

The series that started
it all has a fresh new look!

HARLEQUIN
Romance

The tender stories you've always loved now feature a
brand-new cover you'll be sure to notice. Each title in
the Harlequin Romance series will sweep you away to
romantic places and delight you with the special allure
and magic of love.

Look for our new cover wherever you buy
Harlequin books.